P9-DKF-719

BITTERSWEET

China Bayles Mysteries by Susan Wittig Albert

THYME OF DEATH
WITCHES' BANE
HANGMAN'S ROOT
ROSEMARY REMEMBERED
RUEFUL DEATH
LOVE LIES BLEEDING
CHILE DEATH
LAVENDER LIES
MISTLETOE MAN
BLOODROOT
INDIGO DYING
A DILLY OF A DEATH
DEAD MAN'S BONES
BLEEDING HEARTS
SPANISH DAGGER
NIGHTSHADE
WORMWOOD
HOLLY BLUES
MOURNING GLORIA
CAT'S CLAW
WIDOW'S TEARS
DEATH COME QUICKLY
BITTERSWEET

AN UNTHYMELY DEATH
CHINA BAYLES' BOOK OF DAYS

Cottage Tales of Beatrix Potter Mysteries by Susan Wittig Albert

THE TALE OF HILL TOP FARM
THE TALE OF HOLLY HOW
THE TALE OF CUCKOO BROW WOOD
THE TALE OF HAWTHORN HOUSE
THE TALE OF BRIAR BANK
THE TALE OF APPLEBECK ORCHARD
THE TALE OF OAT CAKE CRAG
THE TALE OF CASTLE COTTAGE

Darling Dahlias Mysteries by Susan Wittig Albert

THE DARLING DAHLIAS AND THE CUCUMBER TREE
THE DARLING DAHLIAS AND THE NAKED LADIES
THE DARLING DAHLIAS AND THE CONFEDERATE ROSE
THE DARLING DAHLIAS AND THE TEXAS STAR
THE DARLING DAHLIAS AND THE SILVER DOLLAR BUSH

With her husband, Bill Albert, writing as Robin Paige

DEATH AT BISHOP'S KEEP
DEATH AT GALLOWS GREEN
DEATH AT DAISY'S FOLLY
DEATH AT DEVIL'S BRIDGE
DEATH AT ROTTINGDEAN
DEATH AT WHITECHAPEL
DEATH AT EPSOM DOWNS
DEATH AT DARTMOOR
DEATH AT GLAMIS CASTLE
DEATH IN HYDE PARK
DEATH AT BLENHEIM PALACE
DEATH ON THE LIZARD

Other books by Susan Wittig Albert

WRITING FROM LIFE
WORK OF HER OWN
A WILDER ROSE

Susan Wittig Albert

Bittersweet

BERKLEY PRIME CRIME, NEW YORK

THE BERKLEY PUBLISHING GROUP
Published by the Penguin Group
Penguin Group (USA) LLC
375 Hudson Street, New York, New York 10014

USA • Canada • UK • Ireland • Australia • New Zealand • India • South Africa • China

penguin.com

A Penguin Random House Company

This book is an original publication of The Berkley Publishing Group.

Library of Congress Cataloging-in-Publication Data

Albert, Susan Wittig.
Bittersweet / by Susan Wittig Albert.—First edition.
pages ; cm
ISBN 978-0-425-25562-9 (hardback)
I. Title.
PS3551.L2637B56 2015
813'.54—dc23
2014043791

FIRST EDITION: April 2015

PRINTED IN THE UNITED STATES OF AMERICA

10 9 8 7 6 5 4 3 2 1

Cover illustration copyright © by Joe Burleson.
Cover design by Judith Murello.
Interior text design by Tiffany Estreicher.

BITTERSWEET

Prologue

The blue and white Cessna 172 dropped out of the gray November sky. The pilot banked sharply, slowing to eighty knots, then turned on the carburetor heat and powered back to 1500 rpm. When he made the field, he extended another ten degrees of flaps, dropped his airspeed to seventy, and corrected for the crosswind that blew off the cliff to the west. He powered back, leveled off, and touched down at the end of the grassy north-south strip. The landing was bumpy but no rougher than usual. He regularly mowed the private strip tucked into the Bee Creek valley at the foot of Sycamore Mountain and knew where to avoid the worst of the hummocks and dips. He powered down, braked lightly, and taxied the short distance to the Quonset hut that served as an airplane hangar. Glad to be back in Texas, he climbed out and was greeted by the man who had just come out of the barn.

"Where the hell you been?" the man demanded angrily. "I been expecting you for hours." He shook his head. "Ever' time you go up in that antique bolt-bucket, you could come home in a body bag."

"Hey," the pilot said. "She may be an antique, but she's still in the air. And I don't notice her condition keeping you from taking her up whenever you feel like it." It was true. Both of them flew the plane, although its certification had lapsed long ago. The pilot paused to flick a light to his cigarette. "Stopped off outside of Lubbock to say hi to a little girl I know there. Took longer than I thought. Sorry," he added. "Shoulda called." He grinned, remembering. "Guess I had something else on my mind."

The two men were brothers, but there was no family resemblance. In his late thirties, the pilot was sandy-haired, short, and barrel-chested, broad and heavy across the shoulders. His younger brother was thin and dark, with a disfiguring knife scar that ran across his narrow cheek and under his ear, earned in a barroom fight in Corpus Christi a few years before. Both wore cowboy hats and jackets—the pilot denim, his brother a green army field jacket—jeans, and scuffed cowboy boots.

"Lubbock," his brother grunted. "I just might have to shoot you." Both men laughed. They pushed the plane into the hangar and went swiftly through the usual postflight items. They were both good fliers, both good mechanics. Had to be, since they didn't have the money to pay somebody else to keep the plane flying.

"You heard from the truck?" the pilot asked as they closed the big doors. "Jack loaded up and got off before dawn. I told him to phone you with updates." Jack was their partner. He worked on another ranch, but he'd taken a few days off to do the job.

"Phoned twice. Last time he'd got as far as Lampasas, coming down 281. Should be pulling in—" He looked at his watch, "Give him another hour, maybe. That trailer work out okay?"

"It loads better than the old one and rides smoother, but six white-tails are still more than I like to handle. Those animals panic real easy." The pilot paused, considering. "This was a real good batch, though. Big, solid bucks, hundred seventy pounds each, maybe fifty percent bigger than the wild bucks on the range around here."

Size was the thing, of course. If you were trying to establish a game ranch, the native deer made pretty sorry breeding stock. Bucks averaged around eighty-five, ninety pounds on good range, and with the drought, most range was only fair to poor. So you either laid out big dollars to rent stud bucks from the breeders or bought their semen at seven, eight thousand dollars a pop.

But he and his brother didn't have that kind of money. Their dad would rise up out of his grave and come gunning for them if he knew they had mortgaged the family land to high fence most of it. When they got enough money together, they could finish the job and apply for their deer breeder permit. Which was why they were bringing in the Oklahoma animals. And that was taking a big risk, since Texas had passed a law a few years ago making it a felony to haul deer in from other states. Scared of "wasting disease," they claimed, although everybody knew it was just the big white-tail breeders protecting their business from out-of-state competition. The feds had gotten in on the act, too, and passed a law against illegally transporting deer.

But first they had to catch you. The pilot figured the chances of that were pretty slim, all things considered. He knew of a team up in North Texas that had been running a similar black market operation for the past five years, bringing in deer from up north, from Indiana, Illinois, Wisconsin. They were still in business, making money hand over fist. All he and his brother needed were a couple of good trips to stock the ranch, and then they'd have their herd and could make it legal.

"Antlers?" his brother asked.

"Jack's bringing them." The antlers were always removed for transport, to keep the animals from injuring themselves or one another. "Impressive racks, obviously superior genetics." That was the buzzword, what everybody was talking about these days. Superior genetics, meaning genes for monster racks that hunters would pay big money for.

"I figure we can keep the best buck," the pilot added, "and find breeders who'll pay six thousand apiece for the rest, easy. Seven or eight, maybe more, once they see those racks." There were breeders out there who had more money than sense and were perfectly willing—eager, even—to buy black-market animals. And there was almost no risk. They knew they could simply launder those deer into the herds already on their hunting compounds, where they'd bring tens of thousands of dollars.

His brother nodded. "About time for a beer, wouldn't you say? You can tell me all about that little girl in Lubbock."

"I'll drink to that," the pilot replied, and the two headed up the hill toward the ranch house, their boots kicking up dry dust. It had rained in the valley over the weekend, but not up here on the mountain. That was the way in this drought. Hit-and-miss, mostly miss.

The tin-roofed clapboard house was weathered to a dull, nondescript gray. It had served as the family ranch house for four generations now, going back to the days when the only way to get to the Bar Bee was to ride your horse or drive your wagon from the main road up the limestone bed of the shallow Frio River to the spot where the ranch road headed off up Bee Creek. When the river was in flood, you stayed where you were until it was down again. Now, it was paved from the highway near Concan almost all the way up to the Bar Bee, and some of the old ranches were now gated communities with riverfront parks and underground electricity. The pilot hated the thought, but there was no denying it. Pretty quick, they were going to run out of country.

The two men went in through the back door. Inside, the house reflected its occupancy by a pair of bachelors, neither of whom bothered to make beds or wash dishes on a regular schedule. The kitchen table still held the remains of the previous day's meals, and the sink was piled with dirty pots and pans. The main feature in the living room was a gigantic HDTV, with a pair of brown La-Z-Boys parked in front of it, a table between them topped with an overflowing ashtray and a couple of empty beer bottles.

They took Lone Star longnecks out of the fridge, then went to sit in the rocking chairs on the front porch, propping their boots on the rail. From this vantage point, they could look out over the nearly two thousand acres of the old ranch, hillsides densely wooded with mesquite, cedar, and oak, the creek bottom with sycamore, pecan, and cypress, and enough open grazing to support a couple of hundred cows. Their dad and granddad had been cattle ranchers, so the whole place was low fenced—high fenced now to confine the deer herd they were intent on building. This was the southern rim of the Edwards Plateau and good land, all of it, prime habitat for wild turkey, dove, feral hogs, and white-tailed deer. When they were boys, the brothers had hunted every inch of it. There was no other place on earth that either of them would ever want to be, and when their dad was dying, they'd promised him that they would keep the land.

But cattle ranching was a losing proposition these days. Beef was bringing a good price, but the years-long drought had reduced the amount of hay they could raise to feed their cows, so they'd had to sell off most of the calves. The pilot had even thought of selling the plane, but he knew they wouldn't get what it was worth to them. He and his brother had talked the subject up one end and down the other and had come to the conclusion that they either had to sell the land to a developer or turn it into a trophy-hunting ranch, like the one Jack worked for. Which was what they were doing. Give them another two years and enough black-market deer to pay for the rest of the fencing, and they'd be in business.

"So what's the stock count now, with this batch coming in?" the pilot asked.

"Eleven from out of state, plus those four fawns Jack brought over. We sold off five of the Oklahoma bucks already."

The pilot frowned. Jack, who was experienced at working with white-tails, was buying into their project on shares, with breeder fawns and other stuff: supplies, tools, equipment.

"Those fawns," he said, "they're a problem. Once the Oklahoma white-tails are inside our fence, they could be native to the place and legal, far as anybody can tell. But I don't care how big a rack their daddy carries, those fawns were a mistake."

"Yeah. Those ear tattoos. Since it's the genetics we're after, we won't need the animals themselves, once we've got their offspring. We can get rid of them. And when Jack brings the next batch come spring, they better be unmarked. No more tattooed ears."

"I'll go for that," the pilot said, and tipped his bottle. "You told him, I reckon."

"Yes, but he's got another problem, too. His wife is pissed off about what he's doing." The brother's voice had a jagged edge. "I told him he'd better keep her in line, or else." His laugh was raspy. "Women. They got their uses, but they're never happy, no matter what. It's always something with them. Always something."

Or else what, the pilot wondered uneasily, trying not to remember the details of that bad scene in Corpus that had ended with his brother spending five years in jail for manslaughter, plus probation. He eyed the Cooper's hawk circling over the meadow that sloped down to the creek below and watched as it arched into a steep, stooping dive, pulling up sharply with a struggling shape in its brutal claws. Or else what?

With a shiver, he stopped remembering Corpus and thought instead about Jack's wife, who was a tempting dish. "Always something," he agreed mildly.

His brother pulled out a can of Red Man and poked a wad of tobacco into his cheek. "You got it. Well, there's more. The day you and Jack left for Oklahoma, I had to get the vet out here. Not our regular, but the old guy. The one Dad used to go fishing with."

"Oh yeah. Him and Dad was real close. Which cow?"

"The red heifer. She twinned."

"It go okay?" The pilot thought it probably had, even though it was a first birth. They had grown up with cows and knew how to deal with most situations. Must have been a tough one for his brother to call in a vet.

"Nope. The bull calf died—the vet's damn fault, although he wouldn't own up to it." He narrowed his eyes. "And there's worse. While he was here, I think he got a look at those fawns."

The pilot sat up straight, feeling a twist of uneasiness. "A good look?"

His brother shrugged. "That old man is shrewd, and he knows our place from way back." There was that jagged edge again. "He likely knows we ain't got a permit."

The pilot didn't say anything for a moment. Then, casual and soothing, he said, "Well, I don't reckon he'll say anything. Not his business."

The brother picked up a rusty can and spit a stream of tobacco juice into it. "I been thinking of having a little talk with him."

The pilot didn't answer for a moment. Then, carefully, trying to be cool, he said, "I don't think you should do that. Maybe he didn't—"

"Leave it to me, bro. I'll take care of it."

"Okay," the pilot said reluctantly. "Well, okay."

The hawk was back in the air, circling for another kill. He thought again of Corpus Christi.

Chapter One

American bittersweet, *Celastrus scandens*, is a climbing vine that can grow to twenty feet. A native, it is reported to occur throughout most of the eastern two-thirds of North America, from Canada to Texas. Other common names include climbing bittersweet, false bittersweet, climbing orangeroot, fevertwig, fever-twitch, staff vine, and Jacob's ladder. It prefers a sunny location and neutral soil. As a climber, it is a valuable ornamental landscape plant that can control erosion and harbor wildlife. Its orange berrylike fruits are produced in late summer and autumn, in hanging clusters that provide winter food for grouse, pheasant, quail, rabbit, squirrel, and deer. Fruit-bearing branches and twigs are prized for holiday wreaths and dried arrangements.

If you plan to add this vine to your landscape, be sure to choose the native American bittersweet, rather than the invasive pest Oriental bittersweet (*Celastrus orbiculatus*), which is sometimes sold in nurseries. Aggressive Oriental bittersweet vines can girdle and smother trees and shrubs and have overwhelmed entire plant communities. This imported plant bully not only outcompetes and displaces our indigenous American bittersweet, but can also hybridize with it. Widespread hybridization could genetically disrupt the native bittersweet population to the point of extinction. In some states, Oriental bittersweet has been listed as a prohibited noxious weed and targeted for eradication.

China Bayles
"Native Plants for Wildlife Gardens"
Pecan Springs Enterprise

Sometimes it's hard to know just when and where a particular story begins. Once you know the ending, you can trace it back to a dozen different starting points, places where you can say, "It all started here," or "This is where it began." But that's not the whole of it, either—because each of those starting points is the ending of another story, which has a beginning somewhere else, which is the ending of yet another story. It's like a vine. Sometimes you can't untangle it.

So when I tell you that this story begins on the Monday morning of Thanksgiving week, it's because I have to start somewhere, and that day is as good as any other. I remember that particular day because my herb shop is closed on Mondays and I was taking the opportunity to do some restocking and decorating for the coming holiday season. Up until that moment, it had been a very ordinary day, full of the ordinary kinds of Monday things. I was standing on the stepladder, making room on the wall for the half-dozen wreaths that had just arrived, when the phone rang—the phone call that pulled me into a chain of events that wouldn't end until three people were dead.

Over my shoulder, I called to Ruby Wilcox, who was unpacking a big box beside the counter. "Hey, Ruby, get that, would you?"

"Why?" Ruby asked, taking a box cutter to a large cardboard carton. "We're closed. Let the machine pick up."

"It could be Brian. I called to remind him about Thanksgiving dinner at the ranch." My stepson is a freshman at the University of Texas, and corralling him for family get-togethers is not an easy business. I have to make a date with him weeks ahead, and then remind him—more than once. In this case, though, I knew he wanted to be reminded. Thanksgiving at my mother's South Texas ranch has become a family tradition. It's something we look forward to.

"On it," Ruby said, and reached for the phone.

I cocked my head to one side, surveying the wall, pleased that I'd been able to clear enough space to hang at least four of the six beautiful twenty-four-inch bittersweet wreaths that Ruby was unpacking. They'd been sent by a Michigan wreath maker I had recently met online, and I was anxious to put them up. Bittersweet isn't available locally, and these were gorgeous. They would probably be gone by the weekend.

I straightened a holly wreath, tweaked a burlap bow, then climbed back down the ladder. "Brian?" I mouthed to Ruby, who was holding the cordless phone to her ear.

She shook her head, said, "Here she is, Leatha," and handed me the phone, then went tactfully back to work.

"Hey, Mom." I leaned against the counter. "What's up?"

There was a time when a telephone call from my mother would have sent me into a near-fatal tailspin. My childhood memories of her are blurry, as if I'm seeing her in a foggy mirror, but my grownup bitterness was sharp edged and painful. All that stuff you read about difficult, dysfunctional mother-daughter relationships? It's all true, what you've heard, at least where mine was concerned. It was dysfunctional to the core. My mother was an alcoholic.

But as Leatha would say, she is a *recovering* alcoholic, and we've become closer since she went clean and straight. We survived a terrifying family crisis a few years ago, when we discovered that Leatha's aunt Tully was suffering from Huntington's disease, a fatal genetic neurological disorder, and it looked like my mother and I were in line to inherit it. (Thankfully, not.) There'd been another crisis after that, when some of the mysteries around my father's death—his murder, as it turned out—were exhumed. I learned that I had a half brother I'd never met, the product of my father's decades-long extramarital affair with a woman who wasn't my mother. Leatha and I managed somehow to muddle through all that messy stuff together, and since then, things have been better. Not idyllic, of course. Just . . . better.

"I'm so glad I caught you, China," Leatha said, in that sweet Southern voice that pours through you like warm honey. She grew up in Mississippi, on a plantation in the Delta Country of the Yazoo River. Jordan's Crossing is gone now, sold to pay for Aunt Tully's nursing care. But some part of the place still lives on in my mother. I can hear it in her accent.

Like most Southern women, my mother was taught to keep unpleasantness at bay for as long as possible. But today, she sounded anxious. "I'm afraid I've got bad news," she said, almost as if she were apologizing. "It's . . . it's Sam. He's in the hospital."

My heart began to thump. Sam Richards, my mother's second husband, is the nearest thing I have to a real father. He's thoughtful, affectionate, caring—everything my own father wasn't—and I've grown to love him.

"Uh-oh," I said, pulling in my breath. "Oh, Mom, I'm so sorry. What was it? An accident? Is he going to be all right?"

Leatha and Sam live on a 3,000-acre ranch on the Sabinal River in Uvalde County, not far from the little town of Utopia in south central Texas. Sam inherited the ranch from his father, who for most of his life raised registered cattle, aiming to preserve the breed. In his later years, though, the elder Mr. Richards imported a dozen species of rare African game animals and sold hunting leases—permission to hunt on the land for a day, a specific season (deer season, for example), or a year or more—to wealthy men who wanted the adventure of shooting wild game.

That had been Sam's scheme, too. When he and Leatha got married a few years ago, they added a couple of units to the hunting lodge his father had built on the ranch in the 1970s and began advertising exotic game hunts. It was a successful enterprise until last year, when Sam decided he no longer wanted to be involved with what some people call "canned hunts"—shooting animals that are confined on a fenced game ranch until they're mature enough to be killed for the shooter's trophy collection. He and Leatha named their place the Bittersweet Nature Sanctuary, for the clear, spring-fed Bittersweet Creek that flows into the Sabinal River near the ranch house. They renovated the old lodge, put up a website, and plan to open the new enterprise in the spring to eco-tourists and vacationers who are interested in birding, a passion that Sam and my mother share. Uvalde County, on the southern escarpment of the Edwards Plateau and the northern edge of the South Texas Brush Country, is remarkably eco-diverse. It's a mecca for birders.

"No, it wasn't an accident," my mother replied. I could hear the tautness in her voice, like a violin string pulled tight and vibrating. "It's his heart, China. They did surgery, but there've been . . . well, complications."

His *heart*? Complications? I shuddered. Sam is a strong man, an outdoor man, fit, active, energetic. But a bad heart can cut even a tough guy down to size very quickly. "Where is he? *How* is he? Will he be okay?"

"He's in Kerrville. It's a good hospital, and good doctors. But they won't know how he is, really, for a day or two."

"I'll come down the way we planned," I said, thinking ahead. "But you won't want our bunch for Thanksgiving. It'll be too much." Since she married Sam, my mother had surprised me with her resilience. But I've known her a long time, and I know that she is more fragile than she seems. She has a breaking point. Maybe I don't trust her enough, but I'm always aware that too much pressure might endanger her hard-won sobriety. Worrying about Sam might tip her over the edge.

"No!" she exclaimed. Then, more quietly, "No. Sam is very firm about this, China. He's insisting that we have our family Thanksgiving, just as we always do. He says he'd feel even worse if we cancel just because he can't be there. In fact, we'd already invited another guest—Mackenzie Chambers, our local game warden. Sam met her at a ranchers' meeting a couple of months ago, and we've had her out to the ranch a time or two. When she told me that she'd lived in Pecan Springs, I asked if she knew you and she said yes. She has no family here—and she's looking forward to seeing you again."

"Goes for me, too," I said. Until a few months ago, Mack had been a game warden here in Adams County. I first met her through a friend, Sheila Dawson, the Pecan Springs chief of police, who had a high opinion of Mack's investigative skills. Sheila and Mack had worked together on a case or two. Then Mack and I became friends and saw each other often—in fact, for a while, Brian and I babysat her collection of turtle shells, which her ex-husband Lanny didn't appreciate, in the same way he didn't appreciate most of Mack's interests. Since she moved, we kept in touch via email.

"But I can see Mack later," I went on. "I'm sure we'd all understand if you canceled. You don't have to do this, you know. Or, if it would be easier, I can come down by myself. I want to see Sam."

"But it's Thanksgiving and I want our *family*," she protested. In a more upbeat voice, she added, "Anyway, the worst of it will be over by then. Sam won't be home, but at least he'll be out of the woods. And of course you can see him—although you have something already planned for Friday in Utopia, don't you?"

"Well, yes," I conceded. "I'm supposed to bring a load of plants for Jennie Seale's garden." Jennie is expanding her small restaurant just outside Utopia—Jennie's Kitchen—and plans to have an herb garden all around the patio dining area. We'd already drawn up the planting diagram, and I had special-ordered many of the plants. Most were perennials, and this was the perfect time of year to get them settled in the ground. They'd be rarin' to grow come spring.

"That settles it, then," my mother said firmly. "You and I will go into Kerrville on Thanksgiving morning and visit Sam. We can have our family dinner on Thanksgiving evening. When are you coming?"

"I thought Caitie and I would drive down Wednesday afternoon, so we can help with the pies and other stuff. Oh, and she wants to bring her cat. Is that okay?" Caitie—Caitlin—is my twelve-year-old niece. My husband, Mike McQuaid, and I adopted her a couple of years ago. She's very dear to my mother, even though she's the daughter of my father's illegitimate son. (I know. It's complicated. But then, most families are, aren't they?)

"Of course it's okay," Leatha said. "Are Ruby and Cass minding the shop while you're gone?"

"Yes, with some extra help in the tearoom. We're closed on Thanksgiving, of course, and my friend Sharon Turner is coming in to give them a hand on Friday and Saturday." That's the beauty of having two shops, side by side in the same building with the tearoom. We don't abuse the privilege, but when one of us really needs a break, we stand in for each other. Ruby took off during the long Labor Day weekend. Cass, who does all the cooking, was gone for a couple of weeks in the summer. This week, it was my turn. We also share part-time helpers, like Sharon, whom everyone calls Miss T. Now a retired schoolteacher, Miss T used to be a caterer, so she's a big help in the kitchen and the tearoom, as well as in both our shops. She gave a couple of classes for us last summer in drying herbs and using them in the kitchen.

"McQuaid has an all-day meeting in Austin on Wednesday," I added, "so he'll pick Brian up on the campus and they'll drive down together on Thanksgiving. They need to go back together on Friday, too."

"I can't wait to see y'all," my mother said softly. "Especially you, dear. It's been too long."

"You're right," I said. There wasn't a hint of accusation in her voice, but that didn't blunt the sharp-pointed guilt that jabbed me. It *had* been a while since we were together, which I admit is largely my fault. I've never been a terribly dutiful daughter, and when Sam arrived on the scene and made it clear (very sweetly) that his new wife was *his* responsibility, it was easy to let him have his way. That, and the fact that McQuaid and the kids and the business and the gardens keep me busy all day long, every day. I get annoyed at the cozy mysteries where the shop owner leaves her business for days at a time to go sleuthing. Never think that being your own boss means that you can take off whenever the spirit moves you. It doesn't, and you can't.

"All right, then," my mother said. "I may be at the hospital with Sam when you get there, but you know where to find the key."

"I could stop at the hospital in Kerrville," I said. "It's on our way."

"No, you and Caitie just go on to the ranch and make yourself at home. We'll see Sam on Thanksgiving."

"Okay, then," I said. "And Mom, love and kisses to Sam. Tell him we're all thinking of him and hoping he can go home soon." I put down the phone.

Ruby was lifting a wreath out of the carton. "Is everything okay?" she asked, looking at me with concern. "What's going on with your mother?"

"It's not my mother," I said. "It's Sam. He's—"

But before I finish answering Ruby's question, maybe I'd better fill in some background. I know that some of you are frequent visitors to Ruby's shop and mine, but this may be a first visit for others. If you're new here and feeling puzzled, a little of the backstory may fill in some of the blanks. If you already know all this stuff, feel free to skip the next few paragraphs.

I'm China Bayles, owner and manager of Thyme and Seasons Herb Shop in Pecan Springs, Texas, a small town at the eastern edge of the Texas Hill Country, halfway between Austin and San Antonio. In my previous life, I was a criminal defense attorney for a big law firm in Houston, living a fast-track, dressed-for-success life that was full of close calls, narrow squeaks, and hair-trigger excitement—both in the courtroom and out. There was always something going on—and enough going for me that you'd think I would have been fully satisfied.

But after a few years, the people around me began to seem superficial, artificial, even phony. Nobody said what they meant or meant what they said, and I began to want something genuine, something authentic, something *real*. I wanted real friendships, a real relationship. And real work, where I could put out my hand and touch real things that had their own real lives, not just briefs and pleadings and court documents, words, words, words. Finally, after months of soul searching, I cashed in my retirement fund, kicked off my Pradas, took a deep breath, and jumped ship.

I landed in Pecan Springs, where I bought the herb business I'd been eyeing for some months—a lovely little shop, which is looking particularly festive at the moment. Ceiling-high shelves along the back wall display jars and bottles of dried herbs, salves, and tinctures. There are dozens of herb, gardening, and cookery books on the corner bookshelves, and on a wooden table, I've arranged essential oils, a display of pretty bottles, and aromatherapy supplies. Along another wall are herbal jellies, vinegars, seasoning blends, soaps and lotions and body balms. Baskets of dried herbs are arranged in the corners, bundles of dried plants are tucked into jars and hung from the overhead beams, and holiday wreaths and swags are displayed on the stone walls of the old building. When people walk in, they go "Ahhh," very quietly, and smile. I understand. I live with that lovely "Ahhh" feeling all day long.

A few years after I bought the shop, I married Mike McQuaid, formerly a Houston homicide detective, now a part-time faculty member in the Criminal Justice Department at Central Texas State University and an independent private investigator in McQuaid, Blackwell, and Associates. I knew him as McQuaid when I met him, professionally, and that's what I've continued to call him. A hunk of a guy, really, in spite of his broken nose and the knife scar on his forehead, earned on the mean streets of Houston. He had a young son, Brian, and then Caitlin came along. Life has become *very* full and satisfying.

Okay, that's me. The six-foot-plus, red-haired gal with the box cutter in one hand and the wreath in the other is Ruby Wilcox, my business partner. Ruby's nose is liberally speckled with sandy freckles, her eyes are sometimes brown, sometimes blue or green (depending on which contacts she's wearing), and she has Julia Roberts' mouth. She has two daughters, Shannon Wilcox, who coaches girls' sports at Bowie High in

Austin, and Amy Roth, who lives and works here in Pecan Springs. Amy and her partner, Kate Rodriguez, have a three-year-old girl, Grace, a plump, pretty strawberry blonde who is Ruby's joy and proud delight.

Ruby owns Pecan Springs' only New Age shop, the Crystal Cave, right next door to Thyme and Seasons. The Cave is the place to go if you're looking for books on astrology, runes or crystals for divination, or a class in how to throw the *I Ching*. And if you can't read your tarot card layout or your Ouija board won't answer your questions, Ruby is there to help. Her strong psychic sense—her "gift," people call it, although Ruby herself sometimes sees it as a curse—manifests itself every now and then, as it did recently, when she helped a friend do a little ghost-busting in a mysterious old house way out in the country. I am by nature a logical, rational, skeptical, cut-to-the-chase kind of person, and it's hard for me to swallow most claims of the supernatural. But Ruby has been right so often that when she turns psychic on me, all I can do is shake my head and mutter, "You go, girl." And then stand back and see what happens.

But Ruby is also a practical businesswoman. Thyme for Tea, the tearoom that's located behind our shops, was her idea, and she invited her friend Cass Wilde to sign on as chef. After that, she came up with Party Thyme, our catering service. Then she thought it would be a good plan for us to partner with Cass in a personal chef business called the Thymely Gourmet. "Bundled services" is the way Ruby describes it: offering related products and services to customers who already know and trust us. It's true that I sometimes feel as if I'm one of a trio of maniac clowns who are juggling a half-dozen pins, balls, and rings, trying not very successfully to keep them all in the air at the same time. But Ruby and Cass and I have learned that the more we do, the more we *can* do, and that if we want to stay in business in this challenging economy, we'd better have more up our sleeve than a single trick.

"Sam?" Ruby asked with a frown. "What's going on with him?"

"Heart trouble," I said, and related as much as I knew. "He's insisting that we carry on as usual," I added, "so there's no change in plans on this end. I'll be back Sunday night—at least, if everything goes okay with Sam." I paused, not wanting to think what might happen if things didn't go okay.

"I'm so sorry, China," Ruby said. "Sam has been good for your mother."

"He's been a lifesaver," I said fervently. After a moment, I went on. "I hope you won't be needing Mama over the weekend. I have a load of plants to take down to Utopia for Jennie Seale's garden."

Big Red Mama is the used panel van we bought several years ago to haul our catering stuff, as well as plants. Mama's former owner was a hippie artist named Gerald who was arrested for cooking crystal meth. The Hays County sheriff's office impounded his van, and it ended up in the county's vehicle auction. Ruby and I were attracted to Mama because she was cheap and because of the wild swirl of colorful Art Deco designs that Gerald (probably under the influence of a certain psychoactive herb) painted on her modest red sides. Ruby says that Mama looks like a cross between a Crayola box on wheels and a Sweet Potato Queen float on the way to a parade.

"Nope, Cass and I won't need Mama," Ruby said. "You can take her." She turned the large yellow orange wreath in her hands, eyeing it admiringly. "China, I absolutely *love* this. It's the prettiest bittersweet wreath I've ever seen. Just look—it's simply loaded with berries. I'm going to buy it for my front door at home."

"Hang on a minute," I said, taking the wreath from her and examining it closely. "This is not so good."

"Not so good? What are you talking about?" Ruby snatched the wreath back. "It's extra pretty, don't you think? It's kind of two-tone, with all those bright orange berries and pretty yellow thingies. It looks exactly like the one Martha Stewart made on her TV show. I love it. I want it. Your customers are going to want one, too. You just wait and see."

"They can't have it." I pulled a second wreath out of the carton and looked at it closely, and then a third, and then the rest. "I'm sorry to disappoint you, but Martha Stewart used the wrong bittersweet. All these wreaths are going back to the woman who made them. I'm recommending that she burn them."

"Burn them!" Ruby was staring at me, eyes wide, aghast. "But *why*?"

"Because this isn't American bittersweet. It's *Oriental* bittersweet." I pointed to a berry cluster. "These pretty yellow thingies? They're the capsules that have dried and split open to reveal the orange fruit inside. If this were our native bittersweet, the capsules would be orange, too. And look at the way the fruits are positioned all along the branches, at the leaf nodes. In American bittersweet, the fruits only occur at the tips of the branches."

Ruby rolled her eyes. "Orange, yellow—so what? What's so bad about Oriental bittersweet? You're worried that somebody forgot to pay customs duties? Anyway, I thought these wreaths came from Michigan, not Asia."

"Yep, they do come from Michigan," I said grimly. I was lifting the other wreaths out of the carton. When I had examined them all, I began putting them back again. "Which is really bad, because it's illegal to sell or ship Oriental bittersweet in or out of Michigan—and several other states, as well. This plant is a thug. A bully. A ruthless, aggressive, nonnative species that was introduced as an ornamental around the time of the Civil War and escaped into the wild. It loves to climb up shrubs and trees and smother them. And it hybridizes with the native bittersweet, which makes it even more thuggish."

"Illegal?" Ruby pushed her lips in and out, considering. "Well, maybe. But aren't you overreacting? There's not a chance in the world that this *dried* stuff is going to smother the trees in my yard. It'll just hang quietly on my front door and look pretty." She picked up the top wreath and smiled at me. "I want this one. How much?"

I pulled off a dried berry and held it up. "See that? What is it?"

Ruby frowned. "So it's a berry. So what? It's not poisonous, is it?"

"It's a *seed,* Ruby. This pretty little package is a genetic time bomb."

"A . . . time bomb?" Ruby asked warily.

"Exactly. It's not very likely to go off here in Texas, since this isn't the plant's ideal habitat. But what happens if somebody buys this wreath in my shop and decides to give it to her sister, who lives in Arkansas, or maybe Missouri? The sister hangs it over her mantel until the pretty orange berries begin to drop off, then tosses it on her compost pile. The next year, a dozen little green seedlings pop up. The year after that, a dozen not-so-pretty green vines are twining around the nearest shrub. The year after that, Katy, bar the door. Once this hoodlum moves into the neighborhood, there's no getting rid of it."

Ruby shook her head. "That is too bad. Really."

"Yes, it is. Very bad." I put the wreath back in the box and closed it firmly, to keep those genetic time bombs from escaping. "I think I'll email this woman and tell her that it would be simpler and cheaper if I'd just burn these here. It would save her some shipping. And I'm sure the state of Michigan would prefer never to see them again."

"I guess you know what you're doing." Ruby gave me a rueful look. "Speaking of bombs, I'm sort of in trouble, and I was hoping you could help."

"In trouble?" I chuckled dryly. "So what else is new? You're in trouble at least three times a week."

"Don't be that way," Ruby said.

"What way?" I pulled my laptop out from under the counter and booted it up.

"You know," Ruby replied, wounded. "*That* way."

"I'm sorry," I said, repenting. "That was uncalled-for." True, but uncalled-for. And after all, she was babysitting my shop while I was gone. "I've got your back, sweetie. Tell me what I can do."

"You can go down to city hall and apply for a permit for the yarn bombing on Crockett Street." She pressed her lips together. "The application was due early last week, but I got busy and forgot all about it. The Six Chix have been knitting up a storm, and we're ready to start bombing, but if we don't get that permit, we could get arrested." She shifted uncomfortably. "I'd do it, but they don't like me over there. At city hall, I mean. I'm sure they'll like you better."

"Yarn *bombing*?" I was doubtful. "You have to file an application to bomb yarn? What are you bombing it *with*? *Why* are you bombing it?"

"Yarn bombing is street art. Like graffiti, only with yarn."

"Yarn graffiti? Like, yarn instead of spray paint?"

Ruby nodded. "Grandma graffiti. Guerilla fiber art. It all started over in Houston, when a boutique owner knitted a pink and blue cozy for her shop doorknob. People noticed. Then she knitted a leg warmer for the stop sign on the corner. A lot more people noticed that one."

"I'll bet they did," I muttered. I was looking for the wreath maker's email address.

"She bombed trees and bushes and traffic signs. And then the *New York Times* wrote about her and she began getting corporate commissions to do great big projects, like the Christmas sweater she knitted for a Prius a couple of years ago, and the parking meter cozies she knitted for a downtown shopping district in Brooklyn. Now lots of people are doing yarn bombings."

"A sweater for a Prius?" I asked warily. "I hope you're not thinking of knitting a pullover for Big Red Mama."

Ruby shook her head. "No, we're knitting tree-trunk warmers. You know, like leg warmers, except they're for trees. And it's not just me; it's my knitting group. The Six Chix with Pointy Stix. We're going to bomb some of the trees in this block of Crockett as a holiday project. Everybody gets tired of knitting sweaters and socks, you know."

"I suppose," I conceded. Ah, there was the address of the lady in Michigan, where I'd ordered bittersweet. *American* bittersweet. "Once you've knitted one sock, you've knitted them all. And bombing sounds like a good way to use up your yarn stash."

"Oh, it's that, all right," Ruby agreed enthusiastically. "And I've got a ton of yarn, in all colors of the rainbow. Anyway, the other Chix and I thought we could just *do* it—as an art project, I mean. Something to make everybody smile during the holidays, especially the customers who are shopping on Crockett."

That would be our customers, and customers of the Hobbit House children's bookstore next door, the Craft Emporium on the corner, and the restaurant across the street. Our block of Crockett is host to several attractive venues.

Ruby was continuing. "But then we found out that we had to get a permit at city hall, and when I went to get it, the woman who handles the permits—Mrs. Dillinger—had never heard of yarn bombing. When I told her about it, she decided it was vandalism."

"Ah," I said.

"Or littering. She said she'd never issue a permit for something so adolescent. She was really quite insulting." She made a face. "That's when I got . . . well, sort of excited. I was rude. I . . . yelled at her." When Ruby gets excited and yells, she is awesome.

Ruby went on. "The next day, one of the Chix went to the city council and showed them some photos of yarn-bombed fire hydrants in Seattle and park benches and statues in Chicago. The council overruled Mrs. Dillinger and said that yarn bombing isn't vandalism, it's art. They told her to accept our application." Ruby's shoulders sagged. "I was supposed to get it in by last Friday, but I forgot. And I was . . . well, pretty rude. I'm afraid she's going to hold it against me, personally. She'll use my being late as an excuse to deny the permit."

"So what you want me to do is—"

"Go over to city hall and talk to her. Apologize for being late. Explain that the Chix are ready to start and we really need that permit. And be very nice, would you? Being nice would go a long way toward easing the situation."

"I can be nice," I said, and finished typing my email. It was polite but firm. "Maybe I'd better call first, though, and make sure Mrs. Whatsit is going to be in the office."

"Dillinger, as in the bank robber. Oh, and tell her that you'll be paying the twenty-five-dollar fee. I'll give you a check."

"Works for me." I hit the *Send* button and the email flew off into cyberspace. I was bending over, looking for the phone book under the counter, when I heard the bell over the shop door tinkle. "Sorry, we're closed today," I said, without looking up. I must've forgotten to lock the door when I came in.

"It's just me," a light voice said.

"Oh, hi, Amy," Ruby chirped brightly. "I thought you'd be at work this morning."

I straightened up, the phone book in my hand. "Hello, Amy," I said. "Nice to see you."

It was Ruby's wild child. Amy, now nearly thirty, is her mother's look-alike, although she isn't quite so tall and has many more piercings than Ruby, and several more tattoos. (Actually, Ruby has only one, a fern and flower tattooed across half her chest, where one breast used to be. She sacrificed it to a mastectomy several years ago.) When she was still a teenager, Ruby gave birth to Amy out of wedlock and—at her own mother's behest—gave the baby up for adoption. But when Amy grew up, she did an adoptive search, located her mother, and came back into Ruby's life.

And that was just the beginning, for it turns out that Amy, an animal activist and active conservationist, never does anything the easy, conventional way. It wasn't long before she surprised us with the announcement that she was pregnant and had decided to keep the baby. Ruby was still coming to terms with the fact that she was about to become a grandmother when Amy declared that she was moving in with her friend and lover, Kate Rodriguez. Wild child indeed.

But Amy's relationship with Kate has settled her down. The three of them—Kate, Amy, and Grace—are a family. Kate owns her own successful accounting business, and Amy works as a veterinary assistant at the Hill Country Animal Clinic. The wild child has grown up.

"I'm going in late because I have to work late this evening," Amy said.

"Listen, Mom—I wonder if you'd mind keeping Grace this weekend? Kate has to drive up to Oklahoma City for Thanksgiving with her mother, and I'd like to see a . . . a friend in San Antonio. I'll be back on Sunday."

"There's nothing I'd like better, dear." Ruby spoke without hesitation. "I'll be here at the shop on Saturday, but Grace can come with me. Miss T will be here, and she's always a big help."

Amy grinned. "I like Miss T. I wonder what color her hair will be this time." Sharon is quite a character. Her hair has been white since she was in her twenties, and she changes the color almost as often as some people change their minds.

Ruby nodded. "You'll be with us for Thanksgiving, won't you? Shannon and her fiancé are coming, and I'm roasting a turkey for the gang. But for you, dear, I'm baking a vegan Thanksgiving loaf with lentils, millet, and rice. And a very tasty vegan gravy."

"Of course I'll be there," Amy said with a grin. She was wearing her favorite bloodred *Meat Is Murder* T-shirt, advertising her animal activism. In fact, I first met her when she was trying to shut down an animal experiment at CTSU, along with other protestors from People for the Ethical Treatment of Animals. "And that lentil loaf sounds terrific," she added. "Want me to bring anything?"

"Just yourself—and Grace, of course," Ruby replied. "Who's your friend?" she added in a studiedly offhand tone that didn't quite conceal her curiosity. "The one you're going to see in San Antonio."

Amy colored. "Oh, just . . . just somebody I met through PETA," she said vaguely. "Nobody you know." I got the impression that Amy wasn't anxious to name her friend, but she probably just didn't want to feed her mother's inquisitiveness.

"Well, okay," Ruby said with a little be-that-way shrug. "So I'll see you and Grace on Thursday. And I'll keep Grace over the rest of the weekend. We'll have all kinds of fun."

"Thanks so much, Mom. I really appreciate it. You're a peach." Amy gave her a quick hug and turned to me. "Will you and Mike and the kids be at Mom's for Thanksgiving?"

I shook my head. "We're going down to the ranch." I held up the phone. "Right now, I'd better make this call. I'd hate for your mom to be arrested before she can whomp up your vegan loaf."

"Arrested?" Amy turned to look at Ruby. "Arrested for *what*?"

"Bombing yarn," I said, and went back to the phone book.

"Yarn bombing," Ruby corrected me. "Street art," she said to her daughter. "Grandma graffiti. China is going to get a permit for the Six Chix with Pointy Stix to knit trunk warmers for some of the trees along Crockett Street."

Amy blinked. "O-kay," she said slowly. "If you say so." She headed toward the door. "Have a good one, you guys. And thanks, Mom, for keeping Grace over the weekend."

"I'm glad to," Ruby said cheerfully. But when the door had swung shut behind Amy, she turned to me. "I'm not getting good vibes about this, China," she said uneasily.

"About what?" I asked absently, running my finger down the list of city phone numbers, looking for Mrs. Dillinger, in the yarn-bombing department.

"About Amy's weekend plans. I don't like . . ." She gave me an apprehensive glance. "I don't like this friend. This guy she's going to meet in San Antonio. He's got dangerous ideas. There's going to be trouble. Serious trouble."

I looked up from the phone book, curious. "How do you know he's a he? Amy didn't say—"

"She didn't have to." She gave me a long look, as if she might be about to tell me something, but sighed and turned away.

I understood then. Ruby's gift had given her a glimpse of something she didn't want to see, something that she was afraid might happen over the coming weekend.

But I wasn't going to ask her what it was. To tell the truth, I'd rather not know.

Chapter Two

Rifle in hand, Mackenzie Chambers opened the passenger door of her state-issued Ford F-150 and whistled for Molly. Pink tongue lolling, the blue heeler loped from the bushes where she'd been taking care of her early-morning business and jumped eagerly into the truck. An Australian cattle dog bred to keep the herd moving in the right direction, Molly had a heavy-duty sense of responsibility. She knew when it was time to go to work and had to be reminded when it was time to quit—a little bit like herself, Mack reflected ruefully, as she shut the truck door. A personality characteristic that her former husband, Lanny, hadn't liked and one of the reasons they were now divorced.

Mack walked slowly around the dark green Ford pickup truck, noticing that there was mud on the grill and a big splash on the Texas Parks and Wildlife logo on the driver's door. There'd been rain the previous weekend, and her night patrols had taken her down some sloppy roads. She probably ought to run the truck through the car wash—Utopia's only car wash, at the Pico convenience store, Utopia's only gas station. After a couple of weeks of unseasonably warm temperatures, the November air had a frosty bite, and the clipped grass of her small front yard was glazed with silver in the last light of the full moon that was setting over the wooded hills west of town. The thermometer had dropped to just below freezing during the night.

But the weather guy on KSAT-TV in San Antonio, some seventy crow miles away, was forecasting a high in the upper 50s and partly cloudy skies with scattered showers through the rest of the week—good hunting weather. Deer season was three weeks old, and with the Thanksgiving weekend coming up, she would be patrolling the hills and canyons of northern Uvalde County—her third of the county's nearly 1,600 square miles. The other 1,000 square miles were split between wardens Bert Jenkins and Dusty Ross, her comrades-in-arms. Their District Two boss, headquartered in San Antonio, always talked about them as if they were a team, but their patrol areas were so large that there wasn't much chance for teamwork. Most of the time they were on their own. If one of them radioed for backup, they were likely to get the nearest deputy sheriff.

And vice versa. Just after midnight a couple of weeks ago, a Uvalde County deputy had been alerted to a copper theft in progress at a construction site on the Old Leakey Road, east of Garner State Park. He apprehended two of the thieves, but the third fled in an old black pickup. Happening to be on patrol in the area, Mack had picked up the dispatch on her radio, spotted the suspect with a roll of copper wire in the back of his vehicle, and stopped him. He gave her a little trouble, but her martial arts training came in handy, along with the fact that she was trim and fit from jogging and weight training and he was your basic six-pack-a-day couch potato, two-twenty-plus and slow on his feet. She had him on the ground with her knee in his back and was cuffing him as another deputy arrived on the scene. Last she'd heard, two of the thieves had bonded out, but her guy was still in the county jail charged with copper theft, criminal trespass, and resisting arrest.

Mack didn't much like that part of the job, but it came with the territory. In Texas, wardens and sheriffs' deputies alike were peace officers, with similar duties, similar armament and vehicles, and similar training—except that the deputies didn't have to know as much about the state and federal wildlife regs as the wardens did. In addition to the 600-plus hours Mack had put in to get her peace officer certification, her curriculum included another 750 hours of instruction at the Game Warden Training Academy. And all this on top of her undergraduate major in Criminal Justice and a Wildlife Biology minor from Sam Houston State. Texas Parks and Wildlife liked to brag that its game wardens were the best-trained conservation officers in the entire United States. From what Mack had observed of her fellow wardens in the five years since she'd graduated from the Academy, that was pretty much on the mark.

Next door, the rooster who lorded it over her neighbor's flock of hens noticed the first brush of pink in the sky and cheerfully unfurled his dawn song. From the grassy paddock behind the house (one of the reasons she liked this little place), Cheyenne, Mack's paint quarter horse, nickered softly, and a couple of backyards down the block, a neighbor's sorrel mare replied with a pleasant whinny. The two horses often seemed to communicate, Mack had noticed, like friends gossiping across the back fence about what was going on in the neighborhood. *Did you see that Bartlett kid with his BB gun? Deliberately shot out the garage window and claimed it was an accident. And how about Sam Gruber—drunk again on Saturday night. If I were Mrs. Gruber, I'd leave him.* Cheyenne needed exercise, but since hunting season began, there hadn't been time to ride her—and there wouldn't be time until the hoopla was over, at the end of January.

Mack set her coffee mug into the truck's cup holder. Then she paused beside the open passenger door to do a quick equipment check. The dash-mounted GPS, light-control switch box, and radio were in working order. The console held her log and map folder, spotting scope, binoculars, and flashlight, along with a digital camera, mini-cassette recorder, and first-aid and evidence kits. Her rain gear and highway flares were under the seat, along with a spare flashlight, extra batteries, and a basic truck tool kit. Her AR-15 was already locked into the cab ceiling rack. Like all wardens, she spent most of her waking hours in her truck. She tried to keep stuff stowed neatly and the trash shoveled out.

She opened the door of the rear cab and dropped her insulated lunch pack and thermos of hot chocolate on the floor. Designed to transport prisoners, the truck's rear cab was separated from the front by a sturdy cage-wire panel and a bullet-proof sliding glass pane, and the doors couldn't be opened from the inside. She straightened up and checked her duty belt: her holstered .40 caliber 15-round Glock 22, handcuffs, pepper spray, Maglite, disposable gloves, and handy multi-tool—the Leatherman that had belonged to her father.

Satisfied that she hadn't forgotten anything, she slid onto the seat, flipped open her patrol log, and noted the date (11/22), time (0500), and weather (clear, 30F). She'd gotten into the habit of recording the weather after she discovered that it helped her to remember incidents more clearly when it came time to write up the full report on the computer back in her office, the second bedroom of her tiny, two-bedroom house.

"Ready to hit the road, Molly?" She smiled at the dog perched on the passenger seat. In answer, Molly wagged her butt—like most ranch dogs, her tail had been docked so it wouldn't get stepped on by a cow or a horse or caught in a gate. In this kind of weather, Molly got to do ride-alongs several times a week. Summer was a different story. It was against regulations to leave the truck and the AC running when she made a stop, and the temp in the cab could reach triple digits in a matter of minutes. In the summer, Molly had to stay home.

Mack started the truck and backed out of the driveway. She drove up Oak Street, then turned onto Lee and then onto Main, automatically slowing as she drove past the general store. She noticed the three battered pickups lined up fender to fender in front and guessed that Cal, Jerky, and Butch—three old-timers who started every day but Sunday with a companionable cup of java—were already gathered around the coffeepot in the back of the store, where she could see a faint light.

A couple of doors down, though, the Lost Maples Café was still dark, and there were no vehicles parked in front. In fact, the street was deserted, although in another hour, the café would be doing a land-office business—rightfully so, for the breakfast tacos were pretty good, especially the taco called "The Kitchen Sink." The Sink had everything—generous helpings of eggs, potatoes, cheese, onions, ham, sausage, bacon, and jalapeños, wrapped neatly in a flour tortilla about as big as the hubcap on her truck and served with a salsa that was hot enough to melt the fillings in your teeth. But it was the pie that most folks came for—homemade cherry pie, buttermilk pie, banana cream pie, and more. The laminated legend on the napkin holder said "Pie fixes everything," and Mack agreed.

Mack also agreed with the village motto, "Utopia Is a Paradise: Let's Keep It Nice." It was only a couple of hundred souls. The county seat, Uvalde, was forty-five miles to the southwest, and the nearest city, Kerrville, was sixty miles to the northeast, both on hilly, winding two-lanes. But Mack had no complaints. She had never been a lover of crowded urban-suburban areas, especially after spending several years in Adams County, which was sliced by I-35 and studded with shopping malls and strip centers.

Not coincidentally, the assignment to Uvalde County came the week after her divorce from Lanny and the sale of their condo some seven months before, so moving from Pecan Springs to Utopia had brought a new beginning in more ways than one. She was working in the prettiest county in the whole state (in her opinion), and living in a sweet little rental house, although she'd be the first to admit that she hadn't had time to get proper furniture or even hang curtains at the windows. She'd gotten Cheyenne, her first horse since the gelding she'd shared with her father and two younger brothers. And she'd adopted Molly. (Lanny had been mauled by a neighbor's bulldog as a kid and refused to have a dog in the house.)

And she had met Derek Mitford, a good-looking man with a quirky eyebrow, dark hair that fell over his forehead, and a deep cleft in his chin. His wife, he said, had died of cancer several years ago. He and his daughters had come from a suburb of St. Louis, where he'd worked in an investment bank. They'd just moved into the new house he'd built on a small ranch outside of town.

Mack and Derek had been introduced by Jack Krause at the café several weeks before. A broad-shouldered man with thick, curly brown hair, Jack was the assistant foreman at Three Gates Game Ranch. He had given Mack, the new game warden, the grand tour of Three Gates the month before, showing her the ranch's deer-breeding facilities and the feeding stations and the air-conditioned blinds. The visit was a duty call and Mack was not impressed. She disliked the whole idea of breeding trophy white-tails and charging wealthy hunters thousands of dollars to sit in a blind and shoot them when they showed up at the feeder. She disliked Jack, too, although she couldn't put her finger on why, except that he reminded her of a bully who had given her a hard time back in seventh grade.

But she liked Derek. He might look like a dude rancher in his suede vest and Tony Lama Boots, but he seemed to have an enormous appreciation for the town and everybody in it. "Utopia," he'd mused, after Jack had gone off and they found themselves sitting with coffee and pie (pecan fudge for him and chocolate meringue for her) at the booth in the corner of the café. "I picked this place because of the name. Utopia. Came down here, looked around, and loved it. Perfect name for a perfect little town. Nice to be in a place where everybody's got roots, don't you think? And where everybody knows all about everybody else and all their relatives."

"I like the idea of roots," Mack agreed cautiously, although she was less sure about everybody knowing all about everybody else. She liked her privacy. And while she liked Utopia, she didn't for a moment think it was perfect.

"I couldn't make it way out here in the boonies if it weren't for the Internet, though," Derek had added, picking up his Green Bay Packers coffee mug. Mack's mug was red and said "Shh, there's beer in here." The mugs at the café, like the vintage fifties tables and chairs, were gleefully mismatched. "I've got my office set up so I can be in touch with the financial markets all day long, the way I was in St. Louis. And then I come into this place"—he gestured around the café—"and it's like going back to the 1940s. Best of both worlds." He pointed to the little sign on the table. "Maybe pie really does fix everything," he said with a laugh.

She noticed that his hands and nails were nicely cared for—city hands, she thought. Self-consciously, she hid hers, which were not city hands, by any stretch. And when he asked what she did for a living, she said casually, "I work with Texas Parks and Wildlife." It was her day off, and she was wearing jeans and a yellow plaid shirt instead of her uniform, and her dark hair was loose around her shoulders, instead of skinned back into a ponytail as it was when she was working. Somebody had interrupted them, then, and he hadn't asked for details.

She thought she would probably see him again—Utopia wasn't the kind of place where you could completely lose track of somebody. And sure enough, a few days later they'd bumped into each other at the post office. She'd been in uniform that time, which necessitated an explanation of what exactly she did for Texas Parks and Wildlife. Derek cast a startled glance at the Glock on her hip, and she'd figured that was the end of an interesting beginning.

But to her surprise, he had phoned the next Sunday with a casual invitation to an impromptu afternoon hike along the river with him and his two daughters, aged thirteen and fifteen. It wasn't exactly a comfortable outing, for she'd had a difficult time hiding her surprise at the upscale contemporary luxury of Derek's architect-designed glass-and-stone ranch house, which reminded her uneasily of the world she and Lanny had lived in. The girls were . . . well, they were probably typical teenagers, she thought. They wore tight pants and shirts that showed a lot of skin and shape, and they were far more interested in their smartphones than in the lovely autumn woods along the river. What's more, they made it clear that they didn't like Mack's intrusion into their weekend. She hadn't expected Derek to call after that.

He surprised her again. He'd asked her out for an elegant Saturday night dinner at the ranch. The girls were doing an overnight with friends, and he'd cooked a gourmet meal just for the two of them. She'd worn her one best dress, a short, slim, silky red number with a low V neckline that Lanny had picked out for her to wear to his firm's Christmas party two years before. And she'd worn makeup, which she didn't wear on the job.

Derek had whistled when he helped her off with her coat. "Utopia is full of surprises," he'd said, letting his gaze linger appreciatively on her neckline. He shook his head, faintly amused, and took her hand. "And that's what you're hiding under that game warden's uniform? There oughta be a law, Mackenzie. You should wear a dress like that every day." She didn't tell him that she preferred her uniform, which kept her from having to make decisions about dresses and shoes and stuff like that. But she didn't pull her hand back, either.

"Pie fixes everything," she thought now, as she cruised past the Lost Maples Café and on down the street. Maybe pie was what she needed to patch up that hole in her heart that had been left when her marriage broke up.

Not that she blamed Lanny for what had happened. They had gotten engaged in college, married when she graduated from the Academy, and settled down to a new home and new careers—Lanny as a civil engineer working for a large architectural firm in Austin, Mack as a first-year game warden, responsible for a patrol district in the Hill Country west of Pecan Springs. But Lanny had learned pretty quickly that while his was a nine-to-five job, his wife was on call around the clock, with nighttime patrols routine from September through February and frequent during the summer. For a while, they had loved each other enough to keep trying to make it work, especially when they'd been hopeful enough to imagine fitting a baby into Mack's complicated schedule.

But then a potentially dangerous encounter with a badass hunter had demonstrated to Lanny that his wife's service weapon was not there for show. "I'm sorry, but I just can't live with the fear that you'll leave on patrol one night and won't come home," he'd said disconsolately. Not long after that, he told her he had met somebody else.

Mack didn't fight for the marriage. She wasn't sure there was anything left worth fighting for, and when Lanny made it clear that her career was the price of their reconciliation, she knew what she had to do. She thought about it for all of thirty seconds, offered Lanny his freedom, and put in for a transfer. It didn't much matter where in Texas she went, so long as it was close to what passed for wilderness these days. When the transfer to Uvalde County was offered, she had said an immediate yes.

And that's how she had ended up in Utopia. Now, driving down the shadowy street, appreciating its early-morning peace and quiet, she reached down to the truck's cup holder and picked up the mug of hot coffee. Utopia was one of those blink-and-you-miss-it towns, on a road that didn't go much of anywhere. But from time to time it became a "destination town," and the streets weren't always as quiet as they were this morning. The golf course south of town pulled golfers in for tournaments, and there was the Open Pro Rodeo at the park, the annual Utopia Arts and Crafts Fair, and various barbecue and chili and Dutch oven cook-offs, all of it with plenty of dancing and country music. During dove and deer seasons, weekend hunters wearing camo crowded into the café or picked up supplies at the General Store. There had even been a movie, *Seven Days in Utopia*. Mack hadn't been in Utopia when the film was shot, but she'd heard that it stirred up a potful of excitement—which it would, of course, since it had brought Robert Duvall and Melissa Leo to town. Dozens of Utopians had been employed as extras, and there were snapshots of the stars and the cast and crew plastered all over one of the café's walls.

But the biggest excitement in the past couple of months had been the mountain lion that had added the town to its territory, snatching a puppy out of a resident's backyard and killing a goat tethered to a clothesline. The lion—a young adult male weighing around a hundred pounds—had even been seen prowling along Cypress Street, on the fringes of the town park. People were spooked and rightly so, Mack knew. An adult lion needed eight to ten pounds of meat every day to survive. And a hungry lion might not be particular about who or what was on the menu, as an article in the *Uvalde Leader-News* had recently warned, pointing out that a four-year-old child had been attacked and killed by a mountain lion in the Rio Grande Valley just six months before.

But prowling lions aside, when the movie shoot was over and all the golfers and rodeo riders and tourists and cook-off champs and hunters had left, Utopia was once again transformed into a quiet, modest, back-in-time village—sort of like the mythical Brigadoon that Mack had seen in a movie. It vaulted into the twenty-first century on weekends and slipped back into the nineteenth century during the week.

Like Brigadoon, Utopia had waxed and waned, fading in and out of the gauzy mists that drifted through the Sabinal River Canyon on cool autumn mornings. In the 1790s, the Spanish found silver and dug a mine shaft in Sugarloaf Mountain but hurried back south when the Indians—Comanches, Tonkawas, Kickapoo, and Lipan Apaches—gave them a hard time. The first Anglo settler arrived in 1852. In spite of sporadic Indian raids, more settlers followed, and by 1880, the village boasted 150 citizens and a weekly stage, a post office, a cotton gin, two gristmills, a blacksmith shop, a general merchandise store, three churches, and a half-dozen saloons. The telephone came to town in 1914, and electricity arrived after the Second World War, although paved roads took a while longer. The population dropped to sixty when the decade-long dry spell of the 1950s droughted out many of the old ranches, but the state's rising prosperity in the following decades delivered a recreation boom to the area. Tourism—and Utopia—began to flourish. And so did hunting and fishing, now a fifteen-billion-dollar industry in Texas. Around Utopia these days, a rancher could make more money hawking hunting leases than he could selling beef, wool, or mohair, which had once been the county's cash crops.

But the biggest money of all wasn't in leases. It was in the big-buck breeding and captive hunting ranches, like the 4,200-acre Three Gates Game Ranch where Jack Krause worked. The place was high fenced to ensure that the managed game (which included a dozen exotic species) stayed inside, where they'd get plenty of high-protein supplemental feed. Critics said that these weren't game ranches but deer farms, and that paying upwards of fifteen thousand dollars to sit in an air-conditioned and heated tower blind and shoot a trophy buck that came to feed wasn't hunting at all, but something else. Target practice, maybe.

But like it or not, Texas A&M University had recently reported that white-tailed deer breeding was the fastest-growing rural industry in the United States. In Texas, it was adding some $650 million annually to the economy. And in Uvalde County, the money it brought in wasn't available in any other legal way. It meant jobs. Real jobs that enabled people to feed their families and pay the rent. High-fenced game ranches were a fact of life in a world that turned wild animals into pricey commodities. But that didn't mean she had to like them.

Mack drained her coffee and dropped the empty mug back into the cup holder. Seeing the motion, Molly raised her head alertly, then sat up on her haunches and looked out the window as Mack made a right turn off Main Street onto Farm-to-Market Road 1050 and crossed the Sabinal River. To her right, a hundred yards off the road, was the spot where she and her best friend Karen Wilson—a wildlife biologist from San Antonio with whom she'd roomed during their junior year at college—had set up a lion trap a couple of days ago, baited with a roadkill deer. Karen was conducting a study of mountain lions, and Mack had volunteered to help whenever she could. With luck, they would catch the lion, put on a radio collar, and relocate it to Karen's remote study area.

Mack detoured for a quick check of the trap, which was empty and unsprung, and called Karen to report. Her husband Boyce, sounding half-asleep, answered the phone, and she apologized and asked for Karen.

"No luck this morning," she said, when her friend answered. "I think we're going to need to get some fresh bait. This deer must be three or four days old." She wrinkled her nose at the smell. "It's getting pretty ripe."

"You called me before the sun is up to tell me that, Mackenzie?" Karen demanded sternly.

"Oops, sorry," Mack said, contrite. "I guess I didn't check the time."

"You guess you didn't check the time," Karen repeated in a mocking tone. "You're married to your job, Mack. You are totally, completely uncivilized. No wonder your marriage failed."

"Hey." Mack sighed. "I said I'm sorry." She paused and took another sniff of the deer. "I'll see if I can get a pig or something. For the trap."

"You do that," Karen said dryly. "You get the pig. I'm going back to bed, where Boyce is waiting. Phone me when we've got our lion."

Feeling a little sheepish, Mack rejoined Molly in the truck. "I guess Karen's right, Mol," she muttered. "I'm uncivilized. No wonder Lanny divorced me." Only of course he hadn't. They had divorced each other. But it was true that she was married to her job.

She swung back onto the two-lane heading west in the direction of Garner State Park. This part of the county lay along the southern rim of the heavily eroded Edwards Plateau, with elevations ranging from 200 to 700 feet above sea level. The rolling hills and deep canyons were blanketed with live oak, shinnery oak, red oak, and Ashe juniper, while the clearings were carpeted with buffalo and mesquite grass. To the south, down toward the county seat of Uvalde, the land flattened out into the coastal plains and became more arid, and the brush-covered plains featured thorny vegetation and plenty of guajillo with scattered clusters of post oak and live oak. There was a lot of talk these days about climate change, and Mack knew that if the drought went on for a few more years, it would have a major impact on the wildlife. But there was no use letting the anxiety about tomorrow darken her pleasure in the day. All she could do was concentrate on doing her job—the job she loved—in the best way she knew how.

It was Tuesday, so she was expecting an easy day, although in this business, you never knew. Following a detailed map on which Clyde Brimley, her predecessor, had located the deer camps in her patrol area, she took a right off 1050 at Six-Mile Road and drove up into the hills and canyons along a rocky caliche two-track that skirted the bare ridge above Six-Mile Creek. A few miles in, she pulled off onto a flat shoulder that overlooked a broad reach of rolling tree-covered hills and narrow valleys, the property of Six-Mile Ranch. The owner, Jed Barnes, sold hunting leases and maintained a half-dozen primitive deer camps. Picking up her dad's old Leupold spotting scope, she began to study the terrain below, where one of the camps was half-hidden under a clump of oaks.

Her father, a game warden, was one of the reasons Mack was a warden now. They'd lived in Burnet County, in the central Hill Country.

Spring and summer, he was out on Lake Buchanan or the Lower Colorado River most days, issuing citations for boating while intoxicated and checking fishing licenses, safety equipment, trotlines, and live buckets. During deer season, he was out most days and nights, inspecting hunting licenses and permits and tags, monitoring bag limits, and citing trespassers and jacklighters—people who used illegal spotlights to freeze deer along the road for an easy kill. One dark night, he was shot and killed by a drunken poacher.

Mack pushed the memory as far away as she could—it was an anguished ghost that she could never banish completely—and opened her patrol log. The last time she had checked the camp, it had been occupied by four men with valid licenses. Tarps were spread over the tops and sides of aluminum folding frames for a temporary bunkhouse, cots and sleeping bags arranged beneath. The camp featured all the comforts of home. Off to one side was a portable propane gas grill; four ice chests; four folding chairs around a card table (she had interrupted a poker game); and a laptop. There were several feeders and stands within a couple of hundred yards. One of the hunters had already taken a deer. When she checked, she saw that the tag and harvest log were in order and that his ice chest contained the field-dressed backstraps and quarters. Pointing to a loaded beer cooler, she had given her routine caution against drinking before they went off for their evening hunt and had taken some mild kidding from the guys for being a "girl game warden." She got that occasionally. She didn't like it, but she didn't make an issue of it.

The camp was empty today, and Mack moved on, pulling off the road again at the next camp, about five miles farther on and a couple of hundred feet higher up the canyon. Scoping the stream far below, she spotted a natty black and white crested caracara perched on a dead limb over the creek. The bird was a tropical falcon, a carrion feeder like the vulture that filled the same ecological niche farther north. It cocked its head, peering down, watching a slow, deliberate movement on a half-submerged log. There were two robust splashes in quick succession: a pair of turtles taking to the water, likely red-eared sliders.

Mack peered through the scope at the widening rings left in the silent pool by the disappearing turtles, imagining them foraging among the water weeds on the graveled bottom. She loved the wilderness, loved nature in its wildest, most undisturbed form. The week before, ten miles farther south, she had happened on a docile, slow-moving Texas tortoise feeding on shriveled tuna, the ruby-colored fruit of the prickly pear cactus. Listed as a threatened species in the state, the tortoise was the first live one she had ever seen, although her father had once brought her a saucer-size yellowish orange tortoise shell. She had scrubbed it and brushed on several coats of clear polyurethane and put it on the shelf over her bed with her other prized turtle shells, some she had found along the creek near their house, some her father had brought her. Lanny had objected to her collection ("What do you want with those ugly old things?"), so her friend China Bayles had kept it for her. But when she moved to Utopia, she brought the shells with her and arranged them with several interesting rocks and lichens on a shelf under the kitchen window where she could see them every day, lovely icons of wilderness in her home.

Startled, the caracara gave a hollow, rattling call, lifted its wide black and white wings—at least a four-foot span—and flapped into the air. Mack shifted her scope to the deer camp on the side of the creek nearest the road and saw that two pup tents were pitched there. A small fire burned in a cleared spot on the creek bank, a low metal grill propped on rocks over the flames, a cast-iron pot on the grill. A thickset man was adding a couple of sticks to the fire. In contrast to the previous camp, this one was primitive.

She started the truck again and drove thirty yards up the road, to the head of the faint trail that led down to Six-Mile Creek and the camp. Parked at the trailhead was a rusty red GMC pickup with Texas plates and an empty rifle rack in the back window of the cab. Mack called in her 10-20 to Dispatch (a precaution she always took when she was leaving her vehicle in an isolated area), locked Molly in the truck, and hiked a hundred yards down the steep hillside to the creek at the bottom. She felt the hair on the back of her neck prickle with apprehension as she approached the camp. These encounters were a test of alertness, experience, and judgment, for you never knew what you were going to walk into. All you could be sure of was that every man on the site would be fully armed, might be drunk as a skunk (like the man who had killed her father), and was ready to shoot at anything that moved. She loosened her Glock in its holster.

"Hello the camp," she called as she stepped out of the woods and into the clearing along the creek. "Game warden." Some wardens didn't announce themselves. She did. She'd hate to get shot because of mistaken identity.

The man at the fire straightened up and turned around. Short and hefty, he was wearing a Harley cap and a baggy camo vest. He hadn't shaved in a couple of days. A second man—tall, rail thin, and bearded—crawled out of one of the tents, a heavy throwing knife in one hand.

"Morning, guys," she said pleasantly. "I'm Warden Chambers. I need to see your hunting licenses, please."

"Got mine on me," Short-and-Hefty said, and produced it out of a pocket. Tall-and-Thin crawled back into the tent and came out with his wallet and license—and without the knife. They even had a much folded and creased copy of their signed hunting lease agreement, something that many hunters failed to carry.

Mack handed back the papers back. "Had any luck yet?"

"We just got here last night," Tall-and-Thin said, scratching his chin. "We was out still-hunting early this morning but didn't get anything."

"You know how that goes, I reckon." Short-and-Hefty chuckled wryly. "Still-hunting ain't the quickest way to get your venison."

"There are easier ways to punch a tag," Mack agreed. Her father had been a still hunter, tracking Indian-style through the woods, rather than crouching in a blind waiting for the deer to come to a feeding station. She had begun still-hunting with him the winter before he was killed, on another warden's ranch in Lampasas County, miles from anywhere.

"Fair and square hunting," he had called it. "You're on the deer's home turf, and he knows the landscape infinitely better than you do. He can see and hear and smell better than you can, too. He has all the advantages, so you have to be smarter. You have to be a *real* hunter." She didn't have time to hunt these days and she didn't need the meat. But if she did, that's how she'd do it.

"We was out lookin' for the eight-pointer we saw last time we was here," Tall-and-Thin offered with a grin that showed stained, crooked teeth.

"Worth lookin' for," Short-and-Hefty put in. "But if we don't get him tonight or tomorrow morning, it's okay. We got a spike buck last week for the freezer, and we'll be back."

Mack nodded. She respected hunters who hunted for their tables. In fact, she felt that, for those who could, hunting was better than buying factory-farmed beef and pork in cellophane packages at the supermarket.

She thought people who ate meat should be aware of the fact that an animal had died to feed them. Vegetarians and vegans she understood and respected as well—principle was important, after all—but she could only shake her head at the hypocrisy of those who insisted that killing a deer for food was wrong and then went around the corner and chowed down on a double bacon burger.

"After all," Short-and-Hefty added with a knowing look at Mack, "it's *our* deer. Ever durn one of them deer out there belongs to the people of Texas, don't it?" He aimed a squirt of tobacco juice off to one side. "If one of them Frankenbucks goes rogue and hops over his fence onto our lease, we can take him. Ain't that right?" Frankenbuck was the term some people used to describe the genetically modified deer with massive antlers that were bred on the game ranches.

"The deer are a natural resource, yes." Mack chose her words carefully. "They belong to the people of Texas."

She was avoiding the man's specific question about the escaped buck, which was at the heart of a huge argument brewing in the state legislature. By Texas law, all wild animals belonged to the people of Texas. This did not make the deer breeders happy, since they had a massive capital investment in fences, buildings, and animals—especially in the animals. As far as they were concerned, the deer they bred and raised inside their high fences didn't belong to the state. They were private property, like cows or sheep. The breeders were pushing a slate of bills in the legislature that would essentially change the status of the animals on their game ranches from wildlife to privately owned livestock and move jurisdiction over deer ranching from Parks and Wildlife to the Texas Animal Health Commission. Mack hated this idea with a fierce passion, but she had the bad feeling that the breeders were going to prevail.

Her generic answer seemed to satisfy Short-and-Hefty. "Thought so," he said with satisfaction. "Anyway, we'll be here through the weekend, stalking that buck, if you want to drop in again." He gestured toward the fire. "Or maybe you'd pull up a rock and join us now. We got us a good pot of chili goin'—last year's venison, taken right over there across the creek."

"Thanks for the offer," Mack said, "but I've got a sandwich in the truck—if my dog hasn't helped herself to it." She touched two fingers to the bill of her tan cap. "Y'all have a good one, guys. Hope you get what you came for."

On her way back to her truck, she noted the GMC's license place and jotted it and a couple of other details about the encounter in her log. She checked in with Dispatch again, then got her lunch pack and hot chocolate out of the rear cab and ate the baloney and cheese sandwich, listening idly to the radio traffic and sharing the crusts with Molly but keeping the granola bar for herself. She poured a cup of chocolate from the thermos, then splashed some water into the plastic bowl she kept under the seat for Molly. When they were both finished, she let the dog out to do her business, watching her and calling her back quickly when she was finished. Molly was obedient, but a heeler who spotted a squirrel was a gone heeler, and she didn't want the dog disturbing the hunters in the camp below. Still hunters, in her view, deserved all the breaks they could get.

The rest of the day was uneventful, the stops at the camps routine. When she crossed Highway 83 and headed west toward Reagan Wells, she checked for messages on her cell phone and found one from Derek. Returning his call, she heard him say that the Panhandle weather looked bad for the weekend—an ice storm was predicted. He and his daughters had decided not to drive to Abilene to visit the girls' grandmother for Thanksgiving, as they had planned.

"We're having Thanksgiving at home instead," he said, in that husky, intimate voice—a bedroom voice—that gave Mack a momentary shiver.

They'd made love twice, the first time the night of the gourmet dinner at Derek's place, the second time a week later, at her place. Neither time had been all that great, for her at least. It hadn't been Derek's fault, certainly. He was experienced and skillful and had all the right moves, from start to finish. But she'd been ambushed by her lack of . . . well, passion. She'd wound up putting on an act, which made her feel uncomfortable, even dishonest, especially since she'd never had to do that before. It definitely hadn't been that way with Lanny—she'd felt plenty of passionate desire, right up to the last time they'd made love, a couple of days before she found out about the other woman in her husband's life.

So what was the problem? She wasn't still carrying a torch for Lanny, was she? She didn't think so, but she supposed it might be possible, somewhere deep down in her subconscious. But it had been a long while since she'd made love. Maybe she was just out of practice, although you'd think it would go the other way. The longer the abstinence, the greater the desire.

"It would be great if you'd join us for dinner," he went on. "I'm sure the girls would love it. Please say you will, Mackenzie." *Mackenzie.* She liked it that he used her full name. He seemed to say it with a special, soft intonation.

Mack hesitated. "I'd like to," she said, "but I've already promised to have dinner with Sam and Leatha Richards. We're eating at four." Derek knew the Richardses through the local ranchers' association, to which nearly everybody belonged. "Leatha's daughter will be there, too, from Pecan Springs," she added. She and China stayed in touch by email, but she hadn't seen her for months. She was looking forward to spending some time with her.

And just as importantly, she was pretty sure that Derek's daughters, Elise and Margaret, wouldn't be enthusiastic about her butting into their family Thanksgiving. The previous time they'd all been together, she'd gotten the idea that they viewed her as an interloper. She had been a girl herself once, and although that seemed like a distant country, she remembered her girlfriends expressing disdain and dislike through eye rolling, smirking, and shoulder shrugs. She'd seen Elise and Margaret sending several of those signals to each other—when they weren't engrossed in their smartphones, that is.

"Sam Richards?" Derek paused, his voice sober. "I heard at the general store this morning that he's in the hospital over in Kerrville. Heart attack."

"Uh-oh," Mack said softly, suddenly concerned. Sam reminded her of her father. "I wonder if—" She hesitated. "I'd better call Leatha and see if the dinner is still on."

But Derek wasn't going to let her off the hook. "Even if it is, would it kill you to have two Thanksgiving meals?" He sounded amused, and she imagined one dark eyebrow quirking. "Tell you what. We'll move ours up a couple of hours and call it a Thanksgiving brunch. How's that?"

Mack considered. "Well, okay," she said. "But remember I'm on call. Want me to bring anything?" Quickly she amended, "And I'm on patrol tomorrow night, so it'll have to be something I can pick up at the store, like a can of cranberry sauce or a box of instant rice. I won't have time to cook." That had been another of Lanny's complaints during their marriage.

"Just bring yourself. The girls and I will do the rest." He chuckled. "Well, more likely me. I can't seem to interest them in the fine art of cooking. They'd rather be on Facebook, or wherever it is that kids hang out these days." He paused. "How about ten thirty?"

"Works for me," she said. "See you then."

He paused again and his voice seemed to change. "Where are you?"

"West of 83, north of Garner State Park," she replied. "Why?"

"No reason," he said lightly. But when he added, "I guess I just worry about you, out there on patrol all by yourself," she heard the concern in his voice. "I mean, you might run into something unexpected. So I worry."

"That's why I put in all those hours at the Academy," she countered lightly. "Training for the unexpected. Don't worry, Derek." She bit her lip, thinking of Lanny, who'd fretted when she was on night patrol. *Please, please don't worry, Derek,* she said silently. *You'll spoil it.*

"If you say so," Derek said, dragging it out. "I know you're trained and all that. And you've got a gun. But be careful."

"Always am," she replied briskly. "See you on Thursday."

"Thursday, ten thirty," he echoed. "Looking forward to it."

But as it turned out, she would be seeing him sooner than that. And it wouldn't be Mack who couldn't handle an unexpected situation. It would be Derek.

Chapter Three

Carolina buckthorn (*Rhamnus caroliniana,* also *Frangula caroliniana*) is an attractive, drought-tolerant plant that deserves to be used more widely in landscapes in Zones 5–9. The foliage of this small, shrubby tree is a glossy green, turning in autumn to a bright yellow gold and a deeper bronze. The quarter-inch berries that appear in clusters ripen from pink to red to a dark blue purple—beautiful in a Thanksgiving display. The Delaware Indians of Oklahoma used a decoction of the bark as a treatment for jaundice and as an emetic or strong laxative. The fruits of most species of buckthorn contain a yellow dye, and the seeds are high in protein. In China, oils from buckthorn seeds have been used to make soap, printing ink, and lubricant. The leaves and bark are browsed by deer.

Yaupon holly (*Ilex vomitoria*), is the only native North American plant (Zones 7–9) that contains caffeine. It also contains antioxidants and theobromine, the plant chemical found in chocolate. Yaupon tea was brewed by the indigenous people of the Southeast as a stimulant beverage, medicine, and ritual drink. The dried leaves and twigs were roasted and boiled into a rich, dark tea known to European explorers and colonists as "black drink." Medicinally, a stronger decoction was drunk as a laxative and purgative, while a weak tea made from the bark was used as an eyewash. During tribal ceremonies, high-status males drank a much stronger brew as an intoxicant and purgative. Yaupon is a popular landscape shrub, and its bright red berries are attractive to birds and wildlife. It has another important asset, too. Deer don't seem to like it.

China Bayles
"Native Plants for Wildlife Gardens"
Pecan Springs Enterprise

I had promised Leatha that Caitie and I would be at the ranch by midafternoon on Wednesday, but we got a late start. It was past one by the time we'd loaded Big Red Mama with plants for Jennie Seale's garden and set out on our way. When we reached Wildseed Farms on 290 outside of Fredericksburg, I stopped to check on a bulk order of wildflower seed for the shop. (If you've never been to Wildseed Farms, do put it on your bucket list. But plan your visit for April and early May—wildflower season in the Hill Country. Wildseed's fields are acres of scrumptious blooms, depending on the season: bluebonnets, gaillardia, poppies, cosmos, black-eyed Susans, monarda, and more. Much more.)

Back in the van, we headed down toward Uvalde County. The hills—the people who live here call them mountains—were draped with dense growths of dark green cedar, with softer traces of color folded into the canyons. In the road cuts, layers of sedimentary rocks, the relics of ancient seas, piled one on another high into the sky. And on the heights, we could look out over a rolling landscape, brightened by the afternoon sun, with playful puffs of white clouds chasing their own shadows across the distant view.

I'd been looking forward to the drive because it would give me some quiet, mom-and-kid time with Caitlin. Dark haired, pixielike, and small for her age, Caitie is still recovering from the twin tragedies of her mother's accidental drowning and her father's murder, at a time when most girls are playing with My Little Ponies. She isn't nearly as withdrawn as she was when she first joined our family, and her aptitude for the violin has given her a new and delightful confidence in herself. Last week, for her intermediate recital, she played Bohm's Sarabande in G Minor. I'm no music aficionado, but I was moved to tears by what seemed to me to be an extraordinary performance. She didn't just get the notes right, she *felt* the music, and in feeling it herself, made her audience feel it, too. Even Sandra Trevor, her teacher, was impressed. And that takes some doing.

Caitie is a good passenger, but her cat, Mr. P, is not. Heaven only knows how many miles that scruffy old orange tomcat traveled to get to our house, where he showed up one evening, sore-pawed and starved, and purred his way into Caitie's compassionate heart. At the time, I tried to convince her that a cuddly kitten would be a more appropriate pet for a little girl, but no dice. "He's just like me when I first came to live here," she'd said, defiantly clutching the crafty, battle-scarred reprobate in her arms. "He doesn't have any family. He needs somebody to adopt him. He needs *me*."

And that was that. Mr. P (his full name is Mr. Pumpkin) yowled from his crate behind our seats for nearly an hour before he gave it up as a bad job and went sulkily to sleep. After that, I kept Caitie entertained by pointing out the sights along the way and—as we drove down into Uvalde County—telling her some of the history of the area. "Travel is educational" is my motto.

"All this land," I said, pointing to the hills that thrust abruptly against the horizon to the west and south, "was once hunted by Indians—Comanche, Tonkawa, and Apache."

"Really?" Caitie sat up straight and looked out the window as if she expected to see a hunting party picking its way through the shrubby cedars and shinnery oak, on the trail of a deer for dinner.

"Yes, really," I said. "The Spanish got here first, in the 1600s, but the Indians chased them out. When Mexico won independence from Spain in 1821, more settlers began to move in, which seriously annoyed the

Indians and led to raids and killings and such. Meanwhile, a little farther that way"—I pointed to the east—"in San Antonio, the Mexican army under a general named Santa Anna was taking the garrison at—"

"I know!" Caitie exclaimed eagerly. "At the Alamo! The Texans lost and everybody was afraid of Santa Anna, because he gave no quarter. That means," she added in an explanatory tone, "that he killed everybody, whether they were waving a white flag or not."

"Bloodthirsty," I remarked.

"Yes," she said seriously. "Soldiers aren't supposed to do that. But Sam Houston had the Twin Sisters, so he beat Santa Anna at San Jacinto. That was in 1836. We learned about it in fourth grade," she added, "but I still remember."

"Good for you," I said admiringly, slowing to pilot Mama around a pair of tractors mowing the roadsides. "But who are the Twin Sisters? I don't think I know about them."

"They're two big cannons that were made in Ohio and shipped down the Mississippi to help the Texans," Caitie replied. "But the Texas soldiers didn't have any cannonballs, so they loaded them with handfuls of musket balls and broken glass and horseshoes."

"No kidding?" I said, widening my eyes. "Horseshoes? That's amazing!"

Caitie nodded. "But the thing is, nobody knows what happened to the Sisters. They totally disappeared. Poof." She waved her hand to illustrate a cannon vanishing. "It's a mystery, where they went."

"Sounds like." I shifted down so Mama could climb the hill up ahead with greater confidence. "So what happened to Texas after Sam Houston beat Santa Anna?"

"Well, after that it was a republic, with a president and an army and everything, until people decided it should be a state. That was in 1845. It was a slave state," she added darkly. "Mostly, the slaves were in East Texas, where people grew a lot of cotton and some sugar, too. But some slaves worked on ranches. I guess they were cowboys."

"Uh-oh," I said. "Not good at all. What happened after Texas became a state?"

"I don't know," she confessed. "We stopped there. My teacher said we'll do the rest in seventh grade."

"Well, *I* know," I said, "since I'm past seventh grade." That got a giggle out of her, and I went on. "When the Civil War broke out, Texas seceded from the Union and joined the Confederacy. But some Texans supported the North, and after the fighting was over and people came back home, there was a lot of fighting between the Confederates and Unionists. Down here in Uvalde County, violence was such an everyday event that the county tax assessor had to hire armed guards, and there were a couple of years when they couldn't find anybody brave enough to pin on the sheriff's star."

"The Wild West," Caitie put in. "Awesome."

"Really wild," I agreed. "Desperadoes, smugglers, horse thieves, cattle rustlers. They liked to hide out in places like that canyon over there." I pointed to the steep-sided canyon we were passing, opening out into a meadow along the road. "They would wait until the stagecoach came along and rob the passengers. And there were cattle rustlers, too. They were after the maverick long-horned cattle that had been abandoned by the first Spanish settlers back in the 1600s. When they gave up and went back to Mexico, they left their cows behind."

Now it was Caitie's turn to widen her eyes. "They just *left* them? Poor things! They had nobody to feed and water them."

"Oh, but these cows were tough, Caitie. With those long horns, they could defend themselves and their calves against the mountain lions, so they got along just fine all by themselves. And since the range was pretty much open, if you wanted a couple of hundred cows to sell, you and your cowboys would round them up and head out for New Orleans or Kansas City. If rustlers showed up to take them away from you . . . well, there'd be a shoot-out."

"That's when there were cowboys and trail drives on the Chisholm Trail." Caitie leaned forward. "I saw it on television. The cowboys would drive the Longhorns up to the railroad in Kansas City, where they'd be shipped east."

"Exactly," I said. "Although the people back east weren't real crazy about eating Longhorns. No matter how you cooked it, the meat was as tough as shoe leather, especially after the cow had walked all the way from Texas to Kansas City. And that's where Sam's ranch comes into the story. And Sam's great-grandfather, Ezekiel Richards. Want to hear it?"

"Sure," Caitie said, settling back into her seat. "Sam is a really neat guy. But I've never heard about his great-grandfather before."

"Here we go, then. In 1872, Ezekiel moved to Uvalde County from Dallas and started a ranch on the Sabinal River—the place that Sam and your grandmother call the Bittersweet Nature Sanctuary. But just about the time Ezekiel got started in ranching, something big happened that changed everything."

"What?" Caitie was paying serious attention.

"Barbed wire."

Caitie turned to stare at me. "Barbed wire? You mean, like in a fence?"

I nodded. "Barbed wire came to South Texas in 1875, when a guy named Bet-a-Million Gates convinced the San Antonio city council to let him build a barbed-wire corral on the plaza in front of the Alamo. He drove some long-horned cows into the corral to demonstrate that barbed wire could contain animals as big and tough as the wild cattle. He bragged that the new fence was 'light as air, stronger than whiskey, and cheap as dirt.'" I chuckled. "Old Bet-a-Million was pretty much right. And that was the end of the open range. The end of the wild Longhorns, too, as it turned out."

Caitie frowned. "I guess I don't see—"

"Sam's great-grandfather bought enough of the new barbed wire to fence his entire ranch. Once he did that, he could put his own brand on the best of the Longhorns he rounded up and keep them *inside* the fence. Then he bought some cows from up north and added them to his herd, to improve it by selective breeding."

"Oh, like breeding chickens!" Caitie exclaimed.

In her spare time—that is, when she's not playing her violin—my daughter is a chicken fancier. She started with three Rhode Island Red chicks and three white leghorn chicks who grew into six highly productive laying hens, blessing us with more eggs than a small family can eat. (At Caitie's insistence, we were bringing two dozen to share with her grandmother.) Then came Rooster Boy, a handsome red-feathered fellow with an iridescent ruff and a sweep of colorful tail. Rooster Boy's first seven offspring are just beginning to display their curiously mixed red and white heritage, and Caitie has had fun speculating which babies came from which moms. Chicken Breeding 101.

"Yes," I said, pleased that she saw the analogy. "Like breeding chickens, except that the process takes a little longer. Ezekiel's northern cows had more meat and fat on their bones, and the fat made the beef taste better. Breeding them with the wild long-horned animals, he got cows that were strong and adaptable and tasted better. And that was the beginning of the ranch."

"Wow," Caitie said with satisfaction. "That's a great story. Maybe Sam knows more."

Sam. I bit my lip, and the apprehension that had been hovering at the back of my mind all during the drive suddenly flooded through me. His surgery, followed by "complications." I wished I had pressed Leatha for more information. What was his prognosis? Was he going to be okay? If there was more trouble, how would Leatha handle it? Would she—

"I'll ask him," Caitie said, unburdened by any of these worries. She knew that Sam was in the hospital, but she had no idea how serious it was. She began digging in her pink nylon backpack and pulled out a book. "I brought *Harry Potter and the Deathly Hallows*. It's a great story, too. Is it okay if I read for a while now?"

"Perfectly okay," I said. I'm not exactly crazy about Harry Potter, but anytime one of my kids wants to read a book, any book, I'm all for it. I flicked on the radio and found some country music—an old Waylon Jennings song, "Ladies Love Outlaws." It seemed to fit the territory.

A little later, we were turning off the highway, Route 187 south of the village of Utopia, and onto the ranch road. The turnoff was marked by a large painted sign that said "Bittersweet Nature Sanctuary on the Sabinal River—A Birder's Paradise." Beneath that: *Fishing, Swimming, Hiking. Come for the day or for a long stay*, with the address of the ranch website and a phone number. A paper banner announced: *Opens January 1!* I was surprised by the sign, and especially by the announced opening date. Together, they gave the project a worrisome reality. If Sam couldn't help, how was Leatha going to manage all this?

The gravel lane was lined with the brightly festive autumn foliage of

Carolina buckthorn and yaupon holly. As we drove up, I saw that Leatha—already back from the hospital—was standing on the porch of the old ranch house that she and Sam had remodeled when they were first married. The house stood at the top of a long slope that led down to the Sabinal River. Off to the right was another long, low structure: the guest lodge that Sam's father built when he ran the place as a game ranch. Leatha and Sam had remodeled it in the past few months in preparation for their birder guests.

Leatha held out her arms as Caitie jumped out of the car and raced toward her.

"Gramma!" Caitie cried excitedly. "We're here, Gramma!"

"My little girl," she said, burying her face in Caitie's hair. "My dear, sweet little girl. How very glad I am to see you, baby."

I walked toward the porch slowly, feeling the tears come to my eyes, although you have to know some of the story in order to appreciate why. It's rather like a soap opera, I'm afraid, but families are messy and real life is often chaotic, with love and lust and old dishonesties and deceptions all tangled together. Caitie is the daughter of my half brother, Miles, the illegitimate son of our father, attorney Robert Bayles, and Laura Danforth, his legal secretary and longtime mistress. Both are now dead.

My mother hadn't known about Laura or her son. In fact, she hadn't known any of this story until Miles brought to light the old, dark mysteries around my father's murder. Then Miles was murdered, too, leaving Caitie both fatherless and motherless. The little girl came to us, to McQuaid and Brian and me. We're now a family.

I hadn't known how Leatha would react to Caitie. If you'd asked me, I would have said that she was likely to reject the daughter of her husband's illegitimate son, or at least, not to welcome her—and I suppose I wouldn't have blamed her if she had. My father had rejected her for another woman. Rejecting his granddaughter would be tit for tat, an extra fillip of sweet posthumous revenge.

But that isn't what happened. How she did it is a mystery to me, but Leatha found it in her heart to embrace Caitie exactly as she would her very own granddaughter. And I'm grateful, for Caitie's sake and for my own, especially at family holidays like Thanksgiving and Christmas. These are bittersweet holidays because so much has happened to divide us, and yet so much has brought us together.

Now, Leatha raised her head, her eyes filled with tears. One arm around Caitie, she held the other hand out to me. "I'm so glad you could come, China," she said, in that soft Southern honey voice of hers. "I needed to see you."

I noticed that she was wearing corduroy slacks, a blue plaid shirt, and loafers, and that she hadn't had her hair done recently or paid much attention to her makeup or her manicure. In fact, her nails looked as if she'd been doing the outdoor work on her own for the past week. She was no longer the carefully groomed socialite I had known growing up. She looked drawn and weary.

I kissed her cheek. "How's Sam?" I asked. "What about those complications?"

"It looks like he's out of the woods for now." Leatha put on a bright smile. "I stayed all night at the hospital and only got home a little bit ago. He's doing fairly well, the doctor says. In fact, he sent me home. He knew I was just dyin' to see the two of you." She cuddled Caitie against her. "Especially this one." She lifted her eyes to mine. "Let's go inside, dear. I've made some chili for our supper, and you can put a salad together for us. And then, if you want, we can get started on those pies for tomorrow's dinner. Pumpkin, of course. Mincemeat, too—and there's one jar left of the Fredericksburg peaches I canned last summer. I was saving it for Brian. He always says he loves my peach pie."

I'm always surprised when my mother reveals her domestic talents. When I was growing up, she never cooked a single meal. She didn't have to. She had plenty of household help in our large home in the affluent Houston suburb of River Oaks—and anyway, from the cocktail hour on, she was always so soused she wouldn't have been able to scramble eggs. I was left to eat my suppers alone, since my father invariably worked late—or, as I now knew, spent the evening with Miles' mother. He hated Leatha's drinking as much as I did, which was probably why she did it.

"Oh, let's make a peach pie," Caitie said excitedly. "But I have to get Mr. P out of the car first. He wants to have some supper, too. You don't need to worry about what to feed him, though, Gramma. I brought his food. Oh, and I brought you some eggs from the girls. Two whole dozen!"

"Fresh eggs? Oh, that's wonderful, Caitie!" my mother said, beaming. "What a treat! You can put Mr. P's dishes and litter pan in the laundry room. I'm sure he'll want to sleep with you, though. You're in the room at the end of the hall, where you slept last time you were here."

As Caitie raced off to the car, she shook her head. "What a lovely, lovely child," she said softly. "I hate what your father did, but I just have to love that child." She smiled. "Enough of that. We've got a lot of catching up to do, China. I don't want to waste a single minute. Come on!"

She opened the screen door and led the way into the house. Nestled beside a clump of sheltering live oaks, it's a comfortable old place, low and sprawling, with oak floors throughout, a native stone fireplace in the living room, and a kitchen roomy enough to feed not just the family but all the ranch hands.

"I want to hear about Sam," I said. "How did you find out about his heart problem? And how long has it be going on?"

He'd been experiencing chest pains for several months, she told me as we went down the hall to the kitchen. The doctor had warned him to slow down and take things easy. But Sam was used to setting his own pace. With all the work and planning for the sanctuary, he had plenty on his plate and wasn't inclined to follow orders. The first attack had come in early September.

"September!" I exclaimed. "But this is the first I've heard of it."

"We didn't tell you," Leatha said, "because we didn't want you to worry."

The second attack had come on Sunday night. He was rushed to the hospital, where the surgeon put in a stent. But the abdominal artery was compromised, they said, and there was more repair work to be done—soon, they thought. When he recovered, he would have to take better care of himself and "substantially moderate" his activity.

"Which won't be even a little bit easy," Leatha admitted, standing in front of the wide, ceiling-high window at one end of the kitchen. Her hands were clasped, her knuckles white. "That man is as stubborn as a Mississippi mule." She smiled, but I guessed that she was trying to hide her fear behind that sweet Southern smile. When she grew up, women were taught to control themselves, whatever they felt or feared: "A real lady always stays calm and cool, even when that mean ol' General Sherman is burnin' her house to the ground right in front of her." Then she turned, pointing. "Look at the deer! They're lovely, aren't they?" She sighed. "Oh, I do love this place, China. I thought I would never love another place after Jordan's Crossing, but I was wrong. I'm at home here at Bittersweet, at last, and loving it."

Joining her at the window, I could see why. The view opened out onto an expanse of meadow, bordered on one side by Bittersweet Creek and on the other by junipers, mesquite, and several large live oaks. The late-afternoon shadows embraced a pair of white-tailed does, each with twin yearling fawns, grazing without fear.

"They're beautiful," I said, and then did a double take. "Whoa! What are *those* guys? They're huge!"

Those guys were a half-dozen large deer with orange coats and a generous spattering of white spots. They had drifted out of the shadows to join the white-tails. The single male had large-tined antlers; the five females were smaller. They were gorgeous, muscular animals, significantly larger than the deer they were grazing with. The male must have weighed well over two hundred pounds, and the females were twice the weight of the white-tailed does.

Leatha gave a heavy sigh. "They're axis deer, escaped from the exotic game ranches in the area." A sober look crossed her face, and she turned down her mouth. "They're beautiful, yes, but I'm afraid they're a terrible nuisance—worse than that, really. They compete for forage with the native white-tails. And they're more prolific, so there are more of them every year. The ranchers and farmers around here just hate them."

"Invasive exotic species," I said, shaking my head. "I know plenty about that where plants are concerned—kudzu, for instance, and Oriental bittersweet, vines that can smother everything. Trees, too, like chinaberries." The chinaberry tree, which was brought to Mexico and the American Southwest in the 1840s, certainly has its uses. Mashed, the fruits produce a cleansing lather—in Mexico, it's called the "soap tree." In its native Asia, the toxic seeds were pulverized and used to stun fish for an easy catch. In Chinese medicine, the seeds are used to treat liver and intestinal ailments. But the tree, introduced as an ornamental in the 1830s, is on the Texas Forestry Association's "dirty dozen" list of exotic pests because it forms dense clumps that outcompete native species. I added, "I hadn't thought about invasives in terms of animals."

Leatha turned away from the window. "We think a lot about that around here, I'm afraid. The ranchers shoot the axis deer and net them, and those who can't use the meat donate it to Hunters for the Hungry. If we could get rid of them totally, we would. It was a terrible mistake to introduce them. They don't belong here."

I went back to the subject. "You mentioned that Sam would have to 'substantially moderate' his activity. What does that mean in practical terms?"

She turned away from the window and went to the fridge, taking out a large container of homemade venison chili. "Well, I imagine it means he won't be able to do as much, physically," she said cheerily, and got out some lettuce, a couple of tomatoes, an avocado, a cucumber, and some green onions. "Here are the salad fixings, China. The bowl is in the cupboard beside the sink. We could have an oil-and-vinegar dressing with some of that delicious herbal vinegar you sent for my birthday."

Obediently, I opened the cupboard and got out the salad bowl. But I wasn't going to let it go. "Will he be able to work around the ranch?"

Leatha was spooning the chili into a pan. Reluctantly, and in a more cautious tone, she said, "I suppose it means he'll have to slow down some. Which he won't."

I began tearing lettuce into bite-size pieces. I knew that Leatha didn't want to discuss this—she probably didn't even want to *think* about it. But she needed to look ahead. I didn't want to borrow trouble or worry her unnecessarily, but what would she do if he wasn't able to do very much—or, worst case, if he wasn't around?

"I'm asking," I said carefully, "because I'm wondering how you'll manage. I saw your new sign beside the main highway, and I know you're planning to open January first. You've renovated the old guest lodge. And Sam told me he was putting in new trails and observation points. He even mentioned building a tower or something."

"Oh, yes," she said brightly. "I can't wait to show you the new observation tower, China. It has two platforms, one at fifteen feet, the other at forty, with a great view of the Sabinal River. You walk up to it on a two-hundred-foot-long ramp that takes you up through the trees." She put the pan of venison chili on the stove and turned on the burner. "It was a big job, and we didn't get it finished as quick as he wanted because . . ." She sighed. "Because of the attack he had in September. But I found somebody who could help him with the heavy work—the things I couldn't manage. And I posted the photos on the website just last week. I'm sure it's going to be a big attraction for our guests."

I began chopping tomatoes. "So you and Sam are going ahead with your project—in spite of his heart surgery?"

"Of course we're going ahead. Actually, we're counting on the income. It's been . . . well, a little rough lately. You know, hard times."

I was startled. I'd never inquired deeply into my mother's financial business. My father left her well-off, and Sam had plenty, as well as this ranch. But of course things change, and the economy wasn't in the best shape. Had their situation changed, too? Did they actually *need* the money this venture would bring in?

She was going on. "When I checked the computer this morning, I found another January reservation—four people, two guest rooms, for a full week. Sam will be thrilled to hear it. He says he expects the lodge to be fully booked before the birding season gets under way. The spring migration doesn't start until late March, but there are plenty of resident birds that people will be thrilled to see. Why, just yesterday, I saw a vermillion flycatcher and a beautiful belted kingfisher. I hope you and Caitie brought your binoculars so you can—"

I put down my knife. It was time to face facts. "Mom," I said quietly, "how in the world are you going to manage? I mean, it's entirely possible that Sam won't be able to help with the guest rooms, not to mention the cooking and the logistics. You're going to need somebody here on the ranch to do the heavy work and help with the guests and—"

"Oh, that." She waved her hand dismissively. "Don't worry about it, dear. I've already got it all figured out."

"Figured out how?" I asked, trying not to sound as worried as I felt. I didn't want to discourage her, just to make her look at things realistically. The sanctuary was a beautiful place, and I was sure it would attract plenty of guests. But except for the little town of Utopia some fifteen miles away, it's isolated. Leatha and Sam would find it difficult to hire anybody to come in by day, and the chances of locating live-in help were slim, at least at the wages they could afford. And they would need help, lots of it. Leatha was past sixty-five now, and Sam . . . well, to put it in the best light, Sam was recovering from serious heart surgery.

But if Leatha had heard my worry, she was ignoring it. She took a large spoon out of a drawer and began stirring the chili. "It was a stroke of luck, actually. Lucky for us, I mean—not for her. I hate to take advantage of somebody else's heartache, but in this case, we're helping each other out of a tight spot." She put down the spoon and turned to face me.

"Sue Ellen Krause is going to move into the lodge and give us a hand until Sam is back on his feet."

"Sue Ellen Krause?" I frowned. The name was familiar, but I couldn't place her.

"I've mentioned her before, but I don't think you've met her. She's been at the Three Gates Game Ranch for five or six years, managing the guest lodge there. She's had a *lot* of experience dealing with guests. I know she'll be a big help."

I began slicing the cucumber. I visited Three Gates a couple of years ago with Sam. At 4,200 acres, it's one of the largest game ranches in Uvalde County. Completely surrounded by an eight-foot high-tensile galvanized wildlife fence, it's located five or six miles south, between the Sabinal River and Blanco Creek. It belongs to three Gateses: Jim Gates, Houston's most famous brain surgeon, and his two sons, Benny and Alec, lawyers practicing in San Antonio.

The ranch isn't the Gates family's home on the range, though. It's strictly an investment. A *humongous* investment, when you figure in all the costs. I looked up the ranch on the Internet after my visit there and found that they have trophy white-tails, which are bred on the ranch, as well as elk, axis deer, fallow deer, sika deer, buffalo, and several other high-dollar exotics. Then there's the the hunting lodge, the swimming pool, the fishing lake, and the payroll for the staff it takes to maintain and service the place. And that fence. At twenty thousand dollars a mile, the fence alone would've set the three Gateses back by almost a quarter of a million dollars. All those costs can be written off against their income. Even a brain surgeon and a pair of lawyers can figure out that a hunting ranch doesn't have to make money to make money, when it comes to what they owe Uncle Sam on April 15.

I dumped the sliced cucumber into the salad and started to work on the avocado. "If Sue Ellen Krause is coming to work for you, she must've left Three Gates. How come?"

Leatha gave a little sigh. "She and her husband, Jack, are getting a divorce—that's the heartache. He's the assistant foreman at the ranch. He's been making things . . . well, difficult." Putting place mats, plates, and large soup bowls on the table in front of the window, she added, "The situation has gotten too intense, so she's decided it's time to get away." She looked up at the clock over the sink. "In fact, she'll be here any minute. She's coming for supper."

"Tonight?" I asked in surprise, then noticed that Leatha had laid out *four* red plaid place mats and was putting down four plates and bowls.

"Uh-huh." Leatha got a handful of silverware out of a drawer. "She phoned me this morning and said that she and Jack had a big fight and asked if she could move in this evening instead of next week, as we were planning. I'm sure the ranch manager at Three Gates must hate to see her go, especially during hunting season. They're probably booked full. I hope he doesn't think that Sam and I have hired her away." She paused, surveying the table. "Of course, we won't have any real work for her until the guests start arriving in January."

"But she can help you get set up," I said. To myself, I added, *And she would be here, in case . . . well, in case Sam's recuperation didn't go as well as we all hoped.*

"Of course, we can't pay her what she's worth." Leatha began laying the silverware beside the plates. "But we can give her a safe, rent-free place to stay for as long as she needs it, which is what matters most right now. She's really sweet, China—and so kind and thoughtful. She always calls to let me know she's going shopping down in Uvalde and asks me what she can get for us or what errands she can run. She's a local girl, so she knows her way around. And she's been such a help to me."

"That's nice," I murmured. I felt vaguely uncomfortable at the thought that another woman was running my mother's errands for her—and then wondered why I felt that way. I hoped I wasn't jealous. Shouldn't I be glad?

"It *is* nice. It's such a neighborly thing, not something you expect from most young women these days." Leatha put four red napkins down, one beside each setting. "She brings me little gifts—you know, candy and soap, even my favorite perfume. And she called right away when she heard about Sam, wanting to know what she could do to help." She looked up at me and smiled in that twinkly way of hers. "Sue Ellen can't begin to take the place of my dear daughter China, but it'll be good to have her living here with us, even if it's only for a few months. And she's looking forward to meeting you." She put salt and pepper shakers on the table. "She might even have some questions for you about her divorce. She seemed especially interested when I told her that you're a lawyer."

"I'm not *that* kind of lawyer, Mom," I protested. In my former incarnation, I was a criminal defense attorney. I know next to nothing about family law.

"Of course, dear," Leatha replied soothingly. "But you may be able to answer some of Sue Ellen's questions. And I'm sure that just talking to you will help her feel better. Please do what you can, China—she's been so helpful to me."

I know my mother wasn't trying to make me feel guilty, but I couldn't help feeling guilty anyway—which may be the lot of *all* daughters, for all I know. I reminded myself that I ought to be thrilled to learn that my mother had somebody she could turn to when her daughter wasn't around (which was almost all the time). Sue Ellen could be the heaven-sent answer to my worry about how Leatha was going to manage.

"Of course I'll be glad to talk to her," I replied. "And I'm relieved to know that you'll have some experienced help here."

"I am, too," Leatha said. "She may not stay more than a few months, though. She plans to go to college. She knows she needs a degree to get ahead in this world."

"Good for her," I said heartily. "But I hope she stays long enough for you to get this new enterprise under way. And for Sam to get a nice, long rest."

When I talked to Sue Ellen that evening, I'd be sure to make that point.

Chapter Four

Mack had been out on patrol until after 2 a.m. on Wednesday morning, and since she was off duty for the day, she was hoping to sleep a little later. But her cell phone woke her at seven fifteen. They had a lion.

Before she went out the night before, she had met Gene Murray, the Utopia constable, at the mountain lion trap. They replaced the overripe deer carcass with a feral hog that Gene's brother-in-law had shot on his ranch south of town. The nonnative wild pigs were the offspring of pigs brought by early Spanish settlers. Remarkably prolific and incredibly damaging, they rooted up crops, killed young livestock, and were a threat to native wildlife and the environment. Young pigs were excellent eating, although the old boar that Gene's brother-in-law had shot would be gamey and tough as tanned cowhide. But he turned out to be just what the mountain lion was looking for. Gene was calling to tell Mack there was a lion in her trap.

Mack climbed into jeans, boots, and a green hoodie over a couple of sweaters—it was cold now, but by midmorning the temperature would be in the sixties and she'd be peeling off the layers. While her coffee was brewing, she called Karen and told her the news. ("Yes, it's a lion. Honest. Get here as quick as you can.") She consoled Molly, who wanted to ride along, then grabbed a to-go mug of hot coffee and backed her old blue Toyota pickup out of the single-car garage. She was reluctant to take it because it was running rough, hesitating when she was accelerating, surging when she was idling. But Karen didn't have a truck they could use, and this morning's job was definitely not official business. She needed to use her own vehicle, not the state truck, and was crossing her fingers that the Toyota wouldn't give her any trouble.

Karen, an athletic young woman with gold-rimmed glasses and short-clipped, spiky blond hair, met Mack at the trap an hour later. "Hey, nice!" she said, getting a good look at the lion, a handsome, healthy-looking young male with tawny fur. She sedated him. Then, working quickly and efficiently, she and Mack fitted him with a GPS radio collar, weighed and measured him, and collected blood, DNA, and feces samples.

The prep work done, the two women loaded the cage into the back of Mack's Toyota and drove it some thirty miles to Karen's study area at the far northwestern corner of the county, wild hill-and-savannah country on the far side of Boiling Mountain, where there would be plenty of prey. They unloaded the cage beside a clear creek, and Karen turned on her tracking gear and checked the radio collar's transmission, a steady *beep-beep-beep*. Then Mack released the lion while Karen snapped photos. The two of them retreated to the safety of the truck and watched as the groggy animal got to his feet and stumbled off into the brush. He could be expected to live for another eight years or so, but he might not live out his natural life. Karen had collared and released seven other lions in the past several years. Two of them had been struck by vehicles, and three of them had been shot.

"Damn shame," Karen had said when she told Mack about it. "The lions cull the weaker deer and keep the exotic population down. But you can't convince the ranchers of that. They shoot on sight, even when there's no evidence of predation."

Mack, as a conservationist, hated the situation. Texas was the only state in the union where the killing of mountain lions was unregulated. There were no bag limits, no permit requirements. All you had to do was aim and fire. You didn't even need to report your kills. In Mack's opinion, it was time to start implementing a plan to maintain a viable population. By helping Karen, she was doing what she could.

Mission accomplished, Mack started the truck and they drove off, bouncing along the gravel track barely etched out in the short grass along a dry creek bed. Karen glanced at her.

"I've been meaning to ask. How's it going with your new guy, what's-his-name?" Karen was the matchmaker who had brought Mack and Lanny together, back in college. Since the divorce, she had taken an interest in Mack's love life—or rather, the lack thereof.

"His name is Derek," Mack said, and hesitated. Karen was the closest thing to a best friend she'd ever had, and rooming with her in college had been fun. But growing up, she had spent more time with guys—her father, her brothers, their friends. She'd never really learned the easy girl-talk that other girls seemed to know instinctively, especially when the subject was boys and sex. "It's going okay, I guess," she added. "And I've met his daughters. Two. Teens." She made a little face. "I can't say that I was a big hit with them."

"Daughters are tough," Karen said with sympathy. "Especially teens. They tend to be possessive of fathers. Been to bed with him yet?" She chuckled at the look on Mack's face. "Just thought I'd ask, Mack. You don't have to tell, if it's a state secret. But don't forget—I used to be a girl. And I was standing right beside you when you and Lanny got married."

"It's not a secret, exactly," Mack said, feeling the heat rise up her neck and trying to hide her embarrassment. "It's just that . . . I mean, yeah, maybe we did, a couple of times."

"*Maybe* you did?" Karen rolled her eyes.

"Okay, we did. Twice. But I'm not sure I . . ." Mack's voice trailed off.

"Hey." Karen laughed, crinkling her nose. "I'm just teasing. And it's okay. Not every guy can be a super stud right out of the starting gate. Some of them just need a little encouragement, especially the first time or two. He'll get better at it."

Mack colored. "It's not Derek," she said. "He's fine. I mean, he's really good." Remembering, she had to admit that this was true. He *had* been really good; expert, even. That wasn't the problem. "It's me. I just didn't feel . . . well, turned on. The tingle was sort of missing." She managed a little shrug, as careless as she could make it, which wasn't very. "I guess maybe I'm just out of practice. Or—" She stopped.

"Or maybe you're still hot for Lanny?" Karen inquired gently.

"I don't think so," Mack said, trying very hard to be honest. "If that's true, my conscious mind doesn't know anything about it."

But even while she was denying it, she felt a little panicky. Was some part of her still in love with Lanny? Was her past marriage, her *failed* marriage, going to get in the way of her future relationships—with Derek or anybody else?

"Well, don't push yourself if it doesn't feel right," Karen cautioned in a practical tone. "I'm of the opinion that sex is a pretty good barometer of a relationship. You can keep trying, but if the chemistry isn't working, there's probably a reason. You'll figure it out when it's time." She paused, slanting Mack a look. "On the other hand, maybe you're just not ready to get crazy about another guy. You think?"

Mack pictured Derek, with his quirky eyebrow, his quick laugh, his concern for her safety, which was both touching and troublesome. Was there a reason—a *real* reason—she wasn't already crazy about him? But if there were answers to these questions, Mack didn't know what they were.

To Mack's relief, the Toyota made the trip with only a couple of rough-running episodes, and they were back in Utopia by lunchtime. Mack pulled up next to Karen's car, which they'd left on Main Street, across from the café. "Want to get a sandwich before you go back to San Antonio?" she asked.

"I'll have to take a rain check," Karen said. "I've got Boyce's family coming for Thanksgiving tomorrow, and I need to go home and get started doing turkey stuff." She put her hand on Mack's arm. "Hey, if you don't already have an invitation, why don't you drive to San Antonio and eat with us? My brother will be there. He's single again, and he's a pretty hunky guy. I think you'd like him." She grinned. "I *know* he'd like you, especially if you wore that red dress Lanny got you a couple of Christmases ago."

"Thanks, but I've already got two invitations," Mack said. "Derek asked me to his place for brunch, and I'm supposed to have dinner with some friends at four. If I tried to squeeze in another meal, I wouldn't be able to waddle. Anyway, I'm on call, so I need to stay in the county. And being on call means that the dress is out." She chuckled at the thought of apprehending a jacklighter in that sinfully tight red dress. He'd think she was soliciting.

Karen raised her eyebrows. "You're laughing?" she demanded. "You think it's funny to be on patrol every night and on call on Thanksgiving Day?" She shook her head, frowning. "My life can be a little nuts sometimes, but yours is downright crazy, girl—*all* the time. You will never find a guy who'll put up with it."

"Maybe," Mack said ruefully. "It's a good thing I'm not dying for a guy." Which was true, she told herself. Derek was okay, and they might even make it together. But love and marriage—or love and sex, or even just sex—were not at the top of her priority list. "At least, not until the end of hunting season," she added, with a crooked grin. "Maybe I'll take a rain check on meeting your hunky brother. The load gets lighter in January."

"Atta girl," Karen said. "Just remember that I'm here for you." She reached for the door handle then stopped, peering through the windshield. "Whoa." She gave a low whistle. "Talk about hunky. Who the devil is *that*, Mackenzie?"

Mack glanced at the dark-haired, uniformed man who had just gotten out of the white sheriff's department pickup parked in front of the café. He turned around, got his white Stetson out of the truck, and put it on. As he did, he looked up and saw Mack, squinted as if he wasn't quite sure who she was, then waved.

Surprised that he had recognized her, Mack waved back. "That's Ethan Conroy. He's the new deputy sheriff. He's been on the job for a month or so. We've met, but we haven't had a chance to work together yet. He's been mostly working the middle of the county, and I'm mostly up here."

"Well, you should make an effort," Karen pressed, following him with her glance. "Unless of course he's married. Is he?"

"No idea," Mack replied. "I heard that he lives in Sabinal." She watched as the deputy opened the café door and went in. She hadn't really noticed until Karen pointed it out, but he was pretty good-looking. Tall, broad shouldered, and lean, he wore an air of personal authority that was emphasized by the .357 on his hip.

"You ought to find out." Karen raised an eyebrow suggestively. "I mean, if you and Derek aren't going to hit it off." When Mack rolled her eyes, she added hastily, "Hey, I'm just offering a recommendation. You know how you are, Mackenzie. If I hadn't made you get your nose out of your textbook and comb your hair and put on some makeup, you and Lanny would never have gotten together."

Mack had to admit that there was some justice in that last remark. She had been a conscientious student, and studying was a higher priority than dating. Even with Karen's encouragement, the thing with Lanny hadn't been quick and certainly not easy. He'd seemed confident from the beginning, but it had been over a year before she was sure that they were right together. When that had finally happened, she had found herself open and eager and absolutely positive that they could work out any obstacle the future might throw in their path. And look where that had gotten her.

Karen was going on. "And now you've got Molly and Cheyenne and your house in Utopia and the dream territory you always wanted, and you think everything's perfect. You think you don't need a guy in your life. And you're wrong."

"Oh, I don't know," Mack said, trying to ignore the irritation that bubbled up in her. Really. Why was Karen pushing her on this?

"I *mean* it," Karen insisted. "And if you want to know what I really think, it's that you're holding back with this guy Derek because you're afraid of getting blindsided again. What Lanny did to you, I mean. Cheating. Betrayal."

Blindsided? "It wasn't—" Mack stopped, biting her lip. "Don't blame Lanny, Karen. Whatever he did, he did because I made him unhappy. I mean, I wasn't . . . I wasn't right for him, as things turned out. I loved my job and he wanted me to—"

"He wanted you to quit because he couldn't take the competition," Karen put in.

Mack frowned. "No. Really, Karen. When Lanny and I got married, I hadn't gotten started on my career. He didn't sign on for the way that turned out. The hours, I mean, and the fear and uncertainty, and—"

"Bull *feathers*," Karen said emphatically. "Look, Mack. The truth is that Lanny likes to be the big star in everybody's universe, and when he's not, he gets his nose out of joint in a hurry. I didn't know that about him when I introduced the two of you, but I found it out pretty quick. And I was very proud of you when you told him to kiss off. In my opinion, he'd had it coming for quite a while."

Mack was startled. "But I didn't tell him to—"

"Yes, you did." Karen reached for Mack's hand and gave it a hard squeeze. "That's exactly what you did, and you ought to take the credit. You had to do it because Lanny wasn't special enough. It's going to take a really special guy to love you *and* love what you do—because you very much are what you *do*, you know. In ways other women probably aren't."

Not special enough? Mack ducked her head, feeling confused and uncertain but at the same time grateful. Yes, grateful. She and Karen had known each other for a long time, and she trusted her. If Karen saw the situation that way, maybe she should try out that point of view.

"Thanks," she said softly. "I'll . . . I'll think about it."

"See that you do," Karen directed. "And while you're at it, check out that hunky deputy. He looks pretty cool."

Mack nodded, but she was thinking of something else. "When you go up to your study area again, let me know and I'll try to go with you. I'd like to know more about those lions and what you're doing up there."

"Sure thing," Karen said, opening the truck door. "We can make it an overnight, just us girls. And if you hear about any more lions, give me a call."

"I will," Mack said. "I'd much rather trap and release than trap and kill." Which was what Parks and Wildlife did when a lion began hanging around a populated area and making a nuisance of itself.

"Yeah. That policy stinks." Karen made a face. "Killing is what happens in the end, though, by vehicle or by rifle. There are too many of us humans living in the lions' habitat."

A few minutes later, Mack was letting herself into her house, aiming to have lunch, then spend the next couple of hours catching up on the pile of paperwork on her desk. Molly greeted her with delight and followed her into the kitchen, tail nub wagging an ecstatic welcome. Mack poked her head out of the back door to check on Cheyenne, who pawed the ground at her paddock gate and gave her an inquisitive—and impatient—nicker.

Mack considered for a moment, and then said, "Maybe tomorrow, huh, girl? You could go out to Derek's place with me and we could give the girls a ride." Molly pushed with her nose at the back of Mack's knee, and she laughed down at the dog. "You, too, Mol?" Derek's daughters seemed to be more into their smartphones than the great outdoors, but maybe that was just because they hadn't been introduced to horses or dogs. All girls loved horses, didn't they? *She* had, when she was a girl.

Mack made herself a quick cheese and lunch meat sandwich, poured a glass of milk, and snagged some chips and a couple of cookies. Trailed by Molly, she took her lunch into her office and settled down to work. She started by picking up the messages on her office answering machine: a couple regarding holiday changes in the district meeting schedule, one from fellow warden Dusty Ross about some equipment he was trying out, and one from a woman named Amy Roth, calling from Pecan Springs. She identified herself as a member of PETA—People for the Ethical Treatment of Animals—and said that she wanted to talk about a project she and Chris Griffin were working on involving the use of drones.

Mack frowned as she noted the number where Amy Roth could be reached. The name Chris Griffin rang a bell, although she couldn't quite place him. Something to do with drones? What she did know, though, was that the legislature was considering a bill (cannily titled the Texas Privacy Act) that would make the private use of drone aircraft illegal by individual citizens, by journalists, or by organizations like PETA. It was said to be the most restrictive law in the United States.

But the bill hadn't yet gotten out of committee, and for the moment, at least, Texas citizens could still fly drones. Parks and Wildlife was using them, too, to track bird habitat in Galveston Bay, monitor invasive tamarisk on Texas rivers, and survey fly-fisherman on the Guadalupe River. Parks and Wildlife hoped that the drones would eventually replace helicopters, which were both costly and dangerous. In fact, three years before, they'd lost an aircraft and air crew to an accident. If they could replace the helicopters with drones, there would be no more risk of fatalities.

Mack was interested in drones, and curious, both personally and professionally. When she was a kid, her brothers had built radio-controlled model airplanes, and they'd let her fly them. Flying a drone must be a torqued-up version of flying a model plane, she thought, and the idea of being able to get a bird's-eye view of the landscape intrigued her. She could think of a dozen ways that conservationists could use drones—for research, not as spies in the skies. Karen's mountain lion, for instance. The tracking equipment was cumbersome, and it had to be carried on foot, over difficult terrain. What if she and Karen could fly a drone over the study area? It could pick up the radio signals from the lion's collar and report the animal's whereabouts, maybe even get video of it.

Mack keyed Ms. Roth's number into her cell phone. She had worked with PETA members on a couple of projects when she was an undergraduate. They were an important force for the protection of animals, and they often weighed in on Texas wildlife conservation issues—mostly on the right side, in Mack's opinion. But they could be pretty aggressive in their methods, and they sometimes crossed the line. She had the feeling that she'd better find out about Roth's drone project, whatever it was.

But it looked like they were going to play telephone tag. Her call was routed to voice mail, so she left a brief and reasonably cordial message saying that she was interested in learning more about the project and went back to her work. She had opened her report file on her computer and was beginning to update it from her log book when her cell phone dinged. She saw that the caller was Derek, and when he spoke, she could hear that he was clearly upset.

"I've just found six dead white-tailed deer in the pasture, Mack." His voice was strained. "Can you come out and take a look? I have no idea what's going on. What in hell am I supposed to do with all these dead deer? Do you know somebody who could haul them to the landfill for me?"

She frowned. *Six dead deer?* "Dead how?" she asked. "Were they shot? Are they all in one place? Have the backstraps been taken?" Every hunting season since she'd been a game warden, she came across one or two deer that had been shot by hunters, licensed or otherwise, who took only the best meat, the so-called venison filet mignon, and left the rest for the scavengers. But *six*?

"They're all in one place," he replied impatiently, "pretty close together. And no, they weren't shot or butchered or anything like that. I mean, there's maybe a little blood, but I don't see any bullet holes or any sign that they've been killed by an animal—like that mountain lion that's running loose, I mean."

"What do they look like?" Mack asked. "Malnourished? Normal?"

It wasn't an idle question. CWD, or chronic wasting disease, had recently cropped up in a couple of mule deer taken in far west Texas. Related to mad cow disease and epidemic among deer herds in nineteen other states and in Canada, CWD was the primary reason that deer breeders were prohibited from importing deer into Texas or moving breeder deer around the state without a permit. One infected deer could infect an entire captive herd. If an infected deer escaped, it could infect the wild deer. And if CWD got into the wild population, it could make a huge dent in Texas' two-billion-dollar-a-year hunting industry. But the chances of deer dying of CWD as a group were remote at best.

"No, I wouldn't say they're malnourished," Derek replied. "One of them is a good-size buck. They're just . . . dead, that's all. Six of them, not very far from where I'm putting in that new pond." He sounded petulant. "Dead wild animals. This is a job for a game warden, isn't it?"

"Definitely," she said, in the I'll-take-care-of-it voice that she used to soothe upset citizens. "I'm glad you called, Derek—you did the right thing. I'll meet you at your house in, say, twenty minutes, and you can take me to the site. Meanwhile, don't touch the animals. Okay?"

"Don't touch them?" he repeated, now sounding uncertain. "Why? You're thinking some kind of disease, maybe? But if it's a disease, it must be pretty damn contagious. I mean, there are *six* of them out there, and who knows how many out in the woods." He gulped audibly. "Whatever it is, could it infect people? Maybe I should round up the girls and take them to a motel for a couple of days?"

She thought that was going overboard, but she only said, gently, "How about if we don't worry until we know what we're dealing with? See you in twenty minutes."

Mack clicked off the call and immediately phoned Doc Masters, who ran a vet clinic on Highway 187 a couple of miles north of town. He was often out of the office on calls to outlying ranches, but luckily, she caught him in. She described the situation without any additional comment and asked him to meet her at Derek's ranch. She already had her suspicions about the cause of the deaths, but the vet would be the one to take samples and send them to the Veterinary Medical Diagnostic Laboratory in College Station, where the lab analysis would be done.

"I've got things to do this afternoon," the vet said grumpily. "You sure this can't wait?"

"Tomorrow's a holiday," Mack said. "We'd better get this done today."

"Twenty minutes," the vet said and clicked off.

Mack had been introduced to Doc Masters at the café and had bumped into him at the General Store, but she hadn't yet had a chance to work with him. To tell the truth, she'd been apprehensive about it. The old vet—gray-headed and gray-bearded—was known to be crusty and bad-tempered, and he didn't suffer fools gladly. In fact, he didn't suffer fools at all and was reputed to have no love for game wardens, especially female game wardens. Mack's predecessor, Clyde Brimley, had warned her of the need to convince Doc Masters that she knew her stuff.

"He'll make life tough for you if you don't," Clyde had cautioned. "Master's a shrewd old buzzard. He knows all the ranchers in this part of the county, and you need him on your side. But he's got this thing about game wardens, like he thinks we're not well trained or something. I never did figure that one out."

All Mack could do was shrug. She'd run into the anti-woman attitude before, and it always took some extra patience to keep from telling the guy, whoever he was, to go fly a kite. But Masters was the only vet in northeast Uvalde County. And a good working relationship with the local vet was as important as a good working relationship with the local law enforcement officials.

"Not today, Mol," Mack said, when Molly begged to go with her. "You can come tomorrow, for Thanksgiving, and we'll take Cheyenne, for the girls to ride." She bent over and rubbed the heeler's ears. "But if this is what I think it is, it's not going to be pleasant. And I don't want you near it." Then, thinking about the possibilities, she got a can of gasoline and a propane torch out of the garage, stowed them in the back of her truck along with a couple of extra rakes, and headed out to Derek's ranch.

When she pulled up in front of the impressive glass-and-stone ranch house, Doc Masters was already there, talking to Derek, who was wearing baggy shorts, flip-flops, and a Hawaiian print shirt. A slight, stooped man in his late sixties, the vet was dressed in stained khaki pants and a baggy vest with multiple pockets and wore a maroon Texas A&M baseball cap pulled down tight over his gray buzz cut. Nodding curtly to Mack, he put his bag in her truck and the two of them followed Derek's red ATV over a rutted ranch road. After Mack's greeting and Masters' grunted response, the old man refused Mack's efforts at conversation. Mack's heart sank. They weren't exactly getting off to a strong start.

The sun had ducked behind a band of pewter gray clouds, and the wind was picking up ahead of a cold front that was predicted to slide through the county that evening, bringing wind and maybe some rain. After a fifteen-minute drive, Derek stopped his ATV and Mack pulled up alongside him. She could see vultures clustered around the dead animals, which seemed to be scattered across about a half acre of grassland, at the foot of a steep limestone cliff near a small creek. Not far away, a big bulldozer was sitting idle beside a deep, wide basin and a pile of scooped-up soil and rock.

"I counted six dead," Derek said, swatting at a bug on his bare leg. In his shorts and flip-flops, he looked out of place in the rough country. He gestured toward the bulldozer. "I spotted them when I drove out to check on the pond I'm having built."

Mack followed Doc Masters to the nearest dead animal, a young doe. Peering over the tops of his round, metal-rimmed glasses, he looked as if he had seen almost everything in his long career—and he probably had. He had certainly seen *this* before, Mack knew, as she stood beside him, gazing at the scattered group of six dead deer, five does and a buck, in short grass. The carcasses were fairly fresh, but the day had turned warm and they were already pretty ripe. The vultures lifted noisily from their lunch and flapped off to watch from a couple of nearby hackberry trees. The dead animals showed little or no rigor, and in spite of the vulture depredation, Mack could see that small amounts of dark blood had oozed from their mouths and noses. A textbook case, she thought.

Masters hunkered down for a closer look at the doe, then straightened up. He gave Mack a testing glance. "You want to hazard a guess, Miz Warden-lady?" There was a slightly mocking tone in his grainy voice. "What killed 'em?"

Mack met his eyes, steady and sure. "It's late in the year for anthrax, but that's what it looks like to me. What do you think?"

"Looks that way to me, too," the vet agreed with a brusque nod. "Glad to see they're teaching something useful at warden school these days. But o' course we'll have to see what they say about it over at College Station. They may have a different idea."

"I'll bet they'll agree with your diagnosis," Mack said, suppressing a grin. She could have told him that she'd worked on anthrax during her junior field study summer and had been dispatched to two different epidemic sites. But that would have spoiled the old man's fun.

Derek was standing some distance away, his hands in his pockets, watching and listening. "Anthrax!" he exclaimed loudly, sounding panicked. "Anthrax? You think? Omigod! Where did it come from? Are we . . . is it some kind of terrorist attack? What should we *do*?"

Mack turned around, surprised at his alarm. But he was new to this part of the country, she reminded herself, and to ranching. "You don't have to worry," she told him reassuringly. "We need to be careful, of course, but it's not that kind of anthrax."

"What do you mean, it's not that kind of anthrax?" Derek's voice was shrill and barely under control. "Anthrax is anthrax, isn't it? It gets into people's lungs and kills them, doesn't it? And it's a hundred percent fatal, from what I've read. Shouldn't we try to get some vaccine or something? Won't it—"

"No, it won't," Mack said firmly. "You're thinking of aerosolized anthrax, Derek. Weaponized anthrax, the kind that makes the news. And yes, when people breathe it in, it's nearly always fatal. The anthrax we have here in Texas is caused by the same bacterium, but it lives in the soil. We see occasional cases of wildlife and livestock poisoning, especially in the summer. We might even see a few cases of human anthrax across a decade, but nobody has ever died from it—at least, not in modern reporting history, not in Texas." She turned and spoke over her shoulder. "Did I get that right, Doc?"

"Pretty much," the old vet said—grudgingly, Mack thought. "The last human case I heard about was a man over near Del Rio, who got cutaneous anthrax from skinning a buffalo. Fella recovered without a problem." He eyed Derek, who was now pacing nervously back and forth. "You won't have a problem, either, son, long as you don't go skinning these critters. Or harvesting the antlers." Sternly, he pointed to the buck, an eight-pointer. "Consider this an official warning. You leave that rack right where it is. Don't even think about hanging it on your wall."

"But I don't understand where the anthrax could have come from,"

Derek protested. He stopped pacing, bewildered. "Did somebody *do* this? Did somebody poison them?"

Doc Masters grunted. "Somebody sure did. You, most likely."

"*Me?*" Derek sputtered, incredulous. "That's crazy. I had nothing to do with this."

Mack nodded toward the bulldozer that Derek had hired to build his new tank, which he'd said he planned to stock with fish so he and the girls could go fishing. "Doc Masters is saying that the guy who was operating that bulldozer could've scraped up an old anthrax grave site, where a previous rancher buried some diseased animals, or where they died and decomposed. Anthrax spores don't need an animal host to reproduce themselves. In the right soil—high in calcium, as this soil is—they can go through their whole life cycle. They just keep replicating themselves."

Derek was regarding her with disbelief. "You're telling me that the dirt around here is loaded with anthrax? The soil is *poisonous*?"

"I wouldn't put it that way, exactly," Mack replied cautiously. "But yes, there are spores in the soil. We got a good hard rain a few weeks back, and the weather was warmer than usual. The dirt your dozer operator turned up could have sprouted a fresh crop of green grass. White-tailed deer don't normally eat a lot of grass, but they might have spotted your salad bar and decided to help themselves. That's where they picked up the spores."

Derek turned to the vet. "This is right?" he asked, frowning. "They died from eating the freakin' *grass*?" It sounded as if he had suddenly discovered some sort of natural treachery, as if the land itself had deliberately sabotaged him.

"Happens," Doc Masters said. "Or they could have got it from infected flies." He opened his bag. "It's late in the year for that, too, but the warm spell Miz Warden was talking about could've maybe caused another tabanid hatch." He took out a pair of plastic gloves and a mask and held them out to Mack.

"Tabanid?" Derek managed.

"Horseflies," Mack said, slipping on the gloves. "Or deerflies, they're sometimes called. When several animals die together, flies can be the cause."

Doc Masters put on his mask and gloves. "Gotta watch them flies," he warned with a sly glance at Derek's bare legs. "They'd just as soon bite people, you know. Bloodthirsty. You might want to reconsider those short pants, son. Most men around here wear long pants and long sleeves, so's they don't get chewed up." He put the slightest emphasis on the word *men*.

Knowing that Masters was baiting Derek, Mack was about to say that the flies very *rarely* bit people. But the vet was taking out a sampling kit and scalpel and a package of syringes. He gestured to Mack. "Warden, if you're not too squeamish, how about you doing the sampling on those three does over there? I'll take the buck and the other two does."

"Sure thing, Doc," Mack said, noticing that he had dropped the *Miz*. They were making progress. She pulled on the mask. "Both anthrax and CWD, right?"

She was sure the animals hadn't been killed by chronic wasting disease, but it was important to test as many deer as they could, because it could remain dormant, but transmissible, for years. She remembered reading about a 1997 shipment of infected Canadian elk imported into South Korea. The disease went undetected for nearly ten years. And now South Korea had CWD.

"Yep, CWD, too," the vet said cheerfully, and they both settled down to work. She took the necessary blood and tissue samples methodically and efficiently, feeling Doc Masters' eyes occasionally on her, watching to see if she was doing it right.

Derek had resumed his pacing. Now, he stopped for a moment and watched as Mack worked, then turned away, his face ashen, beads of sweat popping out on his forehead. "Sorry," he muttered. "This kind of thing is new to me. I never expected to find anything like it here in Utopia." He stepped hurriedly behind a tree. Mack could hear him throwing up.

"City feller," the old vet said with a scornful chuckle. "Folks come out here from Dallas and Houston, thinking that since the town is named Utopia they've arrived in some kind of paradise. Gives 'em a good shock when they find out that old Mother Nature ain't always a pretty lady." He shook his head. "This place isn't Disneyland, that's for sure. There's just as much bad stuff happens here as anywhere else in this blighted world." Closing a sample bag, he muttered, half under his breath, "Maybe more."

Mack finished labeling her samples and gave them to the vet. Derek had rejoined them, his face pale and sweaty. He had tied a white handkerchief over his mouth and nose, as if to protect himself from whatever toxic anthrax spores might come flying in his direction—or maybe from the smell. He stood well back, his shoulders slumped, his hands in his pockets.

Doc Masters packed the samples in his bag and straightened up. To Mack, he said, "If I get right on it, I'll catch the afternoon mail truck at the post office. It takes the lab about twenty-four hours to grow the cultures and another twelve or so to do the analysis, so it'll be early next week before we hear. Meanwhile—"

"Meanwhile," Derek broke in abruptly, "what am I supposed to do with these dead animals? Do you know somebody I can hire to haul them off to the landfill?"

The vet was clearing his throat to say something—probably something sharply impolite—but this time, Mack headed him off.

"I'm afraid that's not possible," she told Derek, pulling off her mask. "Since it's almost certain that these animals were killed by anthrax, the Texas Animal Health Commission requires that you burn the carcasses right here."

"Burn them!" Derek exclaimed, his eyes widening over his handkerchief-mask. "You're not serious, Mackenzie!"

"Afraid so," Mack said ruefully, and stripped off her gloves. "It would be best if that could be done today. You can see that the vultures have already started doing their thing, and if you leave them out overnight, the coyotes and foxes will join the party. The vultures aren't susceptible to anthrax, but the other predators are. That's one of the ways the disease is spread. In any case, the Animal Health Commission requires that it be done within twenty-four hours of discovery."

"I'm friggin' not believing this," Derek muttered darkly.

"I'll be glad to give you a hand," Mack offered. "I brought a can of gasoline and a propane torch. If we get started right away, we'll have the job done by dark. I'll radio the county dispatcher and let her know what we're doing and why, in case somebody sees the smoke and calls it in. There's no burn ban right now, but dry as it is, folks will be keeping a pretty good eye out for wildfires."

Doc Masters grunted. "You're gettin' some special treatment," he said to Derek. "There's no law that says the warden has to help."

But Derek didn't answer. He turned on his heel and headed for the ATV. Mack stared after him, wondering whether he intended to do the burning or not. If he didn't—

"Well, I guess everybody's got to learn somehow, someway," the vet said philosophically. "Why don't you take me back to my vehicle and then you can thump on him about that burning."

"Yeah, sure." Mack sighed, wishing that Derek had made things a little easier. "Let's go."

As they reached Mack's truck, the vet said, in a casual tone, "I heard that you and that biologist woman nabbed yourselves a nice male lion this morning. What'd y'all do with it?"

"News travels fast," Mack said, not quite sure what she should say. She opened the door and got in. Better tell him the truth. "We collared the animal and took it up to Karen Wilson's study area the other side of Boiling Mountain."

The vet slung his bag in the back and climbed into the truck. "Some folks'll be pissed when they hear, but I gotta say I'm glad you didn't shoot that cat. There's not near enough of the wild left in this world, and the big predators have their own part in the general scheme of things. Shoot the cats, and the deer go like gangbusters. Too many deer means that they eat off all the vegetation along the streams, and what you get is erosion. Silt in the water kills the fish and other aquatic life, which—" He slammed the truck door. "When the big cats and the wolves and the grizzlies are all gone, we'll be the only predator left. And we're pretty sorry predators. We kill for the wrong reasons. Nature culls the weak ones. We kill the best of the best."

"You said a true thing there," Mack agreed, putting the key in the ignition. She added, "At least we'll learn something from that cat, as long as that collar functions." She started the truck and swung out to follow Derek's ATV down the two-track to the ranch house.

Doc Masters stretched out his legs in the foot well and leaned back. After a moment, he said, "I've got something chewing at me." He pulled his cap brim down over his nose. "I've been pondering what to do about it. Wondering if maybe you'd have a thought or two on the subject."

Mack wondered if this was another of Doc Masters' tests, or an indication that she had already passed muster. "What's up?"

He chewed on his lower lip. "Well, I'm not just a hundred percent sure. I know it's bothering me, is all." He turned toward Mack, studying her under the brim of his cap. "You seem pretty well trained and reasonably observant, for a warden. You been out to Three Gates yet?"

Trained and observant. Pleased, Mack thought this was probably the best compliment she was going to get out of the old vet.

"The assistant foreman gave me the grand tour a month or so ago," she said. "Quite an impressive setup. I'm not an admirer of deer farming operations, but it looks like the owners have pumped a ton of money into the place—and they've had some advice from the pros." She backed the truck around and began to follow Derek's ATV back to the ranch house. "The barn is definitely state-of-the-art. I understand that Dr. Boise designed it."

The Three Gates deer-handling barn was surrounded on three sides by a system of high-fenced containment pens, where the deer were kept from birth until their release onto the ranch. The two-story barn contained several handling rooms; a cradle designed like a cattle chute to immobilize the deer for various procedures; and a laboratory with all the latest technology for semen collection and storage, artificial insemination, and disease diagnosis and treatment. It even had an observation room on the second floor, where potential buyers could watch the breeder bucks and does in their pens. After she got back to her computer, Mack had done a Google search for Dr. Arthur Boise, who turned out to have outstanding credentials as a deer biologist. He was a member of the team that created Dewey, the first white-tailed deer clone, some twelve years before. Dewey had produced an incredible thirty-eight-point rack—in Mack's opinion, an incredibly grotesque rack, like nothing ever produced in nature.

Grunting sourly, the vet fumbled in his pockets until he found a package of chewing gum. "The Gates family friends of yours, are they?" He offered her a stick but she shook her head.

"Not friends, no. But I felt I ought to see the facility—a duty call, you might say. I don't like designer deer, and I don't have any respect for canned hunts." She was probably saying more than she should, but she couldn't stop herself. "My father taught me to get out in the woods and look for deer on my own two feet, not sit in a comfy blind and point my rifle at the game manager's pet buck wearing antlers the size of the UT goalposts."

Her visit hadn't been an official inspection—that was handled by the people who managed the breeder permits. But she felt she had an obligation to know what was going on in the area she patrolled, and the owners of Three Gates were obviously intent on establishing a reputation for their ranch in the deer breeding and hunting business. They were likely to do that, at least if you went by the numbers. She'd been told that there were ninety-three fawns born that year, forty buck and forty-three doe fawns, all with "superior genetics," which meant the genes for superior headgear. And the animals didn't even get to enjoy having natural sex. Those ninety-three fawns had been conceived entirely by artificial insemination. Not a naturally bred animal in the batch.

"UT goalposts," Doc Masters repeated, darkly amused. "A freak of nature—but they're really not a freak of *nature*, since they're man-made. Not to mention that the fawns are bottle-fed and thoroughly habituated to humans." He doubled up the chewing gum stick and put it in his mouth, heaving a hefty sigh. "I know I'm old-fashioned, but by damn, I hate those genetically engineered animals. Did you see the bucks in the containment pens? God didn't make deer like that. Man doesn't have any business making 'em, either." He took off his baseball cap and rubbed his scalp. "Not to mention that line breeding is in no way healthy for the animals. Breeding for antlers is a quick way to weaken the gene pool."

Mack nodded, not sure where this was going and waiting to see.

After a moment, Doc Masters sat up straighter and squared his shoulders, as if he had made up his mind that Mack—even though she was a woman *and* a game warden—was somebody he could talk to. "When you went to Three Gates, you probably noticed the deer ear tags and tattoos."

"I did, yes." Mack chuckled. "Learned about that at warden school, too."

When a captive fawn was born, the breeder inserted a plastic tag in its right ear, identifying the sex and the year of birth. A few months later (the delay was supposed to take infant mortality into consideration), Texas Parks and Wildlife issued a number. The breeder tattooed it in the fawn's left ear. The three-digit prefix was the facility's identification number, the following digits a unique number issued to each fawn. At the end of the first quarter of every year, the breeder had to turn in a report on all the fawns born in the preceding twelve months in his facility. At the same time, he turned in a mortality report and a report on any deer he had sold as breeding animals. It was a birth-to-death monitoring program. The identification numbers, carrying on the old tradition of cattle brands, were key to making it work.

The breeders complained about all the records they had to maintain, but the system was designed to keep tabs on the increasing numbers of facility-bred deer, which quite obviously did not have the same genetic makeup as the native wild deer population. If an animal escaped into the wild population, the ear tag and the tattoo identified it as a genetically engineered deer.

Keeping track of individual animals and their pedigree was important as far as the bottom line was concerned, too, for some of the bucks were extremely valuable. Mack had learned that Buckaroo, one of the bucks at Three Gates, wore an $800,000 price tag, and his semen went for $10,000 a straw. That was one of the reasons for the expensive fencing that surrounded such ranches. You didn't want a high-dollar buck like Buckaroo out roaming the neighborhood unsupervised, giving it all away when he should be filling those $10,000 semen straws back home in the barn, or being shot for nothing instead of fetching top dollar during hunting season

"Okay, then," the vet said. "So what we've got are fawns with ear tags and fawns with ear tags and tattoos." He put his baseball cap back on and tugged down hard on the bill, pulling it almost down to his nose. "I went out to Three Gates last spring to treat a horse with a hoof infection. I happened to be there when they were tattooing fawns, and I noticed the prefix. Four-thirty-two. Four-three-two. A number that might stick in your mind, right?"

Mack slowed, as a doe bounded gracefully out of the woods and across the narrow gravel track in front of them. She popped into neutral, idling, and as she expected, two yearling deer—last year's fawns—dashed after the doe a moment later. No ear tags, no tattoos, they were beautiful and wild, a natural part of the wilderness, like horseflies, like the mountain lion. Like anthrax. It was all bound up together.

She brought her attention back to Masters. "Four-three-two," she said, shifting back into first and picking up speed again. "The prefix designates the breeding facility." In Texas, there were over a thousand facilities, with more applying for permits every year. And not just Texas. Nationwide, there were eight thousand deer farms, and the number was growing. Deer farming was the next big bubble.

"Exactly," Masters said. He fell silent again, as if he'd lost the thread of his story.

"And?" Mack prompted.

He took a deep breath, let it out again. "Well, a week or so ago, I made a trip to another ranch, over near Sycamore Mountain. I did what I was there to do—help a young cow birth twin calves. Lost one of them, unfortunately. Happens sometimes, with a first birth. Midway through, I took a break to answer a call of nature, and off behind the barn, I happened to see a fair-size pen, high-fenced, with canvas stretched around the fence so you couldn't see what was inside. But one of the corners was flapping loose, and I noticed that there were a half-dozen fawns in the pen. They weren't wearing ear tags, but they were tattooed, which got my attention right off. You understand why?"

"Because the ranch wasn't a permitted breeding facility," Mack replied. Derek was pushing the ATV fast, and she'd lost sight of him around a bend.

"You got it. It's a cattle ranch, not a deer farm. Been a cattle ranch for decades. A good one, once upon a time; maybe not so good now, though. Times are tough." There was a glint in the vet's eye. "So, being a curious sort of fellow, I waited my chance. When the owner was off doing something else, I went back for a better look. The prefix on the tattoos was four-eight-two. Four-*eight*-two. And the eight looked fresher than the four or the two—at least, that's the way it seemed to me. Not that I got a really close look," he added. "I could be wrong."

"But if you're right," Mack said thoughtfully, "you're wondering whether the eight might have been a three, originally. And if the eight was a three, you're thinking that the fawns in that pen may have started life at Three Gates."

"It's been in my mind," he conceded. "But that's if the eight was a three. It could've been something else. A zero, maybe. Smells like the old brand-changing trick."

"But whatever the number, you're thinking that the fawns were illegally moved, since the ranch where you saw them wasn't a licensed facility. And maybe stolen, to boot. And you're telling all this to a game warden." She gave the old man a sidelong look. "So are you going to tell me where this ranch is and who it belongs to?"

There was another long silence while Masters chewed on his gum. "I dunno," he said, finally. "Dunno whether I am or not." He sighed. "I guess maybe I've been talking a little too much. I didn't think this thing through all the way to the end. It's kind of a tricky business, since one of the owners—" He stopped, frowning.

"Is a friend of yours," Mack guessed. She swung around a corner. Derek's ranch house was just ahead, the ATV parked out in front. Derek was nowhere in sight. "Or a regular client. Even a pillar of the community, maybe." Could be somebody—a professional person, a doctor, a lawyer—who couldn't afford to be exposed. And maybe the fawns Doc Masters had seen weren't the only animals involved. The penalties on something like this could add up fast in fines and jail time, especially if there were any Lacey Act violations and the feds got involved.

"Sorry." Masters pulled on his lower lip. "It's complicated, and there's a lot more hanging on it than there seems to be, just right off the bat, especially for one of the—" He stopped. "Reckon I need to think about it a little longer."

"But you're not going to think about it too long, I hope," Mack said, pulling to a stop beside the ATV and turning off the ignition. Derek was coming out of the garage, a gasoline can in one hand and a rake in the other. He had changed from shorts and sandals to jeans and boots.

The vet chuckled dryly, seizing the opportunity to change the subject. "Well, look at that. Guess he's decided a fella's gotta do what he's gotta do."

"We've all gotta do what we've gotta do," Mack said firmly, not letting him off the hook. "But you don't have to be involved, Doc. Deer are my job. Give me a name and a location and I'll take it from here. Nobody needs to know where the information came from."

"I wish it were that easy." Shoulders slumped, the vet gazed out the window. "I'm not saying it's a matter of life and death, but it's serious enough. I'm wishing I hadn't . . ." His voice trailed off.

Somehow, Mack thought, the tables had turned. She was now the one who had to tell the old man what had to be done, and when. "I'm sure you understand the importance of this, Doc. After that big criminal case over in Cherokee County, everybody in the deer-breeding business is aware of the penalties involved with breaking the law."

The case had made national news. A deer breeder in East Texas—one of the two or three biggest in the state—had pleaded guilty to smuggling illegal white-tails from states up north where CWD was rampant. He had paid a million-dollar fine to the feds for violations of the Lacey Act and another half million in restitution to the state of Texas, as well as forfeiting his entire breeding stock, worth more millions.

"That's true," Masters said, and fell silent again.

Mack persisted. "Look. A few illegally transported fawns aren't any big deal. But I need to get out there and take a look. Right away." In fact, if the owner had happened to notice the vet's interest in the fawns, it was likely that he had already moved them. "How about if I call you first thing in the morning and you give me the location so I can do my job?"

The old man tipped up the brim of his cap with a thumb. "In case you haven't heard," he said wryly, "tomorrow's Thanksgiving. If it's all the same to you, I'd just as soon eat turkey and watch some football. How about you call me on Friday morning?"

Not giving her a chance to reply, he opened the truck door and got out, raising his voice so that Derek could hear. "Well, I'll leave you to settle the business of the carcasses, warden. I'll let you know as soon as I hear back from the lab, but my money is on anthrax."

"Yeah," Mack said. "Mine, too."

He ducked down and spoke to her through the open window. "Nice working with you, Mack. I hope there'll be a next time."

She heard the respect in his voice and understood that he was saying something important. "I'm sure there will," she said.

She watched as the old man walked to his car, got in, and drove away. She urgently hoped he wasn't planning on warning someone, but she understood his reluctance to tell her what he knew. He had lived in Utopia his entire life. He knew everybody, and everybody knew him. If word got around that he had blown the whistle on a friend or an upstanding citizen, people might decide he couldn't be trusted. Small-town people could be petty that way.

Derek had gone behind the garage and now came out, pulling a small two-wheeled trailer. He dropped the tongue hitch onto the tow ball at the rear of the ATV and shoved the locking lever down hard. When he straightened up, Mack rolled down her window and called. "Hey, Derek, why don't you put that stuff in the back of the truck and ride with me to the site?"

Derek stopped five feet from the truck. "I can handle this myself, Mack." He looked at her, eyes flinty, jaw thrust out, mouth tight. "Unless you just want to watch and make sure I'm doing the job right. I sure as hell wouldn't want to break any of your game warden rules."

Oh, *damn*, Mack thought, refraining from rolling her eyes. But she only shrugged. "Sure, whatever you want." She smiled and added brightly, "So what time did we say for brunch tomorrow? Ten thirty? Oh, and Cheyenne needs some exercise—I thought I'd bring her out with me and take the girls for a ride. You think they'd like that?"

Derek gave her a hard look. "I think I need to give you a rain check. After I finish barbecuing those dead deer this evening, I doubt I'll be in the mood to cook a holiday meal for company."

Mack stared at him for a moment. "I get it," she said. "Sorry."

She might have said more, but Derek had turned away. She started her truck and drove away, thinking with painful regret how much you could learn about a person when it came to dealing with six dead deer.

And about what Karen had said earlier that day. *It's going to take a really special guy to love you and love what you do—because you very much are what you do, you know. In ways other women probably aren't.*

By the time she got home, her regret had turned to a nagging exasperation. Derek had irrationally blamed her for doing her job. Doc Masters was being uncooperative when he knew that she *had* to do her job.

And she had missed another phone call from that PETA woman, Amy Roth. This time, however, she had left a more detailed message.

"This is Amy Roth," she'd said in a businesslike tone. "With the holiday tomorrow, we may keep missing each other, so here's what I'm calling about. My colleague, Chris Griffin, is a graduate student in environmental studies at the University of Texas in San Antonio. The two of you met at a regional wildlife conservation conference last year, and he mentioned to you that he was building a surveillance drone. At the time, you seemed interested and said you'd maybe like to see it. The drone is ready for a demo. Would you have some time on Friday to take a look at what it can do? Name the time and place, whatever is convenient for you. We'll be glad to meet you there." She signed off with a telephone number.

Now that she was prompted, Mack remembered Griffin, a dark-haired, intense young man who had waylaid her for fifteen minutes with a rambling, disjointed description of a project that had something to do with using a drone to monitor wildlife. She picked up the phone and punched in the number. To her surprise, she connected with Amy and made a date to meet her and Chris Griffin at ten on Friday morning, at the rodeo grounds in Utopia. There was plenty of open space there, and nobody would be around to bother them or ask questions.

She glanced at her watch. A cold front was blowing down from the north, and the wind was picking up, but there was still an hour or two of daylight left. She pulled on a parka and went outdoors to the paddock. She would saddle Cheyenne and whistle for Molly and they would go for a brisk canter along one of the gravel roads that led out of town.

Maybe the exercise in the chilly air would clear whatever lingering regret she might be feeling about Derek.

Chapter Five

Ashe juniper (*Juniperus ashei*) is a drought-tolerant shrubby tree native to the south-central United States, and especially to the Texas Hill Country, where it can be seen everywhere. In the wildlife garden, its berries, foliage, canopy, and bark serve many animals and birds. The endangered golden-cheeked warbler uses soft strips of bark for nest material, and the tree is a larval host for the beautiful Juniper Hairstreak butterfly. Deer prefer not to eat it if they can find anything else.

Native Americans used the smoke from juniper foliage for cleansing and purification rituals, and the bark for baskets and mats. They employed the berries medicinally, as a diuretic, a treatment for canker sores, and (brewed in tea) as a remedy for indigestion. Southwestern tribes used the berries to treat diabetes and as a female contraceptive. Dioscorides, a Roman physician in the time of Nero, also noted that the crushed berries, placed on the penis or in the vagina, were used as a contraceptive.

Juniper berries have long been used in cooking and in drinks. Native Americans used them to counteract the gaminess of wild buffalo and venison. German immigrants used them to flavor sauerkraut, sauces, and stews. In Europe, they are used in marinades for wild boar, venison, and pork, and in poultry stuffing. The berry of *Juniperus communis* still provides the predominant flavoring of gin.

Junipers also have another use. According to legend, a juniper planted beside the front door will keep witches away, for in order

**to pass by a juniper, the witch must stop and count every needle—
a job that would keep her busy for a while.**

China Bayles
"Native Plants for Wildlife Gardens"
Pecan Springs Enterprise

While we were waiting for Sue Ellen Krause to arrive for supper and the evening, Caitie and I put on our jackets and caps and went for a walk beside the Sabinal River, which flows at the foot of a long, grassy slope about fifty yards in front of the ranch house.

The Sabinal is twenty feet wide at the place where it meets the smaller Bittersweet Creek, and the water is shallow and so clear that you can see the tiny minnows darting like glimmers of silver among the rocks and the crawdads peering out of their holes in the gravelly banks. If you're lucky, you may even see the shimmer and flash of a rainbow trout—and if you're a fisherman, you'll itch to cast your favorite fly onto the glimmering surface. Spring-fed, beautiful, and one of the best-kept secrets in Texas, the river rises in Bandera County, about forty miles to the north of the ranch, and flows into the Frio some ten miles south of Sabinal. Much of its sixty-mile length is bordered on both sides by bald cypress trees, so intensely green in the summer that their color seems to saturate the water itself, turning it into a shimmering green ribbon. The early Spanish called the river Arroyo de la Soledad, Stream of Solitude, which has always seemed to me to describe it beautifully.

But this wasn't summer. It was late November, and a cold front was blowing briskly down from the north, shuttering the sun with bands of scudding gray clouds. A month or so before, the cypress trees had turned from green to a bright russet and dropped their needles into the river. Now, their bare branches were like witches' fingers clawing the darkening sky. The tall grasses, hit by a killing frost, were bleached to the color of bones, and as the wind blew, they rubbed together with a hard, dry rasp, like an old man's cough. On the other side of the river, beyond the cypress trees, the Ashe junipers clothed the steep hills in their somber green.

The landscape was beautiful, but it was a subdued, sober turn-of-the-seasons beauty that reminded me that the cheerful, eager joys of spring had slipped into a forgotten past and the year was growing inexorably grayer, colder, older. Or was it that my mother and her dear Sam were growing older, and more fragile, and less able to do what they wanted to do, and that I was worried about them? Lives have seasons, too, and we grow gray, and colder, and older with the years.

But despite my feeling that winter was already blowing down our necks, there were plenty of birds to brighten the landscape. Caitie had brought her binoculars and delighted in naming as many as she recognized and pointing out those she didn't. A golden-fronted woodpecker, beating a rapid tattoo on the rough bark of a nearby hackberry tree. A raucous scrub jay, bright blue with black eye patches. ("And white eyebrows!" Caitie cried ecstatically. "Look at his white eyebrows!") A tidy brown cactus wren, busy among the leaves. A dapper gray and red pyrrhuloxia, a cousin of the northern cardinal, but with a parrotlike yellow bill and an elegant crest that looked like it had been dipped in bright red paint.

And many, many more. There were birds in the trees that I had never seen before, and birds wading in the shallows along the banks, and birds soaring high overhead. Downstream, I glimpsed the outline of the wooden observation tower that Sam had built—Caitie and I would explore it tomorrow. I had no doubt that Leatha and Sam could attract a throng of birders to Bittersweet, who would flock there in large numbers for the sheer pleasure of adding another dozen birds to their life lists.

But then the worry came back again, and I couldn't push it away. Sam was in the hospital, with an uncertain prognosis for the weeks ahead. Sue Ellen Krause would be around to lend a hand for a while; after several years working at Three Gates she probably had the kind of experience that was necessary to ensure that Bittersweet's first birding year got off to a smooth start. But if Sue Ellen was planning to enroll in college, she wouldn't be staying long. And if Sam's heart condition meant that he had to take things easy for the rest of his life, Leatha was going to need more than short-term or part-time help. I'm her only child, and I couldn't help feeling responsible. I couldn't offer anything more than moral support, however, for I have a business and a family and a house back in Pecan Springs. Where would the help come from? It was an unsettling question, as sharp as the wintry wind that was blowing down my neck.

Caitie tugged at my sleeve. "There's the lodge over there," she said, pointing. "I haven't been inside since Gramma and Sam fixed it up. Can we go in and look around?"

"I'm curious, too," I said. "I'm sure it will be okay, as long as it's not locked."

It wasn't. The lodge sat back from the river about forty yards downstream from the ranch house. It was a long, low log building with a green metal roof and a wide covered porch across the front. Roof-high dark green junipers sheltered each end of the building, and rosemary bushes skirted the front. (Strongly resinous, rosemary is one of the shrubs deer don't like, which makes it an ideal landscaping plant in deer-traffic areas.)

There were seven individual guest suites in the lodge, and on this side, each suite had a front door and a wide front window so the guests could enjoy a view of the river. A large wooden sign painted with the words *Bittersweet Lodge* hung in the center of the long front porch, and each of the suites was named: *Sandpiper, Indigo Bunting, Blue Heron*, and so on. There was a framed photo of the bird beside each door.

The lodge's exterior logs were well weathered—as they should be, since the lodge had been built by Sam's father when he opened the ranch to hunting some decades before. But the interiors had been completely remodeled, and very nicely. Gone were the small, dark rooms with their lingering odors of tobacco smoke and wet shoes and fried fish. Newly pine-paneled, the air-conditioned and heated suites featured tidy kitchenettes with microwave ovens, cook-top ranges, mini refrigerators, and dining tables and chairs. Each had a carpeted sitting-sleeping area with a sofa bed, upholstered chair, and coffee table, and a television set. Twin beds were made up with colorful quilts, and there was a folding cot in the closet. The compact bath had a large mirror over the sink and pine cupboards stocked with fluffy towels. The glass door in the back of each sitting area opened onto a private deck furnished with comfortable chairs, tables, and a barbecue grill.

The accommodations seemed just right to me—comfortable, attractive, and perfect for a single, a couple, or even a small family. The thought popped into my mind that maybe McQuaid and I could squeeze in some time to come and relax, but with it came another thought. I wouldn't be relaxing. I'd be here to help my mother. After the guests checked out, somebody was going to have to clean all those kitchenettes and bathrooms and put fresh sheets on the beds and fresh towels on the shelves and run the vacuum over the carpets. (I know about this, because I rent out the stone cottage behind my shop as a B&B, when it's not in use for workshops and other activities. And I'm the one who does the housekeeping.) Seeing that this place was clean and tidy would be a ten-hour-a-week job, at least. Sam and Leatha could handle it. But if Sam couldn't help, could my mother handle it alone? Another thing for me to worry about.

Caitie and I had left the lodge and were heading back to the ranch house when a banged-up red Ford Focus pulled up in the driveway, piled high with boxes and bags. A pretty young woman got out—Sue Ellen Krause, I guessed. A few moments later, we were taking off our coats in the kitchen and my mother was introducing us.

Sue Ellen had the look of a country-and-western singer—a younger version of Reba McEntire, maybe—sparky blue eyes, deep dimples, a sassy mouth, and long auburn hair falling in loose, tousled curls down to her shoulders. She wore a western shirt in a muted blue plaid with pearl snaps down the front, tight Wranglers, and filigreed, fancy-dancin' cowgirl boots. Her complexion was flawless, except for a pale bruise at the corner of her jaw, and she had the kind of figure that most women secretly covet and most men openly lust after. She looked to be in her middle twenties.

"I have been dyin' to meet you, China," she said, extending a hand and briefly clasping mine. Her voice was low and warm and there was a muted chuckle in it. "Your mom has told me so much about you—I feel like I just about know you already. I do truly want to be friends." She held up a bottle of red wine. "And today's a great big red-letter day for me, so I brought this Merlot. Let's all have a glass right now."

"You know I can't do that," Leatha said in a matter-of-fact tone. "But you and China go right ahead, dear. Caitie and I will have iced tea."

Sue Ellen planted a noisy smooch on my mother's cheek. "You can have some of this," she chirped merrily. "And so can Caitie. It's totally nonalcoholic. We can drink as much as we want!" With an easy familiarity, she found wineglasses on the top shelf of the cupboard and a corkscrew in a drawer, and she poured for the four of us, including a half glass for Caitie.

"Here's to new friends," she said, and tipped her glass against mine with that sassy smile. She lifted her glass to Leatha. "And to old and dear ones!"

And by some magic, we became friends almost immediately. While Caitie bustled around, helping my mother get the venison chili, salad, deviled eggs, and hot garlic bread on the table, Sue Ellen and I sat across from each other and sipped our wine. To tell the truth, I was a little surprised at her high spirits. Leatha had said that she had sounded terribly unhappy that morning on the phone, so I was expecting gloom—maybe even tears.

"You said it's a red-letter day for you," I said. "What's going on?"

"I left my husband for good today, and I do mean *good*." Sue Ellen shook her head and her long curls bounced over her shoulder. "I feel so relieved. It's like I'm about to get to the end of a long, hard road." She paused, reflecting, and added in a more sober tone, "At least, I hope it's the end." Over her shoulder to Leatha, she said, "I crammed as much of my stuff in the car as I could and brought it with me, Leatha. You'll have to tell me where you want me to bunk."

"I thought we'd put you in the lodge, in Sandpiper, which is the suite nearest the ranch house," Leatha said, putting down a plate of hot garlic bread. "If you want to invite friends over, or play music or whatever, you'll have plenty of privacy there. China can help you move in after supper." She began ladling chili into our bowls. "I didn't use much chili powder in this, because I know Caitie doesn't like spicy stuff. But I did use a couple of secret ingredients. Tell me what you think, China."

"Oh, let me guess!" Caitie cried, sitting down beside me and picking up her spoon. She tasted, then tasted again, frowning intently. "It's . . . something," she said, puzzled. "But I don't know what it is." She tasted again, and wrinkled her nose. "Cinnamon?" she ventured.

"Good for you, Caitie!" Leatha said, taking her place next to Sue Ellen. "You're right, cinnamon is one of the secret ingredients. She looked inquiringly at me. "What's the other, China?"

I tasted. I frowned. I tasted again. "Juniper berries," I said. "But they're more . . . citrusy than usual." Piney, peppery dried juniper berries are great with wild game, but sometimes the pepper dominates the other flavors.

"That's because they're fresh," Leatha said, pleased. "Right off one of the junipers next to the lodge. What do you think of the chili?"

"I love it," I said promptly, and dug in. "And you're right—fresh makes a big difference. I've always used dried berries in the cabbage and sausage soup that McQuaid likes. I'll make it next week and try the fresh berries. We've certainly got plenty on the trees right now." The dried juniper berries in the grocery store come from the European juniper. Our Texas junipers are *Juniperus ashei* and their berries are more tart. I'd try just two.

"It's great chili, Gran!" Caitie said enthusiastically.

"It's wonderful," Sue Ellen said, and turned to Leatha. "How's Sam? I'll bet he was glad to see you. Is he feeling better?"

"Some," Leatha said guardedly. "We're just taking it day by day." She leaned forward. "Caitie, your mom tells me that you're going to be in your teacher's winter recital. You brought your violin with you, I hope. Will you play your recital piece for me?"

"I won't play that one," Caitie said, very seriously, "because I need the piano accompaniment. But I've been practicing a couple of other pieces to play for you." She helped herself to a piece of garlic bread. "And could we talk about maybe getting me a full-size violin?" she asked tentatively. "Dr. Trevor says I'm ready for it. I've been saving my egg money, but at the rate the girls are laying, it'll be years before I can afford it myself."

Leatha had given Caitie the three-quarter-size violin I scorned when I was her age, and she had done so well with it that her teacher, Sandra Trevor, thought it was time to move up to a full-size instrument. Her grandmother had offered to get it for her, but Caitie had wanted to earn the money herself. Now, Leatha leaned across the table and patted her hand. "You keep on saving your egg money, dear. Christmas is coming in a few weeks, and I'm sure that Santa will be able to get his elves to make a violin just for you."

Caitie clapped her hands with delight. "That's super!" she cried. "I can't wait to tell Dr. Trevor!" She gave up on Santa last year, but that didn't stop her from playing along with her grandmother's little tale.

From there, the conversation turned to family matters. Caitie reported on her ant farm, her project for the science fair. I reported on Brian's first semester at the university, where he was majoring in Personal Independence and minoring in Doing His Own Laundry, and on the holiday events that Ruby and I were planning at the shops and the tea-room. Sue Ellen wanted to hear all about that, since it was her dream to own her own business.

"Did your mom tell you I'm going to college?" she asked eagerly. "I know it's a big dream, but I'm determined. I'm going to get my degree in . . . oh, I don't know—interior design or something like that. I love to change rooms around and have everything nice. I couldn't do that, living over at Three Gates. I'm looking forward to having my own apartment, where I can fix things up however I want." Then she patted my mother's arm. "But I'm going to be right here for a while, helping out. We need to get Sam back on his feet first." She leaned toward me, her blue eyes warm. "I just can't tell you how sweet your mom and dad have been to me in my time of troubles, China. It means the world, having somebody I can talk to and someplace I can come and know I'm safe." She waved her hand. "Oh, heavens. That sounds so silly and dramatic. It's just that— Well, things have been a little rough lately."

"It's wonderful to have you here," Leatha murmured, with a smile for Sue Ellen that she shared—almost as an afterthought, it seemed—with me. I felt a stab of something that I hoped wasn't jealousy. I liked Sue Ellen, and I reminded myself to be grateful for the time she was willing to devote to my mother, who needed someone she could depend on right now. She needed Sue Ellen, actually. And it sounded like Sue Ellen needed her.

I learned more about that after we finished the dishes. Leatha pulled me aside and reminded me that she hoped I would be able to answer Sue Ellen's questions. "And I hope you'll be nice," she added in a low voice.

"I'm always nice," I said, surprised.

She sighed and shook her head. "Sometimes you're . . . well, you're a lawyer."

"Ah," I said. "Well, if she needs to ask a lawyer a question, she needs to get a lawyer's answer, doesn't she?"

"Just be nice," Leatha said, and turned away. "Come on, Caitie. What kind of pie shall we make first? Peach or mincemeat?"

Sue Ellen and I turned on the outdoor light—it was pitch-dark already—and went out to unpack her Ford. It turned out to be loaded with an amazing amount of stuff. Clothes, shoes, books, record albums, a laptop, even a bag of groceries and a gray tabby cat who was not amused—a lot more than you'd think such a little car could hold. I found a wheelbarrow, and we piled it high with boxes and bags and trundled them to the lodge, Sue Ellen cradling her cat, Amarillo, in her arms. It took several trips to empty the car, but at last it was done.

Leatha had given Sue Ellen a key so she could lock the doors when she left, but she dropped it into the drawer of the nightstand beside the bed. "I don't know that I'd even bother locking up here," she said happily, looking around the small suite. "It feels really safe." She made a face. "I don't mean to be harping on that theme, China. It's just that it's kind of important to me right now, after the past week or two."

"Sounds like you've had a tough time." Mildly curious, I stacked my load of cartons on the floor next to the bed. "What's been going on?"

Sue Ellen went into the bathroom with a box of cosmetics. "Oh, just . . . stuff," she said vaguely.

I moved a pile of clothes to the other end of the sofa and sat down. "Leatha says you have some questions you want to ask me."

Sue Ellen came out of the bathroom. "Why do you call your mother Leatha?" she asked curiously. "And I noticed that you call your husband by his last name. Seems a little . . . well, unusual. But that's not one of the questions I wanted to ask," she added hastily. "You don't have to answer if you don't want to."

"My mother and I weren't very close, when I was growing up," I said. "Back then, she wanted me to call her by her first name. I think it made her feel . . . younger, maybe." I didn't want to tell Sue Ellen that the woman she knew now was different from the woman I had known when I was a girl. I propped my feet on the coffee table in front of the sofa and leaned back, clasping my hands behind my head.

"As for McQuaid, when I met him, he was a cop and I was a criminal defense lawyer. Everybody in that business uses last names, so we were Bayles and McQuaid. He's gotten out of the habit, but I like the name McQuaid. It seems to fit him." I brought the subject back to her. "That's my answer. So what are your other questions?"

"Hang on a sec." She stepped into the kitchenette, pulled a couple of soft drink cans out of a six-pack, and stuck the rest into the small fridge. Handing me one of the cans, she plopped into the chair beside the sofa, and we popped our tops in unison.

"Your mom told me you handled criminal cases," she said, as if she were answering me. Amarillo, who had been exploring the premises, saw his chance and jumped onto her lap to get his paws warm.

"That's right. I'm afraid I don't know much about divorce law." I was being nice. "For that, you need to find somebody who specializes in—"

"I know." She stroked Amarillo, who powered up his purr. "I found a lawyer in Uvalde and filed last week. He told me that since Jack was being such a butthead, I should go ahead and move out." She turned her head and touched the bruise on her jaw.

"Ah," I said sympathetically, and my heart hardened toward her husband. There's no excuse for violence. Period. "That's too bad, Sue Ellen."

"Not as bad as this." She rolled up her sleeve and held out her arm so I could see the large purple bruises, then rolled down her sleeve again.

"Did your lawyer suggest a protective order? If you're afraid—"

"He did, but now that I've moved out, I don't think Jack will bother me."

"Maybe," I said slowly. "Still, if he's been violent, a protective order is a good idea, Sue Ellen. The penalty is hefty—up to a year in jail. That by itself could keep him away."

"But it's not just him," she said. "It's his buddies. Duke and Lucky. It's the three of them. I mean, I don't give a damn what happens to those other two guys. They can go straight to hell as far as I'm concerned." She scooted the cat off her lap and began pulling her boots off. "It's Jack I worry about. Duke and Lucky are using him, and he's into something dangerous." She grunted and yanked. "I have always been a totally loyal person, but there's a limit."

"Dangerous? Dangerous how?"

"Oh, just . . . you know." She thought about it for a moment, decided not to tell me, and went on. "Of course, now that I've filed, Jack can do whatever he wants. It's not my business anymore." She dropped the boot.

Maybe yes, maybe no, I thought. "When will your divorce be final?"

"Sixty days after the first hearing." She pulled off the other boot, and both stockings. "That's because there's nothing to fight over," she added, as Amarillo reclaimed her lap. "No kids, no real estate. All I have is my cat, my little red Ford, and my clothes and records and stuff. And what he has, I don't want anything to do with."

"Why?" I asked curiously. "I mean, why don't you want anything—"

"Because Jack is in way over his head in this really bad deal that Duke and Lucky have cooked up." She wiggled her prettily polished bare toes, flexing them. "It's one of the reasons I decided to leave him. Of course there are others—like his drinking and that rodeo queen up in Bandera last summer. But the thing with Duke and Lucky is the main reason. The big one." Her voice had a hard edge to it. "I told him he's going to lose his job if anybody finds out. I looked it up on the Internet and found out that he could be in for a whopping big fine and jail time. That's when I told him he'd have to quit or I was leaving. He blew up and started slapping me around."

"Quit what?" I asked. It seemed like a natural question. And I was still being nice.

She picked up her can and sipped. "What he's doing."

"Which is?" When she hesitated, I helped her out. "For example, is he killing people? Stealing cars? Cooking meth? Smuggling undocumented workers across the border? What?"

She giggled nervously.

"I'm serious. What's he doing, Sue Ellen?" I wasn't asking out of curiosity. If she knew that he was involved in a criminal activity and didn't report it to the authorities, she risked being charged as an accessory. I liked her, yes, and I wanted to keep her out of trouble, if I could. But I confess to having a selfish motive as well, for if she got into serious trouble, she wouldn't be much help to Leatha and Sam.

She thought for a moment, chewing one corner of her lip. "Well, I guess maybe the easiest way to describe it is to say that he's stealing. From . . . from the guys he works for." She wasn't meeting my eyes.

I prompted her. "Stealing what? Stealing money?"

Another pause, more lip chewing. "Well . . . yeah. Money is what it boils down to, I guess. Maybe you could tell me how much time he'd have to spend in jail if he got caught."

Her hesitation led me to think that it could boil down to something else. Still being nice, I gave her the boilerplate answer.

"Okay, then, if it's actual money, the scale is pretty simple. It depends on how much. If he's convicted of taking less than $500, it's misdemeanor theft, which gets him up to a year and a possible $4,000 fine. More than that, we're talking grand theft, and there's a scale. Up to $100,000, it's third degree grand theft, and he can get up to ten years. Up to $200,000, it's second and twenty. Anything over that, first and ninety-nine. On top of the prison time, there's a potential $10,000 fine." I paused. "And don't forget tax evasion. The feds resent it when people steal and don't pay taxes on their ill-gotten gains. And sometimes divorce doesn't untie the knot, where the feds are concerned." I added the last sentence on purpose, but being nice, I tacked on, "Does that answer your question?"

"Oh my God," she whispered. "Ninety-nine years?" She had turned pale, and the freckles stood out on her nose. "Ninety-nine years?"

"He stole over two hundred thousand?" I was moderately surprised. "His employer leaves that much money lying around? Or your husband has access to—"

"Only for the next sixty days," she put in firmly. "After that, he's not. My husband, I mean." She placed both hands on her heart. "And in my heart of hearts, I'm already divorced."

He must be playing the ponies, I thought. Or the stock market. When somebody got into first degree grand theft, it was usually a nickel-and-dime embezzlement that snowballed. I gave her a hard look. "You didn't get a share of his loot? As in dollars or diamonds or Caribbean cruises?"

"Are you kidding?" she asked. "Diamonds? Cruises? That's a laugh."

"No, I'm serious. Did you?"

Now she was indignant. "I did *not*, swear to God, China. Not a nickel. I have no part in anything that creep and his buddies have done. And as soon as we're divorced, I'll be free of all of it."

I shook my head. "But maybe not, Sue Ellen. The feds don't take divorce for an answer to the question of tax evasion. What they look at is your name on the joint return. If he declared his theft, you're okay. If not, you're not."

"I'm not believing this," she said faintly.

"I know. It's really, really cruel, but that's the IRS for you. If he's been stealing and hasn't declared his ill-gotten gains on your joint return, they can come after you, divorced or not. There's a provision called Innocent Spouse Relief, but it's not easy to qualify."

"Damn." Her eyes were big. And scared. "I had no idea . . ." Her voice trailed off.

I was swept by a wave of sympathy. She was a sweet kid who could find herself in big trouble if she didn't watch out. "I get that, Sue Ellen. That's why the more information you give me, the more help I can give you."

She picked up the soft drink can and turned it in her fingers. "Well, maybe I'd better ask you what the cops would do to somebody who knew—" She stopped, not looking at me, and swallowed hard.

"You're asking what would happen to *Sue Ellen* if the authorities found out that *she* knew what her husband and his pals were up to and didn't tell them." It wasn't a question.

Her pretty mouth dropped open. "Well, yes," she managed. "But how did you know what I—"

"Because you're not the first person who's asked me that." I sat forward and propped my folded arms on my knees. "The answer is, 'It depends.'"

"On . . . on what?" Her voice had gotten squeaky.

"On how much you know and how willing you are to cooperate. If you know a *lot* and what you know is important and if you offer it and yourself up voluntarily, your clever and wily defense attorney will use it like a crowbar to pry you out of the hole you've already dug for yourself by obstructing justice and being an accessory before and after the fact."

Her eyes widened and she pulled in her breath. "But I *haven't* obstructed . . . what you said."

"Yes, you have. Anybody who knows of a crime and fails to report it is an accessory—before, after, or both. And by definition, an accessory obstructs justice." I hardened my tone. "If, on the other hand, you know only a little, or the district attorney already knows what you know, or you wait until they track you down and haul you off to jail, you won't have any leverage at all, and your clever and wily defense attorney will be reduced to getting down on his or her knees and begging for crumbs—crawling, even."

She swallowed and tried to say something, but nothing came out.

"So the moral of this story," I added crisply, "is that the sooner you rat these guys out, the more kindly you'll be treated in the DA's office. I would suggest taking a lawyer with you when you go. And if I were you, I'd go soon. Maybe not on Thanksgiving. But the day after that."

I wasn't being very nice now. Sometimes it takes a little shock to shake people into an awareness of their vulnerability. Sometimes it takes an earthquake. Sue Ellen needed to understand the consequences of withholding whatever she was withholding. DAs like to use a little extra muscle on the spouse (metaphorically speaking), since it is assumed that she is privy to all the marital secrets, including where her husband put the money he'd been shoving into his pockets.

She finally got the words out. "Could you . . . would you be my lawyer, if I needed one?"

I shook my head. "I can't. But I can give you a name or two." At the top of the list would be Justine Wyzinski, a.k.a the Whiz, an old friend from law school at the University of Texas. She is tough, mean, and abrasive, but she has a heart, especially for women in trouble. She sometimes does pro bono work, especially if it doesn't involve going to trial. I thought this situation could be handled with a visit or two to the Uvalde County DA's office—if Sue Ellen would cooperate.

Sue Ellen chewed on that for a moment, then came to a conclusion. "Okay, if that's what you think I have to do. Let me get a pencil out of my purse and you can write down her name and number."

I couldn't help feeling relieved. I liked Sue Ellen, and it sounded as if her husband had backed her into a corner. The divorce was the way out of the marriage, but if he was involved in something criminal, it might not take her off the hook. And she couldn't just sit around and wait to see what happened, either.

"Here," she said, coming back into the room with a pencil and a scrap of paper.

I took out my cell phone, pulled up Justine's number. I wrote it down, with her name, as well as my own. "You're going to have to tell Ms. Wyzinski everything," I said, giving her the paper. "She can't help if you're holding back—if you're holding *anything* back." I paused to let that sink in. "Want me to let her know you'll be calling?"

She wrinkled her nose, thinking about that. "I guess," she said finally. "Yeah, sure." But she didn't sound positive.

"Tell you what," I said. "Give me your cell number. I'll talk to Ms. Wyzinski. Then I'll call you and let you know if she's able to take you on. She's good, so she's pretty busy. We might need to look for somebody else." I slid her a glance. "As long as you're really serious about this. Are you?"

She sounded chastened. "I kind of feel like I don't have any choice. If I do it and Jack goes to jail, I'll feel like crap. If I don't, I'm in trouble." She bit her lip. "I guess I gotta just bite the damn bullet and do it."

"Atta girl," I said approvingly. She gave me her cell number and I keyed it into my phone, then drained my soft drink and stood up. "I hope I haven't made life harder for you, but I always think it's better to know where you're going than grope around in the dark. Could be some really bad stuff out there that you don't know about. It could bite you." Of course, it could bite her even if she knew it was there, but that was another story.

"I guess I was hoping I didn't have to be involved. It's all so ugly."

"We all wish that every so often." I smiled crookedly.

She nodded, resigned. "Anyway, thanks for your help, China. I really appreciate it."

"Tit for tat," I said. "I need to thank you for being helpful to my mother. I can see how much she depends on you. And with Sam in the hospital—" I broke off. "I know I should do more to help them, but I'm pretty far away. I'm relieved that you're willing to give them a hand for a few weeks."

"Don't beat yourself up about it," she said in a practical tone. "Leatha understands that you have your own life. She doesn't expect you to spend time here, except when you can. Like on holidays." She frowned. "I'm sure she's aware that she and Sam have bitten off more than they can chew right now."

"You think?" I sighed. "She's always so damned cheerful, it's hard to guess just what she knows."

"I think," Sue Ellen replied firmly. "But anyway, that's not your problem. I can help out for a few weeks, and after that, I know of somebody else who can pitch in."

"Oh, really?" I asked eagerly. "Somebody who can move in here and help?"

"I don't know about moving in," she said, "but she can help. She's my baby sister, Patsy Wilbur. She lives with our mom and dad in Utopia and works at Jennie's Kitchen. She's full-time there right now, because Jennie's cook is out having a baby. But she'll go back to part-time at the first of the year, and she says she'd be glad to come and help your mom maybe three days a week."

"This is great, Sue Ellen. As it happens, I know Jennie. She's expanding her herb garden at the restaurant, and I'm helping. I've brought the plants with me. We're going to put them in on Friday." I was feeling a huge relief. Maybe things weren't as dark as I'd feared. "Have you mentioned Patsy to Leatha yet?"

Sue Ellen shook her head. "Haven't had a chance. I'll tell her tomorrow. It would be good if she could come out so the three of you—you and Leatha and Patsy—can get acquainted. How long are you staying?"

"Until Sunday, I think. McQuaid and Brian—my husband and our son—are coming tomorrow, but they have to go home on Friday morning. Caitie's going back with them." I smiled. "She can't bear to be parted from her chickens for more than a day or two. She's totally dedicated to her girls."

"Maybe Patsy can come over on one day this weekend, then. I'll check with Leatha and find out when would be a good time." Sue Ellen paused. "Your Caitie is such a little doll. Smart, too." She gave a wistful sigh. "I wanted to start a family when Jack and I got married. But living over there at Three Gates, it just didn't feel right. And then—" Another sigh. "Well, after that rodeo queen, I got to thinking he wasn't the man I wanted to be a father to my kids."

"But someday," I said, "after you've got your degree and you're settled in the kind of work you want to do, there'll be time. And you never know what the future might bring. When I was in my thirties, I figured I'd never have children, and now I have Brian and Caitie. So you never can tell."

"You've said a true thing, China." She smiled, and the dimples in her cheeks flashed. "You just never know. Once I manage to get past this bad patch, there'll be plenty of time."

But she wouldn't—and there wasn't.

Chapter Six

Mack went out on patrol at seven on Wednesday night, thinking that it might be a busy time, since the next day was Thanksgiving. But the only call came in at eight, an Operation Game Thief tip that somebody phoned in. A guy who lived in Concan, a village on Route 83 south of the state park, had posted a really dumb question on his Facebook page that afternoon. "I'm new around here, and I just got me a nice big buck. Anybody know where I can get an illegal deer processed in Uvalde County?"

Mack thought about that as she drove to the address the dispatcher had found after cross-checking the local records. People did some pretty stupid things and then bragged about them on Facebook. The previous year, a guy down in South Texas had put up a photo of himself proudly holding a very large redfish, a good three feet long, with eight others of equal size on display on the back of the pickup beside him. The daily bag limit on redfish is three, with a twenty-eight-inch size limit. Other anglers saw the online photo and were understandably outraged, and the Game Thief tips poured in. When the wardens caught up with the guy a couple of days later, they charged him with nine counts of possession of oversize redfish and fishing without a saltwater license. "Greedy and disgusting," the judge said when he sentenced him to nearly $6,000 in fines and civil restitution. Stupid, too, Mack thought—not just to take all those fish but to post them on Facebook. Like leaving a trail of crumbs to his door.

She had no trouble finding the house in Concan. When she knocked, asked for the shooter by name, and told him she wanted to see his illegal buck, the guy was so astonished that he blurted another dumb question. "How the *hell* did you find out?"

"Some of your Facebook friends don't like the idea of taking game illegally," she said. She charged him and photographed the animal, then confiscated it and took it back to Utopia, to a volunteer who would dress the deer and process the meat for the Uvalde Food Pantry. There were plenty of hungry people who would be glad to get it.

And that was it for the evening, for the illegal hunters had apparently decided to stay home where it was warm. The cold front had blown in, dropping the temperature into the thirties, with gusty winds, brief spurts of hard rain, and thick clouds that obscured the moon. As Mack drove along the road, everything was dark and quiet, except for a few deer darting in front of the truck and the occasional gleam of a pair of eyes in the brush along a fence. It was an easy night across the county, too, with only a couple of convenience store robberies and a single car wreck, down south on Route 90 near the fish hatchery. Occasionally one of the deputies checked in with a 10-20 to let Dispatch know where he was, but otherwise there wasn't much radio traffic. Everybody was taking a holiday, she thought, even the evildoers. The idea was reassuring.

It was nearly midnight when Mack pulled off at one of her regular spots, a vantage point that gave her a view of a wide swath of landscape, allowing her to see the headlights of anybody who might be jacklighting or shooting from the ranch roads below. She rolled down her window a couple of inches to catch the sound of gunshots, always a clue to illegal night hunting, then tuned the truck FM radio, low, to an all-night country music station playing songs from the eighties. But the first song was Kenny Rogers and Dolly Parton's "I Will Always Love You," the song she and Lanny had danced to at their wedding. Bittersweet, the lyrics stung, reminding her of how much they had promised to each other, and how each of them had come up short.

She switched the radio off, brushed away the tears, and pushed the seat back so she could stretch out her legs, forcing herself to stop thinking of Lanny. Instead, she thought back over the day—the *long* day. She was glad that she and Karen had been able to give the mountain lion a few more years of wilderness freedom and wondered whether he had found a good meal and a dry place to sleep. And Doc Masters. She had enjoyed meeting the old vet and hoped he would be able to put aside his worry—whatever it was—and give her the name of the rancher who was harboring the fawns with the doctored tattoos. There was obviously something illegal going on. If the situation was allowed to continue, more animals would be involved and more people—inevitably—drawn into it. In the end, there could be a lot worse trouble.

And Derek. She was sorry for what had happened at his ranch that afternoon. The dead deer weren't his fault, even though the bulldozing may have uncovered the anthrax spores that killed them. And she couldn't blame him for feeling that she was pushing him. She *had* pushed him. That was her job. Burning the carcasses, unpleasant as it was, had to be done without delay, and she had offered to help. She had the tools and the knowledge and the skills to do what needed to be done. And if Derek had a problem with that—well, heck. That was *his* problem, not hers.

Except. Except that it was her problem, too, she thought, feeling a kind of bubbling, baffling despair. Men might find her attractive, an interesting companion, even good in bed. But they had a problem with what she did for a living. You'd think she would have learned that lesson, after her marriage to Lanny had foundered on the reef of her career. *It's going to take a really special guy to love you and love what you do—because you very much are what you do,* Karen had said. Did she love what she did well enough to accept the fact that her job was the only love in her life? The way things were headed, that was where she was going to end up—and that would have to be okay.

But was it okay, for the long haul? She thought of something else Karen had said. *And now you've got Molly and Cheyenne and your house in Utopia and the dream territory you always wanted, and you think everything's perfect. You think you don't need a guy in your life. And you're wrong.*

Well, maybe. Or maybe not. Karen could be wrong. Mack sat with that until the momentary despair subsided. The world was uncertain, and a lot of people had to settle for a lot less than she had. Being able to do what you loved and earn a living doing it was a privilege to be cherished and protected. And anyway, just because you loved somebody, there was no guarantee that it would go on forever. Or if it did, that the loving would go on being *right* forever. What was right at one point in your life could be wrong in another. People changed, situations changed, times changed. She knew that from her marriage to Lanny. You had to take things as they came. You couldn't count on—

A pair of headlights bounced into Mack's field of vision a couple of hundred feet below, and she sat up straight, reaching for the night-vision binoculars stowed in the console. Steadying her forearms on the steering wheel, she peered out into the dark. A white pickup with a light bar on top, a county insignia on the passenger door. A Uvalde County deputy sheriff. She watched it slow to a crawl, then stop, and a spotlight came on, aimed toward her, flaring off her windshield. She reached for the headlight switch, flicked it on and off twice, and put the binoculars back in the console. And waited.

Five minutes later, the truck had climbed the hill and pulled to a stop beside her, driver's side to driver's side. The window went down. "How's it going, Mack?" a deep voice asked. She recognized Ethan Conroy, the new deputy sheriff whom she and Karen had seen in Utopia earlier that day, going into the café. The hunky deputy sheriff.

"Nothing much happening," she said. The light from his dash instruments shadowed the planes of his face. A rugged face, not movie-star handsome but lived-in, firm jaw, cleft chin, easy smile. "How about you?"

"Same here. Quiet night, except for a speeder this side of Sabinal. Clocked him at ninety-five on that two-lane." He turned off his ignition, leaned an elbow on the door, and brushed a shock of dark hair out of his eyes. "Say, are you really the one who collared the guy who was stealing the copper wire?"

"Yeah, that's me," she said, wondering where this was going.

He grinned. "I saw him down at the jail. He's big as a house. You must have some moves."

"Just doin' my job," she replied lightly, but she was pleased by the unexpected compliment.

"And I heard on the radio tonight that you cited that jerk over in Concan who bragged about his nice big illegal buck on Facebook. He give you any trouble?"

She shook her head, grinning. "Meek as a lamb. He'd already admitted it was an illegal kill—in writing, to everybody on the Internet. Didn't leave himself any room for denials. Dumb."

"Dumb," Ethan agreed. Their two radios squawked in unison, another deputy with a 10-20 at the intersection of 187 and 90, working a minor collision. When the transmission was over, he remarked, "Was that your Toyota you were driving in Utopia today? I have one of those. Nice trucks. The long bed comes in handy when you're hauling fence posts, brush, that kind of stuff."

"It's mine," she said. "It's a '95 with nearly 200,000 miles on it. It's been good to me, but—" She shook her head with a sigh. "It's running rough, and when it's idling, the RPM will all of a sudden crank up. I'm afraid it's going to need some work, but you know how it is. One of those intermittent things—easy to put off until all of a sudden it quits on you."

"Really? I had a similar problem with mine. Took me a while to figure it out." He paused. "If you want, I'd be glad to take a look at it for you. I mean, I'm no mechanic, but I might be able to spot the problem. Save you a trip to the shop."

"Well, hey, sure," she said, surprised and pleased. "Ask me anything about Parks and Wildlife regs and I'll give you chapter and verse. But open the hood of a truck and I don't have a clue. If you want to take a look, by all means, be my guest."

He chuckled, deep and solid, a nice sound that set off an unexpected tingle somewhere deep inside her. "I'm off tomorrow. One of the girls at the café told me you live in Utopia. That right?"

He had asked at the café? Mack nodded, bemused, not quite sure what was happening because it was happening so fast—but liking it anyway.

"I'm down in Sabinal," he went on. "How about if I drive up in the morning and take a look at the truck? You hard to find?"

"In Utopia? You've got to be kidding." She laughed. "I'm on Oak, second block east of Main, between Lee and Jackson. You'll see the state truck parked out front."

He frowned, tapping his finger on the steering wheel. "No, wait, sorry. I forgot. Tomorrow's Thanksgiving. You've probably got plans."

"I'm having dinner with friends," she said, "but not until late in the afternoon. If you've got the time in the morning, well, sure, come ahead. I'd be grateful for any advice on the truck. I'd like to keep it, but I don't have a lot of dollars to dump into it."

"Understand," he said, with emphasis. "Is nine too early? Or were you planning to sleep in?"

"Nine's good for me." She paused uncertainly. Would he think she was being pushy if she suggested breakfast? Probably, but she went ahead anyway. "I'll cook breakfast, if you don't mind settling for pancakes and eggs." She might not be much of a cook, but her dad had taught her to make killer pancakes, and her next-door neighbor—Mrs. Cook, the owner of the early-rising rooster—had just given her a dozen very fresh eggs. "It's hunting season," she added, "and I haven't had time to stop at the store for bacon and stuff. And it's a holiday, so the café is closed."

"Yeah, hunting season," he said sympathetically. "Parks and Wildlife has probably had you on the road from dawn to dark, every day. But I've got a pound of bacon. And there might be a package of sausages in the fridge freezer. Want me to scrounge around and see what I can come up with?"

"That sounds great," she said, and then hastily added, "Of course, it *is* hunting season, and I never know what might come up." She felt apologetic. "If I get a call and have to go out, how do I reach you?"

"We'd better trade cards," he said.

"Good idea," she replied.

Then, as if it had been choreographed, both of them turned away to fish in their consoles and turned back to hand their business cards through the open windows. As his fingers brushed hers, she was startled to feel—yes, there it was, definitely—a tingle, a tiny jolt of electricity, almost a spark.

If he felt it, he didn't say. "My cell number's on there," he remarked. "If tomorrow doesn't work, we'll give it a try later. Not on the weekend, though. I've pulled both Saturday and Sunday shifts." His smile was crooked, rueful. "Drove my wife crazy. Totally bananas. Always complaining that she couldn't count on me for anything." He added, in a lower voice, "It's hard on the partner."

Mack caught her breath. She heard the past tense, but still— "It was hard on Lanny, too," she said. "My husband."

He raised one dark eyebrow, his eyes on her face. "Uh-huh. It's why Carol's my ex." He let the word hang there for a moment. "Yours?"

"Ex also," Mack said. She could feel her heart beating.

Both radios squawked, and they paused to listen. It was a rollover on 83, south of the state park, about ten miles away. He keyed his mike, spoke briefly, then listened. "Ten-four," he said. To Mack, he added, "Gotta roll. See you in the morning, I hope." He flashed a smile and lifted a hand. "Nice running into you like this. Ships passing in the night, huh?"

"Something like that," she managed. "Be safe now, you hear?"

"I hear," he said. "Mañana." His window went up and he pulled his truck around, spinning his wheels on the gravel.

She watched as his taillights disappeared into the dark night. Her heart was beating harder now, and she felt almost breathless.

MACK would have bet dollars to doughnuts that she'd be called out first thing Thursday morning, or he would. But it didn't happen. She hadn't gotten back from patrol until 3 a.m., so she slept until eight, then jumped in the shower. When she got out, the message light on her answering machine was blinking, and she thought with resignation, *This is it—one of us has to cancel.* But it turned out to be Derek, apologizing for his rudeness the afternoon before and—in that bedroom voice of his—renewing the invitation to brunch with him and the girls. She played the message twice. Then she picked up the phone and punched in Derek's number. When he answered, she said briskly, "Thanks for the invitation, Derek, but I don't think this is going to work. So let's not. Okay?"

When he protested, sounding like a hurt little boy, she interrupted him. "Excuse me. No time to talk—I've got company coming this morning. Have a nice holiday." And she clicked off.

For a moment, she stood with the phone in her hand, wondering if she had done the right thing. Maybe she shouldn't have ended it so firmly. Maybe she should have told him that she was going out on call, and left the future open, to see what might develop. But what would have been the point of that? She knew in her heart that he wasn't special enough—to use Karen's phrase.

Then she decided that she wasn't going to worry about it and put the phone down. She just had time to run a quick comb through her hair and jump into chinos and a red sweater before she heard a knock on the door and went to answer it, Molly at her heels.

It was the first time she'd seen Ethan out of uniform. He was wearing a light brown canvas work jacket, black turtleneck, worn jeans, scuffed boots, and a black Dallas Cowboys cap. At a glance, Mack decided that it wasn't the .357 he usually wore that made him authoritative. It was just who he was, and when he came in, his strong male presence seemed to completely fill the small hallway, wall to wall, floor to ceiling.

Molly gave her usual sharp, suspicious bark—*Who are you, what are you doing in my house, and when are you going to leave?* But when he squatted down and picked up her paw, comrade to comrade, she unbent. When he reached into his pocket, pulled out a dog treat, and told her to sit, she actually did it. Mack was surprised. Molly was usually made of sterner stuff.

"I've got two heelers at home," he said to Mack, straightening up. "Super breed, loyal and smart as the devil but bossy as hell. You have to be top dog. If you let them think they are, they'll eat your lunch."

"Hear that, Molly?" Mack said with a chuckle. "Better watch it, girl—he's got your number."

Laughing, Ethan handed Mack a plastic sack. "Half pound of bacon was all I had, and I couldn't find the sausages. But my aunt sent me some real Vermont maple syrup, so I brought that, in case pancakes are still on the menu." Up close, she saw that his eyes were the color of coffee. Strong coffee. "Toyota first, though," he added. "I work better on an empty stomach."

"Good man," she said approvingly. Leaving his sack in the kitchen, she pulled on a jacket and led him out to the garage. On the way, he glanced at Cheyenne, in her paddock behind the house.

"Nice-looking paint," he remarked. "Ride much?"

"When I can," Mack said, adding ruefully. "During hunting season, not so much. Cheyenne thinks she's been deserted—she's expecting to spend the rest of her life in that paddock, bored out of her mind."

"It's a problem," Ethan acknowledged. "Same with Buddy Holly. Leave him alone too long and he gets cantankerous. Wants to eat the fence."

She laughed. "Buddy Holly?"

"Yeah. You know who he was?"

"Do I know? One of my favorites." Buddy Holly was a Texas musician from the fifties. When she was a kid, she'd had all his records—that was when they were actually *records*, not a file you downloaded from the Internet.

"No kidding? Amazing. I had another horse once named Willie Nelson. Buddy and Willie. Two great Texans." He grinned. "Listen, when your workload eases up, let me know and we'll go riding together. Friend of mine has a ranch over on Blanco Creek. Plenty of open space to work the kinks out of the horses."

Bemused and by now a little breathless, she nodded. In the garage, she handed him the keys to the Toyota. He started the truck and let it idle for a few minutes, during which it obligingly performed its sudden RPM surge. He left it running, got out, and opened the hood. She went to stand beside him as he scanned the engine compartment for a few minutes. He had big hands, she noticed, hardworking hands, with traces of dirt under short-clipped nails. Her glance went to his cheek, where a long, thin scar traced the line of his jaw.

"Ah," he said, bending over the motor. He reached down and wiggled something. "That's not it," he muttered, and wiggled something else. "Not that one, either." He reached deeper and bent closer. "Aha," he said, and appeared to be wrestling with something. Over his shoulder, he said, "Get in and pump the accelerator, would you? Rev it up."

She followed instructions until he stepped back, dropped the hood, and told her to shut off the engine. "Think that's got it," he said. "But it's only a temporary fix. Probably won't last more than a few miles."

"You're kidding," she said, getting out of the truck. "But you didn't do anything. You never even picked up a screwdriver."

He gave her a mock scowl. "What d'you mean, woman? I *fixed* it. For the moment, anyway."

"But all you did was wiggle a thingy or two."

"What I wiggled was your vacuum hoses," he explained patiently. "Those thingies stiffen up over the years and start to leak. The business end of the bad one is cracked and loose and it needs to be replaced—there are probably some other hoses that could do with a replacement, too. Next time I'm anywhere close to an auto parts store, I'll get what you need and put them on for you. Okay?"

Mack found herself thinking that it was a whole lot better than just okay but that it might be dangerous to tell him so. She didn't stop to ask herself exactly what she meant by *dangerous*, but she knew she was right.

"I guess that means you think you're top dog," she said instead. There was a clean shop rag on a shelf and she tossed it to him.

He gave her a hard look as he wiped his hands. "Hey. I saved you from certain highway disaster, and I'll lay odds you don't have Triple A. Is that all the thanks I'm going to get?"

"Of course not," she said, and smiled sweetly. "I'm about to cook breakfast. How do you like your eggs?"

After the chill outside, the kitchen was warm and fragrant with the smell of fresh coffee. Molly came in and curled up on her bed in the corner beside the stove. When Ethan came in, he (like an investigator, Mack thought) began surreptitiously checking the place out, seeing that it was bachelor-girl tidy and comfortable, definitely not *House-Beautiful* pretty.

"Hey," he said, going to her shelf of turtle shells, "you've got a Texas tortoise! Super. Did you do the preservation work on this?" Without waiting for her answer, he picked up another. "And a Texas map turtle—now, that's a nice find."

They talked turtles for a few minutes, then Mack set to work stirring up a batch of pancakes, frying bacon, and making eggs for two—over easy, since that (it turned out) was the way they both liked them.

While she worked, Ethan hung his jacket on the back of a chair and sat down at the table with a cup of coffee, telling her that he had moved from Williamson County because it was crowded: "Too built-up," he said. "A twenty-acre shopping mall at every intersection, and hundreds of square miles of nothing but houses with yards the size of a newspaper." Divorced for a couple of years, he had two children, boys of eight and six who lived with his ex-wife in Round Rock, where he had been a cop for ten years. He took out his cell phone and flipped through a half-dozen photos of smiling, bright-eyed kids for Mack to admire. In his spare time, he said, he fished and hunted and did a little woodworking in the garage of the house he rented. "Cabinets, tables, stuff like that. Nothing spectacular." He tossed it off carelessly, but Mack heard the quiet pride behind the words.

"My dad loved woodworking," she said, as she put the food on the table and poured Ethan's second cup of coffee. "Seems like he was always out there in his workshop, making something for Mom. I loved to hang out and watch him." Which led to telling Ethan about her father, and how she went hunting with him as a girl, and how he had died, and why becoming a game warden had been her career dream—a mission, almost. Which further led to telling him what she loved about her work and what she didn't like so much, and eventually to the mountain lion that she and Karen had trapped and freed the day before.

"But keep that to yourself," she added, putting the second batch of pancakes on the table. "That was an off-the-job thing. Definitely a private project. Not Parks and Wildlife policy."

"Jeez," he said admiringly, forking another pancake onto his plate and soaking it with syrup. "You're either a very brave woman or a freakin' idiot. I can handle a drunk with a gun, but I wouldn't want to be that close to a cougar."

"The lion was sedated," she said, "while a drunk with a gun can be just plain—" She was interrupted by the chirp of Ethan's cell phone lying on the table.

"Damn," he muttered. He picked it up, listened for a moment, then said, "Where?" and "On it." He clicked off and pocketed the phone. "Gotta get to work." He forked up what was left of the last pancake, gulped coffee, and pushed his chair back. "I'm really sorry to screw up a perfectly good breakfast, Mack. Rain check?" He pulled his coat off the back of the chair and shrugged into it.

"Rain check," Mack replied. She heard the sharp disappointment in her voice and blunted it with, "Don't worry about it. We were pretty much finished, anyway." The call wasn't his fault—and how many times had the very same thing happened to her? She followed him out of the kitchen, Molly at her heels. "What's going on?" she asked.

"Somebody broke into Doc Masters' vet clinic north on 187. Likely after drugs. We had one of those down at the south end of the county a couple of weeks ago. They got a big load of narcotics." His voice was terse, clipped. "This time, though, they got the doc."

Mack stared. "Got the . . . doc?" She felt a flutter in her throat. "Doc Masters? Is he—"

"Yeah. He was shot. He's dead." Ethan was shrugging into his coat. "The clinic helper—the kid who comes in to feed the boarding animals—found him." As if in confirmation, they heard the burp and wail of the siren at the volunteer fire department's garage on Main Street, where the local EMS was headquartered.

Mack pulled in her breath, thinking of the last thing the old vet had said to her, through the open window of her truck, at Derek's. *Nice working with you, Mack. I hope there'll be a next time.* She had smiled, glad to have won the respect she heard in his voice. *I'm sure there will* was what she'd said. And then she thought of what else he'd told her. The flutter disappeared, replaced by a numbing cold and a tightness deep in her belly, and she made up her mind.

"I'm coming with you." She reached past the red Windbreaker on the coatrack and took down her green Parks and Wildlife jacket and her duty belt. She wouldn't take the time to put on her uniform, but this was business. Official business.

"Not your side of the street, Mack." He fished in his jeans pocket, pulled out his badge, and pinned it on his coat. "Nothing to do with Parks and Wildlife. It was likely another drug thing, and there'll be deputies swarming all over it. Too bad about the doc, of course. But you don't need to—"

"Yes, I do." She slung her duty belt around her hips and snapped the buckle. "I'm a law enforcement officer, and I have a reason for going to that crime scene." Her gun safe was a step away, in the hallway closet. She unlocked it and took out her Glock. No special need for it, but it was part of her official gear. As she holstered the gun, she glanced at Ethan. "You don't know for sure that it was an actual drug theft."

"All I know is what was reported." He snapped his coat, watching her uneasily. "But no, I don't know for sure, not until I get over there and take a look. But what the hell else—"

Her mouth was dry and she swallowed. "Doc Masters and I worked together for the first time yesterday, on a call about some anthrax-killed deer on a ranch south of town. He told me he had seen some tattooed fawns on a cattle ranch that doesn't have a deer-farming permit from Parks and Wildlife."

Ethan frowned. "Doesn't have—"

She zipped her jacket. "I tried to get Masters to give me a name and a location, but he said he needed to think about it. I figured he was holding back because the rancher is a friend, or a client. Or a guy who's prominent in the community—somebody who's going to face some seriously bad publicity over it." She took her uniform cap off the shelf above the coat rack and put it on. "I told him I'd call him about it first thing tomorrow morning. That I expected him to give me the name."

"Tattooed fawns? You're thinking Masters might've been killed over a few lousy *fawns*?"

"I don't know." She pulled her cap down hard. Her hair was loose around her shoulders, but she didn't want to take the time to skin it back into the ponytail she wore when she was on duty. "Could be just what you said—a drug theft. The doc happened to walk in on a burglary in progress and the thief panicked and shot him. I agree that it's pretty irrational for somebody to kill over a few illegal deer."

Irrational, yes. Improbable, yes. But not impossible. And she needed to know. She had liked Doc Masters, had felt good about earning his respect, and was disappointed when he wouldn't give her the information she asked for. He was dead, and she needed to know *why*.

At her knee, Molly was pressing hard against her and whining, the stub of a tail wagging urgently. Mack reached down and cupped the dog's muzzle in her hand, tipping it up to look in her dark eyes.

"Not today, Molly," she said firmly. "You can't go today. You have to *stay*." Disappointed but knowing that there was no point in arguing, Molly flopped down on the floor and put her muzzle between her paws, looking up under her eyebrows reproachfully. To Ethan, Mack said, "Come on. Let's go."

"Guess we know who's top dog here," Ethan said, glancing from Molly to Mack. "If you're bound and determined, I reckon I can't stop you. But you'd better take your own vehicle. I have no idea how long I'll be at the scene or what happens after that, and you said something about a date later this afternoon."

"Not a date." Mack went to the door. "A late-afternoon dinner with friends. Sam and Leatha Richards and Leatha's family—you know them? Except," she added as an afterthought, "Sam had a heart attack last weekend. He may still be in the hospital. I'd better check and make sure that dinner's still on. But yes, I'll take the state truck." She pulled the door open and was stepping through, but he put out a hand, stopping her and pushing the door shut.

"Not a date." There was a glint in his eyes, and he was close enough that she could smell the faint citrusy scent of aftershave, overlaid by the woodsmoke odor of his canvas jacket. "That's nice to know. I'd just as soon not have any competition. Hate to say it, but I'm not good with competition. It tends to bring out the worst in me."

It wasn't a flirtatious remark, she thought distractedly. He meant it. And it was some kind of declaration. "Don't tell me you're the possessive type," she said, then wished she had said something else, something less coy, less teasing.

"Not usually, no." He put his hands on her shoulders and turned her firmly toward him. "Actually never. I'm a real mild-mannered guy. Except in exceptional circumstances. Except when I know what I want. Then I tend to go after it."

There was that tingle again, and more. She could feel it racing up her spine and across her shoulders. She could feel how near he was and how indescribably, indisputably *male* he was and how suddenly, inexplicably, she wanted—

He put a finger under her chin, tipped up her face, and kissed her. It was direct and impatient and, in an unexpected way, proprietary, not like any first kiss she'd ever tasted. Instinctively she pulled back, thinking in confusion that this was much too soon, too much, too soon, too—

But then she had to stop thinking, because he refused to let her go. His mouth on hers had suddenly become urgent, demanding. He was holding her tight, pinning her full length against him. Her breath quickened and her arms—of their own volition, not hers, she was sure—were going up and around his shoulders. His fingers were in her hair and her cap had fallen off, and she knew that if this went on a moment longer she would never be able to pull away, never, ever.

Summoning her strength, she pulled back again, and this time he stepped back, dropped his arms, and let her go. She couldn't move. His eyes were searching her face, and she knew, with a sudden hot flush of embarrassment, that he was seeing the unmasked desire written there.

After a moment, he cleared his throat. "I think I'd file that under 'exceptional circumstances.'" He bent down, picked up her cap, and handed it to her, a quick, wide grin spreading across his face. "But I'd want to try it again, sometime soon. Just to be sure."

Mack was too breathless to answer. She finally managed, "Yes." And then wasn't sure what she was saying *yes* to. Flustered, she put on her cap. "We'd better be going."

But he put his hand on the door. "Is there any?" he asked, looking down at her, his eyes intent.

"Any what?"

"Competition. Just for the record," he added.

She hesitated, thought briefly of Derek, and then told the truth. "No," she said. "No competition." She took a breath. "But that doesn't mean—"

He opened the door. "I know it doesn't," he said. "Just wanted to know where I stood at the moment, is all." As he looked down at her there was a smile in his eyes.

"Top dog," he said, and touched her face. "Definitely."

Chapter Seven

The uniquely pungent scent and taste of rosemary (*Rosmarinus officinalis*) make it a flavorful culinary herb. It can be used fresh or dried, with meats, vegetables, eggs, and desserts.

But rosemary also has important therapeutic benefits. Its green, needlelike leaves contain volatile oils that can stimulate the immune system, increase circulation, and improve digestion, as well as anti-inflammatory compounds that may reduce the severity of asthma attacks. Rosemary has been shown to increase blood circulation in the head and brain and has long had a reputation for improving the memory. As well, the antioxidant strength of rosemary has made it a favorite preservative. The needle-like leaves contain carnosic and rosmarinic acids, powerful antimicrobials that help to slow decay. Once used by Egyptian mummy makers, the herb is now employed to slow microbial growth on food products and prevent the oxidation of food oils.

Rosemary is also an important landscaping plant in USDA hardiness zones 7–10. One important asset: deer don't like it!

China Bayles
"Rosemary: An Herb for all Seasons, All Reasons"
Pecan Springs Enterprise

I got up early on Thanksgiving morning and picked up the phone to call my friend Justine Wyzinski, who earned her nickname in law school—the Whiz—by being faster, smarter, and *right* far more often than the rest of us second-rate plodders. I managed to earn a nickname, too: Hot Shot. But I wouldn't have worked so hard if I hadn't burned with the mad desire to best the Whiz at her own game. Since I've left the law, I've intentionally slowed down. Hot Shot no longer fits.

But Justine is still the Whiz. She never slows down for anything, not even National Turkey Day. If I knew her (and I do), she was probably going in to her office in downtown San Antonio early this morning, to catch up on a little paperwork while the phone wasn't ringing itself silly. I was right. She was up and at 'em already, and revved up to Mach 2. At least. She spotted the caller ID of my cell phone and picked up on the first ring.

"What, China?" she asked briskly. None of the usual polite niceties, hello, how are you, so glad you called, haven't heard from you in a while. Just *What, China?* The subtext: Strike while the iron is hot; time and tide wait for no woman, so get on it. Now.

I was tempted to remind her that speed kills, but I held my tongue. "Nice to talk to you, too, Justine," I said pleasantly. "I didn't catch you in the middle of something, did I?"

"In the bathroom."

"Ah," I said. Actually, being in the bathroom was good. It meant that the Whiz might be sitting down. Of course, she was probably already multitasking—reading a brief or marking up an interrogatory, while she drank a cup of coffee and checked her email and handled her other morning necessities, with her Bluetooth in her ear.

"I'm out at Bittersweet for Thanksgiving with Leatha and the family," I began, "and I've got a possible pro bono client for you. Her name is Sue Ellen Krause, and her soon-to-be-ex-husband is up to some serious skullduggery. She knows what it is but hasn't let me in on the details, so far. It appears to involve a hefty theft of two hundred thou or more. He's slapped her around some, so she's leaving him. She says she's ready to do the right thing and tell the story to the DA here in Uvalde County, where the crime took place. But I'm thinking that she may get cold feet at the last minute, so she's going to need an escort. And a mouthpiece. Which is where you come in," I added helpfully.

"Pro bono?" Justine was suspicious.

I was ready for that. "Just to set the record straight, the last one I sent you was a paying client. The artist," I added, to help her remember. "From Pecan Springs. Last summer." It had been a fascinating tangle of truth and lies, woven around a sophisticated art fraud and a decade-old cold case, and Justine had handled the plea bargain.

"I remember," she said with satisfaction. "We got a nice deal on that one. Her testimony guaranteed convictions for a killer, an accessory, and an art fence, so the judge let her off the hook with probation." She paused. "This pro bono—is she an artist?"

Justine is at the point in her career where she can pick and choose her clients. She's easily bored, so she goes for the interesting ones. She has a short attention span, so she prefers quickies, especially on pro bono work. Wondering what I could say to tempt her, I thought of the boots and the trophy hunts.

"Not an artist," I said. "A cowgirl." I qualified that. "She looks like a cowgirl, anyway. Or a country-western singer. She's been working on this big ranch that sells high-priced trophy hunts to city guys with a testosterone-fueled urge to hang a pair of monster antlers over the fireplace."

"Oh, yeah?" There was a flushing sound, then the sound of a faucet running. "I might be interested. I've been wanting to look into that business. Did you hear about that deer-smuggling case over in East Texas? Both state and federal violations—Lacey Act. Huge fine and forfeiture. Hot-button conservation issue. Political, too."

We were off on a tangent, but that didn't matter if it interested the Whiz. "Deer smuggling?" I asked. "Haven't we got enough deer in Texas already? Somebody thinks we need *more*?"

"It's not more they're after, Hot Shot, it's *bigger*. Turns out that our true Texas bucks are itty-bitty pikers when it comes to those horny things they grow on their heads. And you know Texas. If it ain't bigger, it ain't good enough. So some enterprising folks are illegally importing bucks with big antlers from out of state. They bring 'em in to improve the herd and then they bring in big-paying clients to shoot 'em."

"Huh," I said. "Sounds like a racket."

"It is. Tell you what . . ." But whatever it was Justine was going to tell me was swallowed by the sound of vigorous tooth brushing, and more water running, then more tooth brushing and a loud whooshing gargle. The Whiz was rinsing.

I waited. When the sounds had faded, I asked, "Tell me what?"

"What?" I heard the medicine cabinet close. "Tell you *what*?"

"When you started brushing your teeth," I replied patiently, "you said you might be interested. Then you said, 'Tell you what.' What was it?"

"Oh. Well, okay." She was going down her hall now, her bedroom slippers flip-flopping on the floor. "You know how I feel about going into a case blind. Tell the cowgirl to tell you whatever she's going to tell the DA. When you know what it is, tell me, and I'll tell you whether I'll take her or not. Got it?"

"Sounds reasonable," I said. "I don't know whether she'll go for it or not, though." And once I heard the story, it might not be the kind of thing that the Whiz would go for, either.

"I'm sure you can persuade her, China," Justine said, and added, "Anyway, no skin off my nose if she doesn't. She can always find a public defender." I heard a drawer open and close. "I suppose you're having turkey today?"

"Of course. But late in the afternoon. Sam's in the hospital. He's had a heart attack. So Leatha and I are kind of working around that." I thought of something. "Hey. You wouldn't want to drive over to Bittersweet and eat with us, would you?" Leatha had invited Justine and Ruby and me for a girls-only summer weekend several years ago, and we had splashed in the river and painted our toenails and laughed a lot. For all I knew, it was the last time the Whiz had taken a vacation. "It's not that far," I reminded her, "and Leatha would love to see you. McQuaid and the kids will be here, and a game warden friend. You could meet the cowgirl, too."

"Love to, but I can't," she said. Another drawer opened, closed. "I'm seeing a client this afternoon. But tell Leatha I'm really sorry to hear about Sam. He's a nice guy. Is he going to be okay?"

"I think so, but we'll know more in a couple of days." A client, on Thanksgiving. That figured. As far as the Whiz is concerned, holidays are for the rest of us. "I'll call you if I can get the cowgirl to tell me her story."

"Do that," Justine said. She added, more cordially, "Happy Thanksgiving, Hot Shot," and clicked off.

Thinking about all this, I pulled on my jeans, a plaid blouse, a blue sweatshirt, and loafers and ran a brush through my hair. I peeked into Caitie's room and saw that she was still sweetly asleep, Mr. P curled up on her pillow. He lifted his head and flicked his orange tail when I opened the door but didn't offer to get up. That cat knows a good thing when he's found her, and he's not letting her out of his sight.

I was still thinking about Justine when I went into the kitchen to give Leatha a hand with breakfast. She wasn't there, but Sue Ellen was stirring a pot of oatmeal at the stove, dressed in jeggings and a body-hugging long-sleeved red T-shirt, her auburn hair twisted carelessly and pinned at the back of her head. The kitchen was fragrant with hot coffee and the scent of breakfast rolls.

"There's coffee," she said, with a nod to the coffeemaker. "Your mom is getting dressed. She decided to go to the hospital this morning and said to tell you she'd like you to go with her, if that works for you. I'll be here, so I can look after Caitie."

I looked at her sharply. "Is there a problem with Sam?"

Sue Ellen took the pan off the burner. "She didn't tell me what's going on, China. The hospital called and she was talking to the nurse on the floor when I came into the kitchen—that's all I know. I told her to go ahead and get ready and I'd handle breakfast. We've got bacon, oatmeal, orange juice, and sticky rolls, and eggs any way you like them. I'm scrambling for Leatha and me. What will Caitie want?"

"Scrambled for me, too," I said. "And Caitie's still asleep, so it's just us for now." I poured a cup of coffee. "Sticky rolls?"

"In the oven." At that moment, a timer went off, and Sue Ellen added, "Ready to come out. Maybe you could do that." She began laying bacon strips into a cast-iron skillet on the other front burner.

I opened the oven and pulled out a pan of rolls that gave off a mouth-watering lemon-rosemary odor. "Omigod," I crooned. "Oh, these smell utterly delicious, Sue Ellen. They look pretty, too."

"Easy peasy," she said. "Refrigerated dough, with a lemon and rosemary filling—although of course you could use a yeast dough if you want. Just roll it out, slather on the filling, and you're done. Except for the icing." She pointed to a small bowl of white frosting. "That's it. Cream cheese, lemon, and confectioner's sugar. If it's a bit too thick, stick it in the microwave for ten seconds, then just drizzle it on. What we don't eat this morning, we can warm up for breakfast tomorrow."

I got to work. As I transferred the buns to a serving plate, I brought up the subject that was on my mind. "I talked to Justine Wyzinski this morning. The lawyer I mentioned last night."

Sue Ellen turned toward me, and I got a good look at her. In the harsh light of morning, her face was pale, with lines around her mouth and blue circles under her eyes. She looked older than she'd seemed last night.

"Did you sleep well?" I asked, concerned. "Your suite is okay?"

"The suite is fine, the bed is comfortable." She turned up the heat under the bacon. "The problem is me. I'm not ready to hit the panic button yet, but what you said kept me awake."

"I'm sorry about the sleep," I said, putting the bowl of glaze into the microwave. "But I'm glad you thought about our conversation."

"This lawyer. What did she say?"

"She's interested in your situation and would like to help. But here's the thing. She can't agree to represent you without knowing the story up front—the full story." I began drizzling the glaze over the buns. "If you'll tell me, I'll relay it to her, and she'll let us know whether she can do it or not."

"What if . . ." Sue Ellen turned a strip of bacon. "What if I don't tell you?"

"She said, and I quote, 'No skin off my nose if she doesn't. She can always find a public defender.' Which is true, of course. If your husband is arrested and you're charged with being an accessory, you can ask the court to appoint somebody who will—"

"I don't want that," Sue Ellen said hastily. "Not one of those guys. I've seen them on TV. They're losers. They always mess up."

That wasn't true, but I wasn't going to argue. "Then you'll probably want to tell me," I said. "So what's the story?"

Sue Ellen turned the other strips of bacon. After a moment, she sighed. "Okay. I guess I gotta do it. The story is that Jack and these two buddies of his, Duke and Lucky, are trying to get into the trophy-hunting business. You know, like they do at Three Gates, but without the fancy lodge and all the extra stuff. A start-up, you might say. On a shoestring. Duke and Lucky already have the land, which is good. But to get the state permit, they have to put in miles and miles of expensive fencing. They've done some of it, but they don't have the money to finish it. So they—" She stopped to take the oatmeal pan off the burner. "So they're bringing in white-tails. And selling them."

I put the plate of glazed buns on the table and began laying out the place mats and silverware at our places, two on one side of the table, two on the other. I was remembering what Justine had told me earlier that morning about the East Texas deer-smuggling case, which had involved both state and federal violations. It sounded like that was what Sue Ellen was talking about. But I needed to hear it from her.

"'Bringing in white-tails'?" I asked. "Exactly what does that mean?"

"It means that they've been trucking in deer from Oklahoma."

"As in . . . smuggling?"

"Yeah, right. As in smuggling." She eyed me. "So I guess you know it's against the law to haul white-tailed deer into Texas." Her mouth was a thin line, twisted down in one corner, as if she were tasting something sour. "Kind of a dumb law, seems to me. I mean, hundreds of deer walk back and forth across the border anytime they want and nobody tries to stop them. But if you load a couple of deer in a truck and drive them across, all of a sudden you're a smuggler, and both the state guys and the feds are after you. Heck, you can't even truck deer around *inside* the state without a permit. You can go to jail."

"Okay," I said. "I get that. And I understand that the penalties for doing that sort of thing are pretty stiff, and that a smuggler can find himself in some serious trouble." I frowned. "But last night, I understood you to be talking about something else. You said that your husband was stealing money from his employer, and you implied that the thefts amounted to a sizable chunk of change. So how is smuggling connected to—"

"I didn't say he was stealing actual *money*," she put in quickly. "I said—"

"You said it boiled down to money," I corrected myself. "So if it isn't money, what is it? Equipment?" But she seemed to think he had taken more than $200,000—what under the sun had he stolen that had that kind of value?

"No, not equipment." She put a folded paper towel on a plate and began forking bacon strips onto it. "When you hear what it is, you're going to think it's nothing much. But that's because you don't know what's going on in deer ranching these days. These animals—"

"Good morning, girls," my mother said cheerily, coming into the kitchen. She was wearing a navy blue wool pantsuit and matching navy heels, with a white scoop-neck top, pearls, and pearl earrings. Her gray hair was attractively swept back, and her face was carefully made up. She might have been going to a charity fund-raiser luncheon at the River Oaks Country Club.

"Good morning," Sue Ellen and I chorused. We traded half-guilty glances, as if Leatha had caught us telling a dirty story, which in a sense she had.

"Oh, my, that coffee smells good!" she exclaimed, coming over to give me a peck on the cheek and bestowing one on Sue Ellen as well. "I think I'll have another cup. China, did Sue Ellen tell you about going to the hospital this morning?"

For the record, I love my mother and I want to be there for her when she needs me. But at that moment I fervently wished she had put off coming into the kitchen until Sue Ellen had finished her sentence. Or her paragraph. Or whatever it took for me to get the story. By the time we were able to return to the subject, she might have changed her mind.

But there were other priorities, of course. "What's happening with Sam?" I asked urgently. "What did you hear from the hospital? Is there a problem?"

As Leatha poured coffee, I saw that her hands were trembling, and I guessed that the hospital hadn't phoned with good news. "They want to do more surgery." She wasn't looking at me. "Today."

"On Thanksgiving?" If they were doing it on a holiday, it must be serious.

She nodded. "Can you go with me?"

"Of course," I replied promptly. I hesitated and added, "What surgery, exactly?"

She glanced at the serving plate on the table. "Oh, look! Glazed buns." She bent to sniff. "Lemon and rosemary! What a wonderful combination!" She took her coffee to the table and sat down. Beneath her makeup, her face was sallow. "I didn't ask for details, China. I just said we'd get there quick as we could. I thought we'd find out soon enough."

Just like my mother, I thought to myself. Queen of Denial, determined to put off knowing about or even acknowledging the bad stuff as long as possible. But I couldn't blame her. What she and Sam were facing was a threat to the life they had built here at Bittersweet. A life they expected to live together for years to come, a life that would be very difficult for her to manage alone. No wonder she didn't want to know the bad news until she had to.

I put my hand on her shoulder. "Oatmeal? Sue Ellen's made a pot of it."

She bent her cheek to my hand. "Just a little, please." She took a deep breath, then began spooning sugar into her coffee. "Sue Ellen, are there any eggs?"

"Coming up," Sue Ellen said cheerily. "And bacon." She glanced at me. *Later*, she mouthed, as she put a plate in front of my mother. "I'll get you some orange juice," she said to Leatha, and went to the fridge.

Stepping close to Sue Ellen, I said in a low voice, "Maybe you and I can talk some more before we have to leave for Kerrville."

"You need to get going," she said, getting out the pitcher. "Anyway, we don't have to do it today, do we?"

"No." I took the pitcher from her and began pouring juice into glasses. "But if you hold off, Justine is likely to think—"

"Happy Thanksgiving, everybody!" Caitie sang, standing in the doorway with Mr. P draped like an orange fur stole over her arm. "Is it time for breakfast?" She was wearing her favorite pink fairy pajamas and fluffy pink bunny-ear house slippers, and her dark hair was tousled. She looked adorable—although I am her mother, and naturally prejudiced. I often find myself wishing that I could keep her safe from the world and at this sweet age forever.

"Breakfast is most definitely ready," Leatha said with a broad smile. She patted the chair beside her. "Come and sit by Gramma, and Sue Ellen will fix you some eggs and bacon. Did you and Mr. P sleep well last night?"

"Oh, yes!" Caitie exclaimed. She found a small bowl and began filling it with milk for the cat.

"Scrambled okay?" Sue Ellen asked.

Caitie nodded. "Did you know that those eggs were laid by my girls?" She put the bowl on the floor, and Mr. P began to lap up the milk, purring throatily and twirling his tail. That cat is such a *ham*.

"They were, truly?" Sue Ellen asked in mock astonishment. "You mean, you have your very own chickens?"

"Six hens, a rooster, and seven little chickens," Caitie boasted, sitting down beside her grandmother. "And the girls' eggs are all *fertile*. That means," she explained in a knowing tone, "that the hen and the rooster had sex, so if a hen sits on the eggs and keeps them warm all day every day for twenty-one days, baby chicks will hatch out. I know this works," she confided, "because one of my hens volunteered. That's how we got the seven little chickens."

I put a glass of orange juice in front of Leatha, watching to see how she would respond to her granddaughter's version of the facts of life. She didn't even raise an eyebrow. "What a well-informed young lady you are," she said, picking up her fork and smiling at Caitie.

Caitie beamed. "Thank you," she said modestly, and launched into a lengthy description of her chicken-raising, egg-selling enterprise, which occupied us for the duration of breakfast. After that, my mother was anxious to get off to the hospital, so there was no more opportunity for Sue Ellen and me to talk. I had the uneasy feeling that she had welcomed the interruption. I knew from experience with clients that the trek to the DA's office can be a scary one, and I wouldn't be surprised if she got cold feet. But I would be sorry. Her knowledge of her husband's guilt—whatever his crime—could come back to haunt her.

Before we left, Leatha and Sue Ellen quickly conferred about the food for Thanksgiving dinner—stuffed turkey with the usual trimmings. The pies had been baked the evening before, and Sue Ellen planned to stuff the turkey and get it into the oven in time for dinner shortly after four. The sky had been cloudless when I got up, but by the time we started out, it was drizzling a little, and from the look of the thick gray bank of clouds hanging low over the northern hills, we might get a downpour at any moment. We took Sam's Impala, but Leatha asked me to drive—an admission, I thought, that she was feeling a little shaky about what we would find when we got to the hospital. We followed 187 north to Utopia, and as we passed the site of Jennie's Kitchen, the restaurant where Jennie and I would be installing the herb garden the next day, I pointed it out.

"I hope it's not raining tomorrow," I added. "Jennie has some people coming in to help, and it would be good to get all the plants in the ground if we can." Leatha nodded but didn't say anything, and I saw that her jaw was clenched tight. Whatever the bad news to come, she was already arming herself against it.

For once, there were no vehicles parked in front of the Lost Maples Café, which was closed for Thanksgiving. The general store was closed, too, and Main Street was empty—until, that is, we reached the northern outskirts of town. On the right-hand side of the road, a half mile past the library, a half-dozen official trucks and cars were parked cattywampus in the asphalt-paved parking lot in front of the Masters Animal Clinic. The EMS ambulance, followed by a sheriff's car, was just pulling out. A woman wearing jeans, a green cap, and a green Parks and Wildlife jacket stepped out onto the road in front of us. She raised her hand, stopping us to allow the official vehicles to make their exit. Since the ambulance was running its lights but not its siren and wasn't flying at warp speed, I guessed that their cargo was bound for the county morgue. And that it wasn't an animal patient.

"Oh, look!" Leatha exclaimed, leaning forward. "That woman—that's Mackenzie! Mackenzie Chambers, our game warden friend."

So it was. Mack stepped back to the right-hand shoulder and motioned to us to drive on. I checked the mirror and saw that there weren't any cars coming up behind us, so I pulled up next to her and hit the button that lowered the passenger-side window.

"Great to see you, Mack," I said, leaning on the steering wheel and speaking across my mother. "It's been too long." I gestured toward the parking lot. "What's going on?"

She bent over to look through the window, did a double take when she saw me, then smiled quickly, showing even, white teeth in a face reddened by the wind. "Oh, hi, China! Yeah, it's been a while, hasn't it? Seven or eight months, at least. Welcome to Utopia." She put out her hand to my mother. "Hello, Leatha. Happy Thanksgiving."

"We're looking forward to seeing you this afternoon," Leatha said, squeezing her hand briefly and releasing it. "We'll be at the hospital in Kerrville this morning, but we're planning dinner sometime after four. Is that still good for you?"

Mack nodded. "I heard about Sam," she said soberly. "I'm sorry. I know how difficult this must be for you. He's going to be okay, isn't he?"

Leatha lifted her chin. "Sam is going to be *fine*," she said with a determined emphasis. "Of course, it may take a while, but he'll be good as new. And if you're thinking that dinner might be too much trouble for us or something silly like that, just stop." She smiled brightly. "Sam insists that we have our holiday as usual, and you're included. I thought of having a stuffed venison roast, but turkey is really easier."

"Turkey will be wonderful," Mack said. "Looking forward to it."

"What's going on?" I repeated, gesturing toward the parking lot. "Looks like a full house, including EMS. Did somebody get hurt?" I didn't ask why she happened to be there, but I wondered. Game wardens are also peace officers, but you don't often see them directing traffic.

Mack's smile vanished. "Doc Masters," she said gravely. "He was shot."

"Shot!" Leatha's hand went to her mouth. "Oh, no! Was it an accident? Is he going to be all right? Phil is such a wonderful, thoughtful man." Turning to me, she explained, "Phillip Masters is a longtime veterinarian and an old friend of Sam's. He's also an expert bird-watcher, and he's offered to come out next spring and lead bird walks along the river for our guests. He can identify every single bird by the song alone."

Mack's mouth was hard and tight, and I could see the pain in her dark eyes. "I'm afraid he's dead," she said, answering my mother's second question. Then, as Leatha gasped, she answered the first. "And it wasn't an accident," she added grimly. "He was murdered. Shot at close range."

"Murdered!" Leatha whispered. Her eyes were wide and disbelieving. "You can't be serious, Mack. Not Phil—and not in Utopia!"

"Afraid so," Mack said. Her loose dark hair blew across her face, and she turned her back to the chill wind.

"Was it a robbery?" I asked. I was remembering that there had been several break-ins at vet hospitals in the Pecan Springs and San Marcos areas. Animal clinics are a tempting target because they stock narcotics—and because some of them don't have the necessary security. "Somebody after drugs?"

Mack gave me a glance I couldn't read. "That's still under investigation," she replied, in a carefully neutral tone I recognized from my conversations with police officers who don't want to let you in on the details. Somehow, though, I got the idea that it might *not* have been a robbery—or at least, that Mack didn't think so.

There was a quick, light tap on a car horn behind us. Straightening, Mack slapped the roof of our car. "Need you to move on now," she said crisply, and softened it with a smile. "Drive safely. See you at four."

I glanced in the mirror. There were several cars behind us, and I quickly drove off, reflecting that there was a gloomy irony here. Bad things could happen anywhere and everywhere, and they did. But when something bad happened in a pretty little town named Utopia, it might seem a great deal worse. Although when you get right down to it, there's nothing worse than taking a human life—unless it's taking more than one.

"I just can't believe it." Leatha shook her head despairingly. "Who would do such a terrible thing—and why? Phil could be a bit crusty and abrupt, but once you got to know him, all that disappeared. He didn't have much use for people who mistreated animals, either, or didn't take care of the land. But when you became friends, there was nothing he wouldn't do for you." She fished in her purse for a tissue and wiped her eyes. "I can't tell Sam about this, I just can't. They were boys together. They've been friends for life. He'll be devastated."

"I'm sorry," I said. There was nothing else to say, really. Leatha fell silent and turned to look out the window.

As if the weather were a barometer of our feelings, it began to rain harder. The wind was blowing from the north, bending the roadside grasses and buffeting the car. After my recent introduction to the business of deer ranching and the problem of exotic species, I found myself paying attention to the eight-foot-high fences that stretched for interminable miles on both sides of the road, with occasional glimpses of herds of deer grazing as peacefully as cattle. I also saw strange-looking sheep with curly horns, an occasional buffalo, and once—quite remarkably, almost as if it were a mythical animal out of a fairy-tale book—a zebra. A zebra? I almost didn't believe it. Why would anybody want to shoot a zebra, a zebra that had been bred and raised simply to be shot?

And there were signs, peppered with exclamation points. *Trophy White-tails Guaranteed! No Kill, No Pay! Live your dream as a deer hunter! Bag a big buck you can brag about back home!* Whatever you might think about the taste of the advertisements or the ethics of canned hunting, it was obviously a burgeoning business. There must be a heckuva lot of money changing hands.

But all this raised a flock of uncomfortable questions in my mind, and I turned them over as we drove along. What went on behind those fences—was it genuine hunting or more like target shooting, more like shooting a pet pig in a pen? When did a big buck—or an exotic sheep or a buffalo or a zebra—stop being a wild animal and become a commercial product, a commodity to be bought and sold?

I knew that, under Texas law, every deer in the state—wild or farmed—was considered a public resource, which meant that they were all state property. But how did that square with the huge amount of private capital that was invested in these commercialized animals, which—grazing quietly along the fence—looked more like livestock living contentedly on a farm than creatures roaming the wild? There were too many inconsistencies here. And too many inviting and convenient opportunities for criminal activity. The whole business was ugly, top to bottom. Whatever crimes Sue Ellen's husband and his friends had committed, I'd lay odds that they weren't the only people who had done so. And who was regulating this industry, anyway? Who was policing it? Game wardens? I made a mental note to ask Mack.

The rain slowed us down, and the drive to Kerrville took over an hour, the steady *whap-whap-whap* of the windshield wipers punctuating my darkening thoughts. When we were nearly there, I got a call from McQuaid, telling me that he and Brian had been delayed and were just leaving Pecan Springs on their way to the ranch. I had talked to him late the night before. Now, I told him where Leatha and I were going and brought him up to date on Sam's situation—as much as we knew, anyway.

I glanced over at my mother, who had fallen asleep, her head resting against the window. In a lower voice, I added, "Something came up last night, with a young woman who's going to be working at Bittersweet, helping Leatha and Sam. It has to do with deer smuggling—something like that, anyway."

I expected him to chuckle, but he didn't. "Deer smuggling is serious business," he said.

"So I'm beginning to understand." The rain had stopped, and I turned off the wipers. "You know something about it?"

"Some, not much. Blackie knows more, although he's not focusing on smuggling." Blackie Blackwell is McQuaid's partner in McQuaid, Blackwell, and Associates, Private Investigators. "He's involved in an investigation at one of the big trophy-hunting ranches down in South Texas. He's looking into semen theft."

I wasn't sure I'd heard that right. "Semen theft?" I asked incredulously. "You're kidding. You mean, semen as in *sex*?"

"Right. Turns out that deer semen is a hot commodity these days. Pricey, too."

"Huh?" I frowned. "I'm not understanding something here. I mean, how can they get a buck to . . . ? On command, that is." I stopped. The mind boggled.

McQuaid chuckled. "That's how much you know, kid. The buck is sedated and milked and the semen is stored in straws, frozen."

"Sedated? You mean, the poor guy doesn't get to enjoy any of this?" I wrinkled my nose, thinking how truly awful that was—disrespectful, degrading, undignified. It seemed to me that a magnificent animal deserved to maintain his dignity.

"Nope. No joy. He's sound asleep during the whole process," McQuaid replied. "And here's something that's right up your alley: they're experimenting with rosemary to extend the semen's viable life."

"Rosemary?" My jaw dropped. "Now I know you're kidding." Rosemary has been used as a preservative for millennia. The Egyptians even used it in the embalming of mummies, and some of those—the mummies, that is—are still around. But to preserve *deer semen*?

"I am telling you a true thing, China. The people who are selling semen do whatever they can to keep it viable as long as possible. Depending on the value of the stud buck—that is, on the size of the rack he wears—it can be worth thousands of dollars, tens of thousands, even."

"Stud buck?" I shook my head. "My education has been neglected. I had no idea."

"Yeah, well, that's the situation Blackie has been investigating. And it's serious, given the current craze for creating big bucks with monster racks. Picture this, babe. Somebody who steals a couple of dozen semen straws at, say, eighty-five hundred a straw, is making off with the equivalent of over two hundred thousand dollars." He chuckled wryly. "We ain't talkin' small change here. People kill for less than that. And the only way to trace it is through a DNA match of the semen or the progeny it produces."

"Who knew?" I murmured. Two hundred thousand. I thought of my conversation with Sue Ellen. She'd said that her husband was stealing from his employer, and she had implied that whatever he was doing was significant enough to warrant a charge of first degree grand theft. He worked at Three Gates, which was a big game ranch. Was it possible that he was stealing—

But I was getting ahead of myself. I didn't know enough to pursue that line of thought. I looked over at my mother, still sleeping, and kept my voice low. "But there's more, I'm afraid. The local vet—a friend of Leatha's and Sam's—was shot to death at his animal hospital last night, or maybe this morning. EMS was taking the body away when we drove past."

"Damn," McQuaid said. "Drug theft?"

"Mackenzie Chambers was at the scene. She seemed to think it was . . . something else."

"Mack? I guess in a small town, anybody with a badge gets involved when there's a serious crime," McQuaid said thoughtfully. "Even game wardens. Mack is savvy. I wonder why she thinks—"

"She's joining us for dinner at the ranch," I said. We were coming up to the intersection where I had to turn, and I needed to pay attention to the traffic. "We can ask her about it then. Drive safely, sweetie. Oh, and call me in a couple of hours, and I'll update you on Sam's situation."

We said good-bye and I clicked off the phone. Deer *semen*? I wanted to laugh. But McQuaid had sounded dead serious. It was something to think about.

WHEN we got to the hospital, we were shown to a small room where we waited—an interminable time, it seemed, but it was really only eight or ten minutes—until a white-coated doctor came in, a stethoscope around his neck and a clipboard in his hand. Leatha introduced him to me as Dr. Mendelsohn, a cardiologist. He was a tall man, stooped, with silver-framed glasses perched on a beak of a nose. He greeted us, then began without preamble, in that businesslike way doctors have when they want to get on with things." Sam's recovery from the stent insertion is going better than expected." He paused to let that sink in, and Leatha and I exchanged relieved grins.

"Oh, that's wonderful," she breathed, letting out a long sigh. "When the hospital called this morning, I thought— Well, I was afraid that . . ." Her voice trailed off. I took her hand. The Queen of Denial had worried unnecessarily because she hadn't asked for details.

The doctor took a ballpoint pen out of his breast pocket and ticked something off on the clipboard. "Well, then. After consultation, Dr. Madison and I think it would be a good idea to go ahead and repair the abdominal aneurysm I told you about. Do you remember?"

Leatha nodded vaguely.

"Good. Sam has agreed. We've scheduled surgery in—" He looked at his watch. "Forty-five minutes."

I was surprised. Leatha gulped and her fingers tightened on mine. "You have to do this *today*?"

"We think it's a good idea," Dr. Mendelsohn repeated. "Sam is an excellent candidate for endovascular surgery." He described what they would be doing and added, "We have every expectation that the procedure will go quickly and well, and that he'll have a full recovery." Tucking his ballpoint back in his pocket, he gave us a reassuring smile. "He's still awake. You can both go in and see him now."

I was heartened by the words "full recovery" but shocked nearly speechless by Sam's appearance. When I had seen him the previous summer, he had been robust and strong, brimming over with energy and plans for the future. Today, he was frail and shrunken, his face lined and gray, and I thought again, almost despairingly, of the challenges that lay ahead for him and Leatha. Even a "full recovery" seemed a fragile hope. Would he ever get back to his old self? How in the world were they going to *manage*?

But his eyes lit up with pleasure when he saw my mother, and he grinned and held out his hand to me.

"Hey, here are my girls," he said in a thin, weak voice. "You're not supposed to worry about any of this. You can't keep a good man down, you know. I'll be back at the ranch before anybody realizes I've been gone."

"I know you will, dear," Leatha said. She took his other hand and held it tightly until they wheeled him away from us. When he was gone, she turned to me. "I'm wondering what's behind this hurry-up surgery—on a holiday. Is there a reason they have to do this *now*? Is there something they're not telling us?"

I was already asking those same questions, and I didn't have any answers. But the procedure went quickly, and by one o'clock, Sam was in the ICU. He had weathered the surgery in what the doctor said was "better-than-expected shape," and Leatha sagged with relief when she heard it.

Leatha settled into a chair beside Sam's bed with the book she had brought. McQuaid called about that time from a few miles north of Kerrville, and I suggested that he and Brian stop at the hospital and pick me up. Leatha could stay with Sam as long as she liked, but now that I knew he was going to be okay, I wanted to go back to the ranch and help with the preparations for our Thanksgiving dinner.

But I also wanted to get Sue Ellen to finish the story she'd started to tell me earlier that morning. I wanted to know what her husband had been up to so I could pass the word along to Justine, with the hope that the Whiz could keep Sue Ellen out of trouble with the law. And now that I knew more about the Texas deer industry, I was curious. What was going on here?

McQuaid and Brian and I got to Bittersweet in time for me to help Sue Ellen with the last of the dinner prep. That part was easy, but I struck out when it came to getting her to tell me her story. I prodded as persuasively as I know how—and I can be pretty persuasive when the occasion warrants. But since I didn't know the details, I didn't have a lot of leverage. And Sue Ellen seemed to have reconsidered her decision to tell me the full story. That worried me. I hated to see her caught in a situation she couldn't handle. And given what I had learned from Justine and McQuaid about the size of the stakes in the trophy buck business, I was beginning to fear that the situation could turn dangerous. If Jack and his buddies viewed Sue Ellen as a serious threat, she could be a target. As if in confirmation of my concern, she got a couple of cell phone calls while we were working on the food. She went outdoors to talk and came back looking pinched and distressed. I tried to tell her that she might be in danger, but I struck out with that, too. She wasn't having any of it.

Leatha got back from the hospital a few minutes before four, and Mack—slim and attractive in a black turtleneck with jeans and a great-looking red leather vest—arrived just as we were ready to put dinner on the table. The star of the show, of course, was the turkey, crisp and brown on the outside, juicy and flavorful on the inside. Caitie was concerned about where the turkey had come from—had Sam shot it in their nature sanctuary? But Leatha reassured her that it had come from the supermarket, which to Caitie's mind seemed to make it more acceptable. I didn't pursue the irony with her. I already had enough on my mind.

Sue Ellen had stuffed the bird with a delicious rosemary and dried cranberry stuffing, and we had mashed potatoes and giblet gravy, sweet potato casserole, ginger and marmalade carrots, slaw with pickled beets and apples, and the peach and pumpkin pies that Leatha and Caitie had made the night before. I stirred up some bourbon-flavored whipped cream to top the peach pie (baked with an interesting hint of rosemary), and everybody raved about the combination.

We ate until we simply couldn't eat another bite, and then sat around the table with our coffee while Brian and Caitie went off to play StarCraft II on Brian's laptop. Brian is a veteran gamer and has initiated his sister into the StarCraft universe. They were so deeply engrossed that we didn't hear another peep out of them for the rest of the day.

While the kids were at the table, we had kept the conversation general. Brian had plenty to tell us about his first semester at the university. Mack told a hilarious story about nabbing a guy who had posted his illegal buck to Facebook and capped it off with a few of the nutty things that people do during hunting season. Sue Ellen joined in with tales about growing up in Utopia, which made us all shake our heads and laugh. The town's name might summon images of the ideal life, but the place itself sounded very much like every other small town in Texas, a mix of the good, the bad, and the simply weird.

But when Brian and Caitie excused themselves and went off to their game, the conversation became more serious. It was good to renew our connection with Mack, and the three of us—Mack, McQuaid, and I—found ourselves involved in a complicated discussion of the ethical and legal issues involved in trophy hunting. Both Mack and McQuaid were longtime hunters, but both were firmly opposed to shooting captive-bred deer when they came to feed, "like shooting fish in a barrel," McQuaid said disgustedly. As they got warmed up, both had plenty to say on the subject, while I was still trying to puzzle through the legal contradictions created by the state's claim to own *all* the deer, both wild and captive-bred, and the private ownership implied by the breeding programs that were given permits by the state. My lawyer-self noted that this conundrum had apparently never been tested in court.

I noticed, though, that Sue Ellen (whose work at Three Gates gave her more direct experience with captive hunting than any of us) said nothing at all during this fairly heated discussion and diligently avoided my glance. When the conversation turned to Doc Masters' murder (I hadn't thought to mention it to her earlier), it was clear that she was shocked. She went suddenly pale, excused herself, and left the table hastily. I was concerned and wanted to go after her. But Leatha put her hand on my arm and shook her head, and then followed Sue Ellen into the kitchen, where I could hear the soothing murmur of my mother's voice and little gulps of sobs from Sue Ellen. Utopia was a small town. I supposed that she had known him.

Mack gave us a little more information about the investigation into the veterinarian's death. The shooting had happened after hours. The vet had parked his truck beside the back door and entered there, leaving the door unlocked. The shooter had apparently used that door as well, since there was no sign of a forced entry, and the front door of the clinic was locked. Doc Masters had been standing in the doorway of his office when he was shot in the chest at close range—a single shot, probably with a .22, since the entrance wound was small and there was no exit wound. A search hadn't turned up the shell casing. The drug storage area in the clinic had been broken into, but the robber—or robbers—hadn't taken much.

"Angie Donaldson, who manages the clinic's office, is going to do an inventory," Mack added. "But at a glance, it looks as if all they took was a carton of pills and a gallon of hydrocodone syrup."

"Sounds like they're planning on getting high and staying there for a while," I said disgustedly.

"Planning to sell it, more likely," McQuaid corrected me, "depending on which pills they took. Some of that stuff is pure gold on the street." In his years as a cop, he saw more than his share of drug busts, as well as robberies, burglaries, homicides, suicides, fights, riots, and chases. His body bears the scars of his close encounters with the dark side. When he comments on criminal activity, I tend to listen.

Now, he frowned. "It's kind of surprising that they didn't take more, though. When one of the Pecan Springs clinics was broken into last month, the burglars parked a truck out back and completely cleaned it out, down to the measuring scales and drug-testing equipment."

Elbows on the table, coffee cup in both hands, Mack was watching him narrowly. "They could have taken more if they'd wanted to, Mike." She was talking cop to cop. "They broke into the closet where the drugs were kept, and there was plenty of good stuff on the shelves. Stuff they could have sold, easily, in San Antonio or up in Austin. There was cash in the office till, too, over a hundred dollars. It wasn't touched."

"No surveillance cameras, I suppose," I said.

Mack shook her head. "No. This kind of thing hasn't happened before—in Utopia, anyway."

Leatha had come back to the table, but there was no sign of Sue Ellen. "It sounds as if Phil came in and panicked them before they could get much," Leatha suggested unhappily. She shook her head, her lips pinched tight. "Such a tragedy. I couldn't bring myself to tell Sam, but he'll have to know, sooner or later. He'll be wondering why Phil doesn't drop in to see him."

McQuaid shook his head at her idea that the vet had interrupted a burglary. "The robber had to know that somebody was in the building, Leatha. Mack told us that the vet's truck was parked out back, and the back door was unlocked. I don't think there was any surprise involved—except for the victim, that is."

"And there's another thing." Mack took a sip of her coffee and put the cup down. "Something came up yesterday when I was out with Doc Masters, and I can't help wondering if it isn't somehow connected."

"Connected with his murder?" I asked.

Mack nodded, but she wasn't replying to me. She was talking to McQuaid. Again, cop to cop. "The doc and I went out on a call to a local ranch. After we finished what we had to do, he told me about a situation he'd run into a few days earlier, involving some stolen deer."

"How did he know they were stolen?" McQuaid asked. It was a very reasonable question, I thought. Some deer are big and some are little. Some have antlers and some don't. But otherwise, one deer looks pretty much like another. To me, anyway.

"The legitimate game ranches have state permits," Mack said. "Fawns born on those ranches are required to have numbers tattooed on their ears. The numbers identify both the ranch and the individual animal and are recorded with Parks and Wildlife as part of our keep-track system."

Ah. So it was Parks and Wildlife that was responsible for regulating the deer-breeding business. There was one question answered.

"I'm not sure I understand," Leatha said, frowning. "Why does anybody need to keep track of them?"

"Because of the potential for the spread of chronic wasting disease," McQuaid replied. "I learned that from Blackie's investigation. It's a major threat."

"And because some of these farm-bred deer may be genetically different from the native population," Mack added. "They're not exotics, exactly, but they are bred for the size of their antlers. And anytime you select for one trait, you're likely to throw other important traits completely out of balance." She pointed at what was left of the roast turkey on the platter in the middle of the table. "For example, that farm-raised turkey and the wild turkeys we see around here are the same species. But the domestic turkeys are genetically modified to gain weight fast. They are genetically designed to eat until they're like sumo wrestlers, supersized and so heavy they can scarcely waddle. Wild turkeys, on the other hand, are lean and alert and fast as lightning. Mix the two, and the wild birds are going to display some of the domestic traits. The wild species could be changed."

"Ah," I said, beginning to put it together. "The genetically different animals could be a threat to the species—or to the environment. Like the axis deer that were imported into Texas for hunting. And kudzu and Oriental bittersweet in the plant world." Plants and animals that didn't belong.

"Exactly," Mack said. "But back to the stolen fawns. Doc Masters told me that he was called out to a ranch—he didn't say where—to handle a birth of twin calves. While he was there, he happened to see some tattooed fawns that he knew didn't belong on the place, because it doesn't have a game ranch permit. I'm responsible for checking reports like that, so I asked him to identify the ranch and its owner. He didn't exactly refuse, but he said he . . ." She looked uncomfortable. "He had to think about it."

"Mmm." McQuaid pulled his dark eyebrows together. "Wonder why."

"I got the impression that the owner was a friend of his, or maybe somebody important in the community," Mack said. "I think he had second thoughts about telling me. Anyway, I told him I would call him first thing tomorrow to find out where those fawns are being held. I made it clear that I wanted the owner's name. And now—" She spread her hands.

"And now he's dead," I said. "And you're thinking there's a connection.

Like, maybe he made a date to talk to the ranch owner about the situation. They were supposed to meet at the clinic."

McQuaid pursed his lips. "Yeah, but I can't see somebody killing a man over a few fawns, can you, China? I mean, seriously, can you?"

At the back of the house, I heard the kitchen screen door slam. My mother got up and left the room again. But I wasn't paying attention to that. I was thinking of what Sue Ellen had started to tell me about the theft her husband was involved in.

"Well, maybe it's not just a few fawns," I said. "Maybe it's bigger than that."

"Bigger?" McQuaid asked. "Like how?"

"Like maybe there's more. More animals. More whatever." I realized my vagueness wasn't helpful. This wasn't a subject I knew much about, and I couldn't think of what "more" there might be. But I was sorting through all the little pieces and wondering what the connections were.

"But still," McQuaid said, "if it's violations of the state game laws, we're only talking fines and some jail time. Not in the same league as a homicide. Just doesn't make sense." He shook his head. "Of course, killing somebody over a carton of pills and a gallon of narcotic doesn't make a helluva lot of sense, either, but drug robberies end badly all the time." He pulled at his lower lip. "Could've been kids, I suppose. They were hanging around in the parking lot, followed him into the clinic, and—" He shrugged.

"Could've happened that way," Mack said flatly. "The stuff about the fawns was maybe only a coincidence. Damn," she muttered. "I wish Doc Masters had told me where he went on that call. Whether or not it has anything to do with his death, I need to locate those fawns and see what's going on."

I thought of my recent trip to the vet so that Mr. P could get his annual vaccinations, and the billing trail that had been left in our wake. "You said Doc Masters was called out for the birth of twin calves? You could get his office manager to check the billing records. Somebody has to have paid for the visit—unless he was in the habit of giving his time away free. Which most vets aren't," I added, remembering the size of Mr. P's vet bill. That cat must have squandered at least eight of his lives before he got to our place, but this time around, he had lucked into a cushy existence.

"Why didn't I think of the billing records?" Mack rolled her eyes. "That's what I'll do, China. Maybe I can go in and have a look tomorrow." She stopped and thought for an instant. "I'll have to do it first thing, though. I'm supposed to meet a couple of kids who want to show me their drone."

"A drone?" McQuaid asked with interest. "I thought the Texas legislature was driving a stake through the heart of drones—at least for ordinary civilians."

"The bill hasn't made it out of committee yet," Mack told him, "so they're still legal. Anyway, I've never seen one of those things up close. I'm curious about the quality of the image, the range, that kind of thing. So I'm meeting them tomorrow at ten, at the rodeo grounds in Utopia."

"I might see you there," I said. "I'm helping Jennie Seale plant an herb garden at her restaurant tomorrow morning. It's not far from the rodeo grounds. And I've been interested in drones, too. They pose some serious privacy issues." I looked at McQuaid. "I'll probably stay here through Sunday, if that's okay with you."

McQuaid nodded. "No problem, far as I'm concerned. Brian and Caitie and I are heading back to Pecan Springs first thing tomorrow.

Brian's got a hot date for tomorrow night, Caitie's got a sleepover, and I need to clean up some paperwork in the office." He looked at Leatha, who had just sat back down at the table. "Unless there's something you need me to do here, Leatha. If there is, I'll be glad to hang around for a couple of hours."

My mother shook her head. "No, dear, you and the children go on. But I do hope you'll come back for Christmas. Sam will be his old self again, I'm sure, and we'd love to have you celebrate the holiday with us." She leaned toward me, a puzzled look on her face, and lowered her voice. "I don't understand it, China. Sue Ellen was talking on her cell phone out in the backyard. I watched her through the window and could see that she was terribly upset. I think she was crying. Then she ran in, got her car keys and purse and coat, and drove off."

"Drove off?" I asked in surprise.

"Without a word. No good-bye, nothing. It's especially odd because we had just been talking about starting the kitchen cleanup. I'm sure something must be terribly wrong."

"I wonder if she went back to Three Gates," I said worriedly. If she had, would her husband be able to persuade her to stay with him? Would he—

Mack's cell phone chirped, and she fished it out of her jeans pocket. "Sorry about this," she said, pushing her chair back. "I'm on call this evening, so I can't turn my phone off. I need to answer." A few moments later, she returned to the table. "I'm afraid I have to leave," she said to Leatha. "A property owner who lives south on 187 just phoned to say that he discovered blood and drag marks across a corner of his field. He followed the trail and found a dead doe, just the backstrap taken. Whoever did it was probably shooting from the road—jacklighting, most likely."

"Jerk," McQuaid growled. "But he's long gone. You don't have much of a chance of getting him."

Mack smiled tightly. "You never can tell. I'll ask around. Maybe a neighbor saw a vehicle. Folks don't like people who do this kind of thing. Hunters especially hate it. They want the guys caught and fined—and named in the local newspaper and on the Internet, for everybody to see." She grinned ruefully. "Publishing names turns out to have a big impact on behavior."

I followed Mack out of the room. While she was putting on her jacket, I said, "I'm sorry you have to leave, Mack. Can we get together before I go back to Pecan Springs? I'd like to catch up on your life." I grinned. "Not your game warden life. Your *other* life. You know. The personal stuff."

"Oh, that." Mack's smile brightened, and a flush rose on her cheeks. "Actually, I might have something interesting to tell you."

"You've met somebody?" Mack had been through a painful time during the last months she was living in Pecan Springs—painful because her husband had been cheating on her and it had taken her a while to catch on. She was a career-first woman who cared deeply about her work and—I suspected—put it first, which doesn't sit well with a lot of guys. She needed somebody who understood her commitment and was willing to support it.

She zipped up her jacket, looking bemused. "Yeah, believe it or not. He's a deputy sheriff. He fixed my truck this morning—a problem with a vacuum hose. I'm thinking that we might actually have a few things in common." She smiled wistfully. "Maybe—just maybe."

"I want to hear more about that guy," I said, thinking that if anybody could understand about the demands of her work, it would be a fellow officer. "Tell you what. If my planting job doesn't take all morning, I'll try to stop by the rodeo grounds and see what's up with that drone. As I said, I'm interested in their use—from a privacy point of view."

Privacy has always been a hot-button issue with me. It used to come up regularly in my criminal defense work, and it's been a concern in my personal life, as well. But drones have raised privacy questions to a whole other level. I had recently happened to talk over some of the issues with a lawyer friend who works with the American Civil Liberties Union. She pointed out that the technology is developing so fast that pretty soon, none of us will have any secrets. For instance, she told me about a tiny drone specifically developed for stealth surveillance. It's smaller than a sparrow, weighs less than a AA battery, and can be parked in the air right outside your second-floor bedroom window. The Federal Aviation Administration is changing airspace rules to make it easier for law enforcement officers to use these little flying marvels, but the new rules don't address privacy protections, and the ACLU is raising plenty of questions. When can drones be used? Can they be deployed without a warrant? How long should the images be kept, and who should have access to them? Can the images be subpoenaed for use in court?

"Works for me," Mack said, fishing in her pocket for a card. "Here's my number. If we miss each other in the morning, give me a call and we'll reschedule."

We said good night, and I went to help Leatha put the dishes in the dishwasher and clean up the kitchen. Then the kids left their game to join us in the living room, and McQuaid and I snuggled together on the sofa to watch the Texas Longhorns play to a tied 7–7 fourth-quarter score against Texas Tech.

"Like kissing your sister," McQuaid grumbled, then sat on the edge of his seat until the Tech quarterback threw an interception and Texas ran the ball back for a touchdown, putting a perfectly satisfactory end to a quiet Thanksgiving evening and—considering Sam's successful surgery—a happy Thanksgiving Day.

Except that Sue Ellen hadn't gotten back by the time McQuaid and I went to bed. As I fell asleep, I couldn't help wondering uneasily where she had gone and why, and hoping that she was okay.

Chapter Eight

Mack woke up early on Friday morning with the bright sun streaming across her face, Molly sprawled across her feet, and Mrs. Cook's rooster crowing lustily under her window. She smiled to herself as she got up and dressed in jeans, a plaid blouse, and a wooly red crewneck sweater. She had a couple of nice things to smile about, too, the first of which was Ethan's phone message, waiting for her on her answering machine when she got home.

"Hey, Mack," he'd said. "Just want you to know that I've been thinking about you. Hope you're having a great Thanksgiving dinner and that you don't have to go out on call. Or if you do, that you nail the bad guy." There was a moment's silence, then his voice warmed. "I was just thinking about those 'exceptional circumstances.' I'd like to give it another try, just to be sure I'm right." She could picture the grin, wide and quick, spreading across his rugged face. "I'll phone you again. Let's see what we can put together."

The other thing she had to smile about was last night's investigation. It had been easier and more successful than she had any right to hope. As it turned out, she didn't need to do a neighborhood canvass, for even though the shooter was long gone (as Mike McQuaid had said), he had left a valuable clue behind. When Mack and the property owner went to take a look at the dead deer, she discovered something lying in the loose dirt beneath the animal, where the shooter had accidentally dropped it in his hurry to take the best of the meat and make a getaway. His cell phone.

She had picked it up and a moment later was talking to the phone's owner, a twenty-three-year-old man who lived on the outskirts of Utopia, not far from Mack's house. He was delighted to learn that his missing phone had been found—until he opened his front door a little later and was confronted by a game warden, phone in hand, who told him where she had found it. And began asking questions.

At first, and with a great deal of extravagant drama, he claimed that his phone had been stolen from him while he'd been at a party. But when Mack pressed him for the location of the party and the name of the host, he began changing his story. Come to think of it, his phone wasn't actually stolen, he'd loaned it to a friend. No, he hadn't loaned it to the friend, he'd gone riding with the friend, and it was the friend who had actually shot the deer. Finally, asked to name the friend, he confessed to shooting the deer himself, from the road, and produced the gun he had used. Mack issued a handful of citations, including hunting without a valid permit, hunting from a vehicle, hunting on a public road, hunting with an artificial light, and failing to retrieve the animal or keep it in an edible condition. As she handed him the sheaf of copies, she thought with satisfaction that—between the fines and the jail time—this was going to be one expensive lesson. She hoped the young man would learn it, and pass along the warning to his buddies.

Now, as she poured coffee, made toast, and nuked a couple of Mrs.

Cook's fresh eggs for breakfast, she thought ahead to the day. She had the morning off, which was why she was wearing civvies. But she needed to call Angie Donaldson and see about getting a look at Doc Masters' billing records, so she could locate the ranch where the vet had seen those fawns. She had agreed to show up at the rodeo grounds at ten to get a look at the drone. And she was on duty in the afternoon and evening. But maybe Ethan would phone and they could—

As if she had conjured it, the phone rang. When she picked up, it was Ethan. "Hey," she said, with pleasure.

"Hey, you." There was that warmth again. She could feel it in her bones, spreading like a honey-sweet glow. She liked it that he went straight to the point, without a lot of preliminary chitchat. "Looks like it's going to be a pretty day. I was thinking that maybe you and Cheyenne and me and Buddy could drive out to my friend's ranch later today and go riding. Maybe trailer separately and meet out there?"

"Can't," she said regretfully. "I'm on duty this afternoon. But I'd love to do it—how about Sunday instead?" Somebody else might enjoy playing hard-to-get, but that had never been her style.

He sighed. "Sorry. I'm on duty this weekend. What's your next free day after that?"

"Tuesday, I think." She checked the calendar on the wall. "Yeah, Tuesday."

"That's good for me, too," he said. "Eleven, say? That would give us plenty of good riding time." He hesitated, adding tentatively, "And maybe we could get burgers at the café after, depending on how we feel." He chuckled. "And if one of us doesn't get called out."

"Works for me," she said, reaching for a pad and pencil. "Directions?"

She jotted them down quickly. "Thanks. Anything new on Doc Masters' murder?"

"Not that I've heard," Ethan said. He paused, and added, "You found out anything more about those tattooed fawns you mentioned? You still following up on that?"

"Some. But not enough to get me the name, if that's what you're asking," Mack said.

"That's what I'm asking." He paused. "If you get a name, would you pass it along to me?"

"I could," she replied cautiously. "As long as you remember that deer are my business. I need to be involved in whatever goes down." She paused. "I'm serious, Ethan. Is it a deal?"

"It's a deal as far as I'm concerned," he said. "But you know I don't call all the shots in this county."

"I know. But if I pick up something and you're in on it, I expect to be in on it, too."

"Works for me." There was a smile in his voice. "Buddy Holly and I are looking forward to Tuesday." He hummed something that sounded vaguely like "I'm Gonna Love You Too," and hung up.

Mack laughed. She didn't think anybody remembered that song these days. She swung into the refrain to "I'm Gonna Love You Too" and danced a little jig. And then, noticing that Molly was regarding her with a worried frown, picked up the dog's forelegs and they danced around the kitchen together. And then she sat down on the floor and gathered Molly into her arms and gave her a huge hug.

"Maybe?" she whispered into the dog's ear. "Just maybe?" And Molly licked her face with a delighted enthusiasm.

Breakfast over, Mack backed her Toyota out of the garage and, a few moments later, was pulling up in front of the vet clinic. She had tried calling, but there was no answer, so she had decided to drive over. She had expected that the clinic might still be a crime scene, but apparently the sheriff had finished the investigation and released it, for the yellow crime scene tape was no longer stretched across the building's entryway. A closed sign hung on the door, however, under a typed note that said, "Friday & Saturday appointments cancelled because of the death of Doc Masters. Please phone on Monday to reschedule."

But as Mack peered through the window next to the door, she saw a light inside. She rapped on the door and after a few minutes, Angie Donaldson opened it. She was a short, stocky woman, middle-aged, with plastic-rimmed glasses and dark, spiky bangs that brushed her eyebrows. Her scrubs were cheerfully printed with yellow and orange kittens, but there was nothing cheerful about her expression. Her eyes were red rimmed and bruised looking, and she was sniffling. She had been crying.

"Doc Masters is dead," she said. "We're not seeing patients today."

"I know," Mack said sympathetically. "You probably don't remember, but I was here with the sheriff's team yesterday. I'm Warden Chambers." She took out her identification and held it up.

Angie peered at her. "Oh. Oh, sorry. Didn't recognize you, Warden. Yesterday was a madhouse."

Mack nodded. "There were a lot of people here, and it must have been very hard for you. Listen, I'm sure you're busy and I don't want to take up your time, but I'm working on a Parks and Wildlife investigation, and it's rather urgent. I need to track down a visit he made recently, to a local ranch. Could I have a look at your billing records? The information I want is probably there."

"Billing records?" Angie was uncertain. "Gosh. I don't know whether I'm supposed to let you . . ."

"I understand," Mack said. "It's pretty simple, really. I'm looking for just one piece of information. But if it would make you more comfortable, I can get a search warrant. It takes a little time is all, and—"

"Oh, heck," Angie said, rolling her eyes. "Who's going to care, now that Doc is gone?" She opened the door. "God, I can't believe I just said that. Can't believe he's dead, either. Just blows my friggin' mind." She wiped her nose with the back of her hand. "Come on in and tell me what you're after."

The office was small and dark, overcrowded, and definitely overheated, and Mack took off her jacket as Angie booted up the computer on the corner of her crowded desk. Mack described what she was looking for. A moment later, she was watching Angie scroll through a list of records on the monitor of the office computer.

"Did he say what day it was that he delivered those calves?" Angie asked. She hunched her shoulders and pulled up another page.

"No. I got the impression that it was fairly recently, though. In the last couple of weeks. And that maybe the owner of the ranch was a friend of his. Or somebody he knew pretty well."

Angie snorted. "That doesn't narrow it down a whole lot. He's got a lot of friends." After another few moments of scrolling, she shook her head. "I'm not finding anything. But then, sometimes Doc gets an emergency call when he's out on the road. He'll go ahead and make the visit, especially if the place is close, then forget to log it into the system when he gets back to the office—unless of course I'm here to nag him about it."

She pulled a tissue out of a box on her desk. "Sorry," she muttered.

"I'm making it sound like he's still alive. I have to start getting used to the fact that he's not." She blew her nose. "He wasn't just my boss, he was a friend, and a damn nice guy at heart. I can't believe that somebody would kill him like that. It . . . it seems so pointless."

"I know," Mack said. "I met him only once, but I liked him. He really knew his stuff." She paused, thinking. "If he made the visit when he was out on the road, how would the billing get handled?"

Angie blew her nose again. "It wouldn't. At least, not until Doc finally remembered it and told me to log it in and send a bill. I kept telling him that we live in the twenty-first century and that we have the tools to do a better job of collecting, if he would only pay attention to that part of the business."

Mack felt a stab of disappointment that made her realize how much she'd been counting on getting the information. "So bottom line, you don't have a record of this twin-calf call. Is that it?"

"Well, *I* don't have a record. In the computer, that is. Which is not to say that there isn't one in his notebook. He might have written it down, meaning to tell me and just forgot. That happens—happened—a lot."

"Okay." Mack straightened. "Where would we find the notebook?"

"Who knows?" Angie pushed back her chair and got up. "Could be anywhere he happened to put it down. We could maybe start with his desk. Come on."

The floor of the dark, narrow hallway was still marked with sticky yellow tape where the body had lain. Angie carefully stepped over the spot as she went into Doc Masters' small office and flicked on the light. Following her, Mack saw that the desk was a formidable heap of papers, medical journals, notes, books, cassette tapes, a pad of sticky notes, paper plates, a half-empty coffee cup. The shelves were a messy hodgepodge of books, journals, and papers, and there were stacks on the floor. A black cat sat on the windowsill.

"Gosh," Mack said, and then couldn't think of anything else to say.

"Yeah." Angie sighed. "But if you need it, you need it. You'll have to dig."

"What am I looking for, specifically?"

"An orange side-spiral notebook, about five by seven, with a wide blue stripe across the front. Sometimes he keeps it in the pocket of his jacket, sometimes he drops it on his desk. Or sticks it in a drawer. Sometimes . . ." She gave a shrug. "Look, I really need to get that drug inventory done this morning so I can tell the sheriff what and how much was taken. And I've got to call Clinker and see if he can get over here this afternoon and repair the drug closet door. Why don't you look around and see if you can find that notebook? If you do, bring it to the office so I can enter the billing. Somebody owes us some money." She turned to go, then paused. "You haven't heard anything from the cops, have you? About the shooting, I mean. Do they have any idea who did it?"

Mack shook her head. "Sorry, I haven't heard a word. But then, I'm not in the loop." If she'd been able to get together with Ethan this afternoon, he might have had some news for her. Otherwise, there'd be no reason for anybody to let her know what was going on.

Mack searched systematically, beginning with the top layers of stuff on the desk and working down to the desktop, disturbing the piles and stacks as little as possible but doing a thorough job. Glancing up, she saw a brown cardigan hanging on a coatrack and checked the pockets—nothing there. She did a cursory examination of the bookshelves, then went back to the desk and began going through the drawers, first on the right side, then on the left.

It was in the top left-hand drawer, and she pounced on it and began paging through. Unfortunately, Doc Masters' handwriting was a nearly indecipherable scribble, and the pages seemed to be a random collection of notes, reminders, even a grocery list. But some of the entries were dated, and at last, she found what she thought she was looking for. *Twin heifer calves, Bar Bee. 3 hours*, with a date. Unless there were two such events in the past month, this must be what she was looking for. She kept on scanning the pages, but it was the only entry that was anywhere close. The Bar Bee had to be the one.

Mack found Angie bent over a shelf in the drug storage closet with a clipboard and inventory sheet. "Found the notebook," she announced. "It was in the top left-hand drawer." She held it up. "The twin calves were born at the Bar Bee. Do you have any idea who owns that ranch, or where it is located?"

"The Bar Bee." Angie straightened up with a frown. "The name doesn't ring a bell. But we can search the billing records. It might be in there from a previous visit."

But it wasn't. And when Angie brought up the browser on her computer and they searched for the name of the ranch, they couldn't find it online, either—or in the telephone book's yellow pages.

"Maybe the tax assessor would know," Mack said. But when she telephoned, she found that the name of the ranch wasn't enough. The county's property records were organized by address, property ID, and owner's name, none of which she had. With a sigh, she hung up the phone.

"Well, I've got a start, anyway," she said. "Thanks, Angie, for letting me hunt for the notebook. I appreciate it very much."

"You're welcome." Angie picked up her inventory clipboard. "You might ask around the café or the general store—about the Bar Bee, I mean. Somebody's bound to know—or bound to know somebody who's bound to know."

Mack nodded, although she wasn't comfortable with the idea of making a public inquiry. She picked up a scrap of paper. "Could you do me a favor? If you happen to think about it when you're at the store or the café, please do, and let me know what you find out. Here's my cell." She jotted down the number and handed it to Angie. "And if you could leave me out of it, that would be great. I'd rather that the owner of the Bar Bee didn't hear that a game warden is trying to locate him." If he did, he'd dispose of those fawns in a hurry.

Angie raised an eyebrow. "Like that, huh?" She pocketed the scrap of paper. "Sure, I'll do it—if you'll keep me posted on the cops' investigation. It's bad enough not knowing whether I'll have a job here at the clinic next week or next month." She shook her head gloomily. "But Doc was the best boss in the world. Not knowing who killed him or why . . . That's a helluva lot worse."

"If I hear anything I can pass along, I'll be in touch," Mack said. She glanced at her watch. "Uh-oh, gotta get going. I promised to meet a couple of people at the rodeo grounds, and I'm late already."

MACK had mixed feelings about rodeos, for she had seen instances of what she considered animal cruelty during and before the performances, and she knew that many animal welfare groups opposed them. But there had been at least some improvements in the way animals were treated, and—like it or not—rodeo was the state sport of Texas. Almost every city, large and small, staged an annual rodeo, counting it high on the list of profitable tourist attractions. Utopia's rodeos were held in the arena on the west side of town, along the shore of Park Lake, a dammed-up section of the Sabinal River bordered by stately cypress trees. A couple of times every summer, the local cowboys and cowgirls (and a handful of professional out-of-town competitors) got together to test their skills in bronc and bull riding, calf roping, wild cow milking, mutton scramble, and barrel racing. Seven tiers of wooden spectators' bleachers lined one side of the fenced infield, with fences and chutes and gates on the opposite side. During the competitions, the grassy outfield and graveled parking lot were filled with pickups, horse and cattle trailers, chuck wagons and church-sponsored food tents, and crowds of men, women, and kids in Western shirts, jeans, boots, and cowboy hats. Sometimes a carnival came to town at the same time, with a Ferris wheel, a merry-go-round, and a half-dozen other rides and carny games. And there was always an evening dance, with a local country and western band. Square dancing, too—and square dance and clogging exhibits. Rodeo weekends brought Utopia to life, Mack thought, like the mythical Brigadoon.

But this was the day after Thanksgiving. The grassy outfield was frost bleached, and the rodeo arena and surrounding outfield were empty, except for a black SUV with dark-tinted windows parked beside the southeastern arena gate and three people tinkering with something at that end of the infield. When Mack parked her truck next to the SUV and got out, she saw that the trio, two young women and a man, were working with an interesting-looking piece of equipment sitting on the ground—the drone. It didn't look anything like the model airplanes she'd flown when she was a girl, though. It looked like a large four-legged spider with a sleek silver central body and outrigger motors at the end of each leg. The spider was about two feet long and two feet across.

Mack recognized one of the two people standing beside the drone—Chris Griffin, a dark-haired, dark-eyed, intense young man wearing chinos, spiffy white tennis shoes, and a blue sweatshirt that advertised his affiliation with People for the Ethical Treatment of Animals. He stepped forward and put out his hand, reminding Mack that they had met at a wildlife conservation conference in San Antonio. He introduced his sister, Sharon, a lively-looking pigtailed blonde of sixteen or seventeen, who was equipped with a video camera. And then he introduced his colleague, Amy Roth, a pretty, willowy redhead in her late twenties. She wore jeans, a denim jacket, and a red T-shirt with the eye-catching words *Meat Is Murder* across the front. She carried an iPad.

"I'm the one you talked with on the phone," Amy said, shaking hands.

Mack glanced at her T-shirt. "Well, I guess we know where you stand on a couple of major issues," she said with a little laugh.

"Absolutely," Amy said lightly. "I like to make my statement up front. That's why I wear it."

Mack nodded. "Listen, guys, speaking of statements, I need to make it clear that I'm doing this because of my own personal interest and not in any official capacity. I have absolutely no input into the use of drones by Parks and Wildlife. I probably should have told you this on the phone, Amy. I hope you haven't come all the way to Utopia on the wrong assumption."

She thought Chris looked a little disappointed, but he only said, "Amy has been wanting to evaluate the drone because of her work with PETA. And Sharon wants to videotape a flight for a science project at school. When we met at that conference, you seemed interested. So I thought we'd put it all together in one package."

"And we were coming this way anyway," Sharon said. "We're planning to use it to watch some people shooting—"

Amy broke in hastily. "Let's just say we're taking it for a practice flight not very far from here, later today."

Mack caught the warning glance Amy had shot at Sharon. She guessed that they were probably going to try out the drone on some sort of surveillance mission and thought she should warn them.

"Just for the record," she said, "I need to remind you that it's illegal to interfere with anyone who is lawfully hunting. I don't want to get a phone call from some irate guy who wants me to throw you in jail because your drone scared away a buck he had in his sights. Or a call from you, yelling that some idiot hunter has shot down your drone."

"What about someone who is *un*lawfully hunting?" Sharon put in. She might have said more, but she subsided when her brother shook his head at her.

"We understand all that," Chris said to Mack. He was scowling. "We've read the regs."

"Yeah, I figured," Mack said with a smile. "I needed to say it, is all." She refrained from calling them kids—they were too old for that, although that's how she thought of them. Kids on a mission, kids with a cause. Kids who could get themselves into some pretty serious trouble if they didn't watch out.

She knelt down to look at the drone. "So tell me what we've got here and how it works. I used to fly my brother's radio-controlled model airplanes. But that was a couple of centuries ago, before all this new technology came along."

"Things are changing fast," Chris said. "This one operates on four motors, one on each of the four outriggers, at twenty-eight thousand rpm in a hover. It has a flight deck containing the flight control system with GPS for navigation, sensors, and receivers. The camera is suspended below the flight deck. It operates on a rechargeable battery." He held up a tablet computer. "This is the pilot's control deck. It's got monitors that show a real-time video streaming, as well as information about the flight: altitude, speed, rate of descent and ascent, and remaining battery life."

"We can see the camera view on other devices, as well," Amy said, holding up her iPad. "There's JPEG photo capture on a thumb drive and live camera views."

"We can watch it on a smartphone, too," Sharon said. "And the video can be uploaded to the Internet."

"Twenty-eight thousand rpm?" Mack asked. "Doesn't that create a lot of vibration? I'd think it would interfere with image transmission."

Chris shook his head. "The camera is foam insulated. You'll see—there's almost no vibration. It's high-definition," he added, "with a wide angle lens. Takes in a lot of territory."

"How much flying time on the battery?" Mack asked.

"About fifteen minutes," Chris said. "As batteries improve, that time will increase."

"Control range?"

"About a hundred eighty feet."

Mack's first thought was that the range wasn't very great. But with greater altitude, you'd still be able to see quite a distance, depending on the camera. "Okay," she said, "let's see it fly. But don't fly it over the town. I don't want to hear complaints from people who think they're being spied on." She gestured. "Fly it to the west, over the lake."

The brilliant blue sky and bright sunshine of the early morning had given way to gray clouds, but there was hardly any wind, which, according to Chris, made it easier to control the flight. For the next several minutes, while Sharon videotaped the demonstration, Chris piloted the drone over the woods and the lake, just over the treetops at an altitude of about thirty feet. Mack and Amy watched the color video feed on Amy's iPad. Mack was surprised at the quality of the image and the resolution, especially given the range. She could see a great blue heron wading in the water and watched it catch and gulp down a fish. On the shore, a squirrel jumped from one branch to another, then swung onto the ground, flicking his tail. With that kind of resolution, Mack thought, you could probably read a license plate number on a vehicle. She could see why people were raising potential privacy concerns.

After about ten minutes, Chris began to recall the drone, swinging it over the field. He was bringing it in for a landing when another vehicle—a red panel van with brightly painted psychedelic swirls on both sides—pulled up and parked beside Mack's truck. China Bayles got out. She was wearing a gray fleece zip-front hoodie over a green Thyme and Seasons T-shirt. There was a pair of garden gloves tucked into the back pocket of her jeans, and the knees were dirty.

"Hey, Mack," she called, and then did a double take. "Amy? My gosh, Amy! What in the world are *you* doing here?"

"Uh-oh," Amy muttered, with a surreptitious look at Chris that Mack couldn't quite decipher. She recomposed her face and smiled. "Hi, China," she said weakly. "What a surprise!"

Mack glanced curiously from Amy to China. "You two know each other?"

"We sure do," China said cheerfully. She slipped an arm around Amy's shoulders and hugged her. "And yes, Amy, big surprise. Mack said she was going to take a look at a drone this morning, but I had no idea that *you* were involved. I was installing a garden at a friend's restaurant on Main Street, and I invited myself to see the drone." She turned to Sharon and put out her hand. "Hi. I'm China Bayles. Amy's mom and I work together."

"Oh, now I get it, Amy," Mack exclaimed. "You're Ruby Wilcox's daughter! I've been in your mother's shop. Really, I should have guessed. You look like her, you know—all that red hair."

"That's my mom," Amy said with a slightly sheepish grin. She turned to Chris. "China, this is my associate, Chris Griffin. You might have met him several years ago, when we were working together on that PETA demonstration at Central Texas State. We've got a different project going here. Sharon is Chris' sister. I'm staying with her this weekend."

"Oh, sure," China said easily. "I understand." To Chris she said, "You must be the drone developer that Mack told me about. Did I miss the demo flight?"

"I just brought it in," Chris said. "Give me a minute to put in a new battery and we'll be ready to fly again."

While Chris was changing the battery, China said to Amy, "I'm spending Thanksgiving with my mom, who lives on a ranch near here. If you're going to be around later this afternoon, why don't you and your friends drop in? She may be at the hospital—her husband is recovering from heart surgery—but I'd be glad to show y'all around. It's a beautiful place, right on the Sabinal River."

Amy shifted uncomfortably. "Uh, sorry. Sharon and Chris and I have . . . uh, something else we need to do. I'm staying in Boerne tonight, with Sharon."

China nodded. "Sure thing—but next time you find yourself in the area, save some time for a stop at the ranch. Bittersweet, it's called. South on 187 about ten miles—watch for the sign on the right. I'm sure Leatha would love to give you the grand tour."

"We're all set for another run," Chris announced, and with a whir, the drone lifted off into the sky over the Sabinal River, as Mack and China watched the images on Amy's iPad. They were so clear that Mack could see the details of leaves, rocks on the shore, a pair of turkey vultures lunching on roadkill on Johnson Street, at the north edge of the park.

"Amazing," China murmured, shaking her head. "Wow. Talk about spies in the skies. No wonder the ACLU is asking privacy questions about these drones."

TWENTY minutes later, Amy, Chris, and Sharon had packed up their gear and driven off, and Mack and China were sitting over complimentary slices of guiche and glasses of iced hibiscus tea at Jennie's restaurant, just off Main Street. The dining area (once the two front rooms of a frame house) was small but homey. The wooden tables were covered with red-checked oilcloth, the chairs were painted red and green, and green plants in red pots hung in front of the uncurtained windows. In warm weather, wide doors opened out onto a brick-paved patio shaded by a green canvas awning and surrounded on three sides by an herb garden. It was still early for lunch, and the dining area was empty. So before they sat down, China and Jennie—a small, delicate woman with a ready smile and a red bandana tied around her dark hair—had given Mack a quick tour of the garden, pointing out the new plants they had settled into the soil that morning: several rosemaries, sage, lavender, thyme, chives and garlic chives, oregano, and Mexican mint marigold.

"That's our Southern substitute for tarragon," China said, pointing to the Mexican mint marigold. "It's too hot in Texas for tarragon, but this plant loves our heat and humidity, and in the fall, it has a pretty marigold-like bloom. There's another bonus, too—the deer won't eat it. In fact, if you scatter a few plants around in the garden, it might even keep them away from the other stuff." She made a face. "Although when it comes to deer, there are never any guarantees."

"China brought us some other pretties to put in, too," Jennie said. "Coreopsis, lantana, Mexican petunia, and several different salvias." She looked around with a smile. "It's going to be lovely here all summer. And I'll have all the herbs I could ever want for cooking. I'm even thinking that I could make up a few packets of fresh herbs for over-the-counter sale during the summer."

"Now, that's a good idea," China said approvingly. "We do that in our tearoom. Rosemary is always popular, but people also snap up our lavender, thyme, and sage. We usually clip a recipe to the package, as well. Sometimes, a recipe for one of our menu items."

"Great!" Jennie exclaimed. "We'll try that." She waved a hand. "And you can't leave without having a slice of our herb quiche. Take a seat and I'll bring some out for you."

Now, at the table, Mack tasted her quiche. "This is so good," she said, and smiled. "Pie fixes everything, you know—at least, that's what they say over at the Lost Maples Café. And quiche is pie, isn't it?"

"Yep," China answered, digging into hers. "A cheese and egg custard with added savories, baked in a pie shell. And yes, I agree. Pie fixes everything." She tasted. "And this quiche is very good. Maybe we should take a piece to Sam. He needs some fixing."

Mack read the concern on China's face. "Have you heard from the hospital today? How is he?"

"Leatha called this morning before she left. The nurse said he was doing 'fairly well,' whatever that means." China's face darkened and her mouth turned down. "I don't mind telling you that I'm worried, Mack. Mom and Sam are committed to this new project of theirs—filling their guest lodge with eco-tourists and birders. It's something they really want to do, and I'd love to see them succeed. But it's going to take a huge amount of work. If Sam's not in shape to help out, I don't know what's going to happen. I'm not sure my mother can handle it alone."

"I thought that's why Sue Ellen was there yesterday. Your mom told me she's going to help out."

"Yes, but it's short-term. She wants to enroll in college. She put me in touch with her sister, Patsy, who's been working here with Jennie. I met Patsy this morning. I like her very much. She seems capable and interested, and I think she'll do a good job." China wrinkled her nose. "But even with help, there's still going to be a strain. I'm worried."

Mack took a bite of quiche. "I think we all worry about our folks," she said. "I know I do. Every time I see my mother, she looks a little older and a little more tired. She works too hard. I tell her to ease up, but she keeps insisting that she's fine. I know she's not telling me the whole truth, but it's not because she's secretive or upset with me or anything like that. She wants me to have my own life. She doesn't want to worry me."

China nodded, understanding. "But there are times when we have to worry. Take Ruby's mother, Doris, for instance. She has Alzheimer's. After a lot of back-and-forth hassle, Ruby and her sister finally got her settled in a facility in Pecan Springs—it's supposed to be the best one. She gets good care there, but she's wandered out a time or two. Ruby and Ramona continually worry about her." She raised her shoulders and lowered them, puffing out a long breath. "Maybe it's simply the lot of daughters to worry about their moms. But at least there are two of them to share the load. Ruby and Ramona, I mean."

"It could be just a daughter thing," Mack said, and chuckled. "I don't notice my brothers complaining about losing any sleep over Mom. As far as they're concerned, everything's copacetic."

"And I'm an only child," China said ruefully. "So maybe I get to lose twice the sleep. You think?"

They were silent for a moment, reflecting on this, then China said, "So tell me about this deputy sheriff, Mack. This wizard guy who knows how to fix loose vacuum hoses in a Toyota."

Mack giggled, then blushed. "There's not much to tell, actually. Ethan—his name is Ethan Conroy—is nice, and he's interested. At least I think he is." She thought of that kiss and her heart raced. "I don't know him very well yet, though. So I guess maybe I shouldn't jump to conclusions."

China was regarding her thoughtfully. "Sometimes it happens fast. You've been going out with somebody else, maybe a couple of somebodies, but you keep finding out that they're not what you thought, they're not important enough to take up your time and soak up your energy. And then this person happens along and you just know, right away."

Not important enough. Mack wondered whether China was reading her mind. But she only said, "Was it like that with you and Mike?"

"Sort of. I mean, yes, I knew. I'd had enough men in my life to know that McQuaid was the right one. But I put up a fight. I loved being with him, but I thought I didn't want to be a couple. And after we finally agreed to be a couple, I loved that, but I thought I didn't want to be a *married* couple. On principle. Nothing against McQuaid, just some silly rule

I'd made for myself, insisting on having my own life, making my own decisions, as a single woman." China rolled her eyes. "Now, looking back on it, I want to say something like, 'You idiot! What did you think you were waiting for?' I shouldn't have wasted any time. I should have dived into it, the minute I was sure. Life is too short."

"I'm nowhere near the point of diving into anything," Mack said with a sigh. "And I have no idea how Ethan feels." But then she remembered that kiss again, urgent and demanding, Ethan's body pressing urgently against hers, and the desire she had felt and couldn't conceal. She flushed. Maybe she was ready. Maybe she *knew*, but she was unwilling—or afraid—to admit it.

China reached across the table and squeezed Mack's hand. "Well, don't dally. That's all I'm saying. Trust yourself to know. And to be right." She paused. "Do you have much in common?"

Mack had to smile at that. "Well, we both have heelers, which is pretty interesting, because that's a breed that doesn't appeal to a lot of people. And Toyota trucks. And we both like our eggs over easy. Oh, and turtles. He even recognized my Texas map turtle."

China chuckled. "Well, that settles it. Turtles. You two are obviously meant for each other."

Mack's smile became a laugh. "And horses," she added. "His is named Buddy Holly. He had another one once, named Willie Nelson."

China forked up the last of her pie. "This guy obviously has the right musical credentials—for a Texan, that is."

That brought another laugh. "He asked me to go riding with him," Mack added, "when we can find the time. Which might be kind of a challenge, between his shifts and mine, and both of us on call."

"Sounds to me like a totally exceptional guy," China said, and her smile widened. "I guess I can stop worrying about your love life and concentrate all my worry on my mom. But do keep me posted on developments."

"I will," Mack promised. After a moment, she added thoughtfully, "Kind of a coincidence, both you and Amy Roth here today. Wouldn't you say?"

"Yes, and a little unsettling, too." China licked her fork. "I got the idea that Amy wasn't at all happy to see me. I wonder if she and Chris have something going on."

"Something going on? You mean, romantically?"

"Just wondering." China pushed back her plate with a sigh. "Amy already has a partner, back in Pecan Springs. They've been together for several years. I like both of them, very much. I'd hate to see their relationship break up."

"Ah," Mack said, understanding. "I'm sure you know her better than I do. I didn't get that kind of impression, though. From something Sharon let slip, I got the idea that the three of them are in on whatever-it-is together. Like maybe planning some sort of surveillance activity. I gave them the standard caution against interfering with lawful hunting." She twisted her mouth. "But they'll probably do it anyway. I won't be surprised if I got a call from some pissed-off hunter—or if Chris or Amy calls to complain that somebody intentionally winged their drone."

China was playing with her fork. "Surveillance activity? Like what?"

"Like spying. They could park along a road adjacent to somebody's deer blind and fly it—to harass the hunter, if nothing else. And they just might happen to catch somebody doing something illegal. Chugging a couple of beers, for instance. It's against the law to drink when you're out hunting."

"And then what?" China asked, both eyebrows raised.

"Exactly," Mack said dryly. "And then what? They can't make an arrest or even detain a violator. They can report what they see through the Game Thief tip line, but by the time one of the wardens got there, the evidence would likely be gone. Whether the surveillance video would be admissible in court is anybody's guess."

"You're right on that count," China said emphatically. "I'd argue against it."

Mack pushed her lips in and out. "Of course, if the legislature approves the bill that's currently under consideration, Chris' drone will be grounded. But Parks and Wildlife will be able to fly them. For patrol or habitat study or anything else." She smiled wryly. "Who knows? Maybe every game warden will be equipped with one of these things someday, like our binoculars and cameras. So instead of patrolling by vehicle, we'll just put up one of these drones. It'll save time, save gas, and help us nab poachers and such."

"Interesting," China said, but Mack got the idea that she wasn't enthusiastic about that kind of wholesale surveillance in the hands of a law enforcement officer. Her friend still thought like a criminal defense attorney.

"Speaking of violators . . ." China fell silent for a moment. "Remember Sue Ellen? The other guest at dinner yesterday?"

"Sure," Mack said. "I'm sorry I didn't get a chance to talk to her. She's Jack Krause's wife, isn't she?"

China folded her arms on the table. She looked troubled. "She is—although she says she's filed for divorce. Do you know him?"

Mack glanced quickly over her shoulder. A couple of women had come in, but they were seated on the far side of the room, out of earshot. From the kitchen came the muted sound of people at work. There was no one to overhear.

"Yes, I've met him," she said. "He's the assistant foreman over at Three Gates, the biggest game ranch in the area." She paused. "Wasn't Sue Ellen working there?"

"Uh-huh. What do you think of him? Confidentially."

"I was afraid you were going to ask me that." Mack sighed. "Well, to tell the truth, he reminds me of a bully who loved to pick on me, way back in seventh grade. It's nothing I can put my finger on exactly. But you know how it is when that happens. You don't get an accurate fix, because you're remembering as much as you're seeing. I may have the guy all wrong."

"I don't think so," China said soberly. "Sue Ellen is wearing bruises. She says he caused them. Actually . . ." She leaned across the table, lowering her voice. "Actually, I'm worried about her, Mack. She left the house yesterday evening as we were finishing dinner. She didn't tell Mom where she was going. And she didn't come back. Her sister, Patsy Wilbur, works at Jennie's Kitchen. I mentioned it to her while we were working on the garden this morning, and she was really concerned. She said she told Sue Ellen she needed to get away from her husband and stay away."

"Did you try calling her cell?"

China shook her head. "I honestly thought she'd be there this morning when I got up. Patsy said she'd try to reach her. But there's something else." She paused, frowning. "I may be talking out of school here, Mack. On the other hand, it might be something you need to know. About those fawns."

Mack was immediately alert. "Those fawns?"

"Right. The fawns you were telling us about at dinner yesterday. The ones you thought might be stolen."

"What about them?"

"There's something going on at Three Gates—something that involves Jack Krause and a couple of his buddies. Sue Ellen knows what it is, or part of it anyway, but she hasn't told me. At least, not yet." She leaned closer, her voice tense. "Those fawns, Mack. I think they might have come from Three Gates."

Mack felt a shiver run up her backbone and across her shoulders. Four-three-two, Doc Masters had said. The number that identified Three Gates as the permit holder for the fawns. And now Doc Masters was dead.

"Did Sue Ellen tell you that?" Mack asked, keeping her voice even.

"Not exactly. She told me that Jack was stealing something from his employer, but she didn't say what. She also said that he and a couple of his buddies are launching a trophy-hunting business of their own. It's a start-up, on a shoestring. They've already got the land, but to get the state permit, they have to put in the fencing, which is an expensive proposition. To finance the operation, they've been trucking in white-tails from Oklahoma."

Of course, Mack thought. The fawns weren't the only black-market animals involved—they were just the only ones that Doc happened to see. "Did Sue Ellen tell you who these guys are?

"Just their first names. Duke and Lucky. Ring a bell?"

"Uh-uh," Mack said. "But I haven't been here very long. One of the other wardens might know."

China pulled her brows together, frowning. "Of course, these are uncorroborated accusations, and vague at that, and Sue Ellen was reluctant to give me the details. But I questioned a lot of people in my previous incarnation as a lawyer, and I can usually pick up signals when somebody is lying to me. I didn't pick up any of those signals from her. Whatever Sue Ellen knows, she believes it's the truth. That's one of the reasons she's opting out of the marriage. That, and the physical abuse."

Mack cocked her head, regarding China closely. "But Sue Ellen didn't tell you what the 'something' is that Jack's stealing from his employer?"

"Nope. That's as far as we got. But McQuaid told me that his PI firm is investigating the theft of some super high-priced deer semen, and then you mentioned the fawns." She paused. "Whatever Jack has been stealing, Sue Ellen thinks it's worth a bundle of money, maybe close to a quarter of a million dollars."

Mack whistled between her teeth. "That's a pretty big chunk of change, China."

"Yes." China shrugged. "Again, she might be wrong, or she might be lying. My money is on her, though. I think she's telling the truth."

The door opened. Mack, who was facing the door, glanced up and saw Angie Donaldson come in, wearing a bulky purple sweater over her cheerful yellow and orange printed scrubs. She stood looking around uncertainly for a moment, spotted Mack, and headed for the table.

"Hi, Warden," she said. "Clinker told me he thought he saw you come in here."

"Hey, Angie," Mack said. "You've got some information for me?" Angie's eyebrows went up, and she glanced at China, questioning. Mack added quickly, "It's okay. China is an old friend from Pecan Springs. China, this is Angie Donaldson. She works at the vet clinic. For Doc Masters."

"Oh," China said. "Then your boss—" She bit her lip. "I'm sorry."

"Me, too," Angie said, pulling down her mouth. "Bummer. Really. Doc was one of the good guys." She looked at Mack. "Yeah, I got something for you. A couple of names."

"That's great! How'd you do that?" Mack asked.

Angie blew out a breath, lifting her dark, spiky bangs. "I had to go to the post office a little while ago to mail a batch of billings. While I was there, I ran into Jimmy Parker. You know him? He drives one of the mail routes."

Mack shook her head.

"He's somebody you should get acquainted with," Angie said. "He's been on the route for a long time, so he knows the names of just about everybody in this part of the county. He can tell you all kinds of stuff about what's going on out there in the boonies, because he's out there every day, driving around. Well, five days a week, anyhoo. They've discontinued Saturday delivery. So I asked him about the Bar Bee, and it turns out that he knows where it is and who lives there. Or who's getting their mail there, anyway." She pulled a torn envelope out of the pocket of her purple sweater. "Here. He wrote it down. He didn't remember the exact address, but he wrote down the directions, sorta." She gave Mack a meaningful look. "I told him I was the one wanting to know, because of the billing. I didn't mention that a game warden was hot on the trail."

"Angie, that's terrific! Thank you." Mack took the envelope and peered at the penciled scribble. Was this the name and address Doc would have given her if he had lived until Friday morning? She frowned. "I can't make out what it says. Did he happen to tell you?"

"He did." She leaned over, squinting. "Good thing, too, because nobody's going to read *that*. Ronald and Thomas Perry is what I remember. Two guys."

"Father and son?" Mack asked.

Angie shrugged. "Dunno. If Jimmy knows, he didn't say. Just two guys with the same last name. Anyway, to get to the Bar Bee, you take 1051 out past Reagan Wells until it forks, then turn left and go for a couple more miles across Bee Creek, up toward Sycamore Mountain. It isn't marked, Jimmy says. There's just a low water crossing and then the mailbox."

"Ah," Mack said. "I know that area. I've been on patrol out there." That land was steep and wooded, cut by deep canyons but with wide swaths of grassy meadows strung along Bee Creek. There were no game ranches in the area, just day and season leases and the occasional poacher and jacklighter. And a gated community three or four miles away.

"Okay. The mailbox has 'Perry' on it, and 'Bar Bee' under that. Jimmy says that there's a road that snakes up along Bee Creek for a ways, which is probably how the ranch got its name. He doesn't go any farther on 1051 because nobody else is getting mail out that way. It's pretty remote." She paused. "So. That's what you're looking for, I guess. That give you something to go on?"

"Sure does," Mack said, pocketing the envelope and feeling grateful for the fact that people in small towns knew everybody and everything, more or less. "Great detective work, Angie. I can't thank you enough." She grinned. "You're going to follow up on this, too, I hope."

"You bet your sweet bippy I am," Angie said firmly. "I'm going back to the clinic right now and write up a bill for three hours of Doc's time for birthing those twin calves, and I'm sending it to those guys. Ronald and Thomas Perry. Meantime, if you get out to the Bar Bee and you find out that it isn't the right place, look around out there and see if there's somebody else who might own up to having a pair of young twin calves, so I can be sure the bill goes to the right place."

"I'll do it," Mack said.

"Good." Angie put one hand on her hip. "And you remember what I said about keeping me posted on that investigation. You owe me, you know. When I find out who the hell shot Doc Masters, I might just go gunnin' for him myself."

"I hope you don't mean that," Mack said, frowning. She didn't think Angie would do something like that, but people fooled you sometimes.

"I mean it more'n half," Angie replied grimly. She glanced at China. "Nice meetin' you, Ms. Bayles. Y'all have a nice day now, you hear?" And with that, she was gone.

"Quite a character," China said, eyebrows raised.

"I'm glad she's on our side," Mack agreed with a wry grin. "Whoever killed Doc should be on the lookout. I have the feeling that she intends to get her man." She paused. "To anticipate your question, no, there's nothing new on the investigation, from what I've heard. But then, I'm not in the loop. For all I know, the cops may have already gotten their guy."

She thought briefly of Ethan. She had promised to let him in on what she learned about the fawns, in case there was some connection to Doc Masters' murder. But maybe she'd better do a little more checking into the situation first, to see if there was anything significant in it. She'd hate to involve him in a wild-goose chase.

China nodded. "If I understood what you and Angie were talking about, you've identified the ranch where Doc Masters saw the fawns."

"Right. I followed up on the twin calves, as you suggested. We didn't find it in the billing records, though. It was in the doc's notebook. No names, just the name of the ranch, the Bar Bee. Angie had to ask around to get the names of the owners." She paused. "Maybe not the owners. Maybe just somebody who lives there."

"Those names." China frowned. "The guys Sue Ellen mentioned are Duke and Lucky. She didn't say anything about men named Ronald or Thomas. Or Perry."

"The white-tails could have been laundered through any number of outfits, legal and illegal," Mack said. "That's one of the bad things about this business. If you're going to game the system, there are a gazillion ways to do it." She pushed her chair back. "I'm glad we had a chance to talk, China, but I need to get going. If you're able to learn any more information from Sue Ellen, please pass it along as quick as you can. Okay?"

China nodded. "You're headed out to the Bar Bee?"

"Yes, but not right now." Mack stood up. "I have to go home and suit up. I'm on patrol this afternoon. I want to get on the state computer system and see what I can find out about these guys before I go out there." She smiled crookedly. "I always kinda like to know what I'm walking into."

"Good idea." China got up, too. "What you do—I know it can be dangerous, Mack. Do you ever take any backup?"

"Not often. But I've got a Glock on my hip and an AR-15 in my truck, and I earned my share of marksmanship medals when I was at the Academy." Mack grinned. "Not to mention the 'Don't Mess with Texas' tattoo on my forehead." She laughed at China's quick, inquisitive glance. "No. No tattoo. Not really. But I scowl a lot. I scare 'em to death."

"I hear you." China didn't laugh. "But just the same, Wonder Woman, you might want to think about taking backup when you go out to that ranch. Sounds like this could be a pretty serious bust, if it happens. Maybe not your average one-woman show. You think?"

"Maybe," Mack said, and grinned. "I'll take it under advisement."

Chapter Nine

Jennie's Herbed Croutons

3 tablespoons olive oil

4 garlic cloves, very finely minced

2 tablespoons finely minced fresh herbs (parsley, thyme, rosemary, sage)

4 cups ¾-inch bread cubes (sourdough is best, about 4 slices, crusts trimmed)

Preheat oven to 325°F. Heat oil in heavy skillet over medium heat. Add garlic, thyme, and rosemary. Sauté about 1 minute. Remove skillet from heat, add parsley and bread cubes and toss with the garlic-herb oil to coat. Spread on baking sheet. Sprinkle with salt and pepper. Stirring occasionally, bake just until croutons are golden, about 15 minutes.

Before I left the restaurant, I went to the kitchen door and knocked. "Just wanted to say thank you for that wonderful quiche," I said, when Jennie came to the door. "Mack and I both loved it. It was the perfect lunch."

"Thank you, China," Jennie replied. She was still wearing the red bandana, but she had tied a red and green apron over her jeans and T-shirt. "It was our pleasure. And thanks so much for helping us out with the garden—and especially for choosing and bringing all those terrific plants. You saved us hours and hours, not to mention a lot of uncertainty when it came to choosing the right plants and knowing where to put them."

"Is that China you're talking to?" a young woman called without turning around. She was working at a counter, arranging torn greens on salad plates. "If it is, I need to tell her something."

"That's who it is, Patsy," Jennie said over her shoulder, and held the door open. "Come on in, China. I'm finishing up the soup." She turned and went to the large commercial stove that stood against one wall of the well-appointed kitchen.

I went over to stand beside Patsy, who was now adding slices of tomato and hard-boiled egg to the salad plates. "What's up?" I asked.

Tall and thin faced, with gingery hair, pale eyebrows and lashes, and freckles on her nose, Patsy wasn't as pretty as Sue Ellen, and she had an air of quiet self-containment that contrasted with her sister's cowgirl vivacity. She was wearing an apron that matched Jennie's. "I finally reached Sue Ellen," she said, sounding mildly irritated. "She said she spent the night at Three Gates. She didn't want to tell me, though. I had to practically wring it out of her."

"Uh-oh." I shook my head. "I don't think that was a very good idea. I hope she hasn't changed her mind—where leaving Jack is concerned, I mean."

"She says she hasn't," Patsy replied. "She asked me to apologize to you for running out on you yesterday. She'll be back at your mom's place in a little while. When I talked to her, she was loading up her car with the rest of her stuff. Sounds like she's really clearing out."

"That's good," I said, with real relief, partly because I didn't like the thought of her staying on at Three Gates, where she might be even further implicated in whatever her husband was up to. And partly because I was hoping—selfishly—that she would settle in at Bittersweet, where she could be a help to Leatha. Knowing that she was there, I could go back to Pecan Springs feeling more comfortable about the situation. Yes, selfish. I admit it.

Patsy finished with the tomato and egg slices and reached for a bowl of herbed croutons. "Try one," she said, handing me the bowl. "I just made these fresh this morning."

"Yum," I said, munching. "Just right."

"Nice with soup, too," Jennie said over her shoulder. "We put containers of these on the tables so people can help themselves."

I touched Patsy's arm. "I hope you don't think I'm butting my nose into your sister's personal business. But I appreciate her willingness to be there for my mother—more than I can say. And I've told her that if she needs legal advice, we can help her find it."

"Which is *good*," Patsy said with emphasis, turning to face me. Her expression was intense. "I've made it my business not to know what's going on out there at Three Gates. The less I know about what Jack Krause is up to, the better. In fact, when Sue Ellen started to tell me some stuff about him and his buddies, I told her I didn't want to be involved. I felt terrible saying that, but I had to protect myself."

"It sounds as if you think something seriously criminal is going on," I said quietly.

She shivered. Her voice was low and so taut that the words seemed to vibrate in the air between us. "I *know* there is, China. And I'll tell you something else. Sue Ellen believes that she's in danger, and she is scared silly. I'm so glad that she has a place where she can just go and be safe. She told me that you're a lawyer. If you can help her get out of this situation and stay out—legally, I mean—I'll be eternally grateful."

I didn't correct her. Technically, I'm still a lawyer. I keep up my credentials with the Texas bar just so I can make that claim—or just in case my business tanks and I have to go back to my profession. "I'll do what I can," I said.

The bell over the restaurant door tinkled. Jennie turned around. "Sounds like the lunch bunch is coming in, Patsy."

"I need to get out of your way," I said. "But before I go—Patsy, did Sue Ellen ask if you would come out this weekend for an hour or so? I want my mother to meet you, and I'd love to show you around her place. You're going to like it out there." At least, I hoped she would. If things went according to plan, she would be out there helping my mother when her sister went off to college.

"Sure," she said. "I'll give Sue Ellen a call when I get off this afternoon. She said she loves her suite in the guest lodge. Maybe I can come out this evening and help her get settled."

"Nice," I said. "We'll probably eat around five or five thirty. Come for supper if you can. It'll be turkey sandwiches, probably, and just the four of us girls—you and Sue Ellen and Mom and me. My family is already headed back to Pecan Springs."

"Thanks," she said warmly. "See you then." She raised her hand. "And thank you for helping Sue Ellen. She's a big girl and she's used to looking out for herself. But I have the feeling that right now, she can use all the help we can give her."

Later, thinking back on our conversation, I would reflect that by the time Patsy said that, it was already too late.

As soon as I got in the car to head back to Bittersweet, I phoned Leatha. She was still at the hospital, where Sam had developed what she called a "little problem." When I offered to drive over, she stopped me. "Thank you, but I wish you wouldn't, dear." Her voice sounded small and thin and far away. "I know you love him, and I'm sure I'm being very selfish. But I'd really rather be here with him, just the two of us. I hope you'll understand."

She sounded near despair, and I was frightened. What was going on? Was Sam *dying*? I should be there with her. But what could I say? He was her husband. They were happy together and she loved him—far more deeply, I felt sure, than she had loved my father. And I understood why she didn't want me to come. I belonged to that other life, the life she'd had before she married Sam. I would be a part of the past, intruding on the present.

"Of course I understand," I replied quickly. "Let me know if you change your mind. I can be there in an hour." I paused. "Kiss Sam for me. I love you, Mom."

"Love you, too, dear," she said. "Don't wait supper for me." And then she was gone.

I clicked off sadly. My mother had lived through so many difficult times—her bouts with alcoholism, my father's long betrayal, Aunt Tully's frightening descent into dementia, the loss of the family plantation that had been the home of her heart. And then she had made a home at Bittersweet, a place where she could at last be the person she wanted to be, where she had a stable and deeply satisfying relationship, a love to center her life.

Now, that stability was threatened. How would she hold up? How would she—how would any of us, come to that—meet the challenge of losing the person she loved most? And if she lost Sam, would she be able to keep the ranch? Or would she lose it, as well?

But all I had were questions. Questions without answers. The answers lay beyond the curtain of time, in the hands of the fates.

I expected to see Sue Ellen's red Ford Focus in the driveway when I got back to the ranch, but it wasn't there, which irritated me a little. I wanted to talk to her, to try to get a clearer fix on what was going on at Three Gates. I was glad that Mack and I had been able to discuss the situation and trade what we knew—and what we suspected. If I was able to squeeze any information out of Sue Ellen, I'd pass it along to Mack. I frowned, thinking of what she was planning and hoping she'd follow my advice and take some backup when she went out to the Bar Bee. It sounded like it might be a volatile situation. Sue Ellen's late arrival left me with some free time. So I put on a jacket, my boots, and a wool cap, slung my binoculars around my neck and stuck my mother's bird book into my pocket, and hiked downriver to Sam's observation tower.

I was still thinking about my mother and Sam as I walked, and wishing regretfully that she had allowed me to be with her at the hospital. But I was glad to have this time to myself. The sun was flickering into cloud, and the sky had the soft sheen of old silver. The air was chilly, and the north breeze had a sharp bite, but I turned up my jacket collar and pulled down my cap and was warm enough. When was the last time I'd been alone beside a river on a wintry afternoon? I couldn't remember.

The woods were very quiet, except for the sound of my boots in the dry leaves and the occasional soft trill of a bird. Every now and then, I looked down, remembering that Sam had once shown me a flint arrowhead lying in the dust of a path not far from here. Long before white people settled here, the Comanche had hunted all through this area, on foot and on horseback, leaving behind a few traces of their time in these woods.

And then, as if by magic, I found another flint arrowhead, its chipped edges perfectly shaped and sharp. Had it been lost in a futile shot from a brave's bow? Or had it felled a deer and been missed when the animal was dressed for eating? Had there been a campfire nearby, where the women and children prepared the food that the hunters brought back? Holding it, I felt that the past was somehow very present, as if the Comanche were somewhere in the woods, watching as I walked along their path, along their river, among their trees. I put it in my pocket, feeling as if I'd found something prized and precious, a relic left by some long-ago hunter for me to discover on this quiet afternoon.

When I climbed the wooden tower, I saw that Sam had sited it so that it offered views in four directions: a view upstream and down; a view of the flat, low-lying, hummocky area behind me; and a view across the river, where I saw a rocky cliff that rose some twenty feet high. The tower platform was nearly level with the top of the cliff and it felt odd, almost intrusive, to watch the birds as they went about their business in the trees around me. Nearby, a flock of a dozen conspicuous cedar waxwings were attacking the purple berries of a juniper. A red-tailed hawk patrolled low above the grassy hummocks, on the lookout for an unwary field mouse. A mourning dove called from somewhere in the distance, and on the limb of a nearby live oak, a robin fussed at me. This tower was in his space. *I* was in his space, and he preferred to live his life without people spying on him.

And then, on the far bank, under the shelter of the cliff, I saw an axis buck wearing a huge rack, much larger than the buck my mother and I had seen from her kitchen window. He was large and imposing and, yes, magnificent and splendid and beautiful. And alien. Watching me, he stood stone-still, sharply outlined against the limestone rock and the dark green of the cedar. Watching him, I held my breath, admiring his size and strength but at the same time understanding that he was a threat, and why, and how, and to what. He was like the white-tails smuggled into Texas for their genes, like kudzu and Oriental bittersweet and chinaberry trees. Like me, a specimen of *Homo sapiens*, the species responsible for all these invasions, the most invasive species of all. It was a bittersweet understanding.

The sun came and went behind skeins of darkening clouds, and when it went for good and the wind began to blow colder, I pocketed the bird guide and headed for the house, thinking domestic thoughts. Sue Ellen would be there by now, and Patsy would be along later, but it hadn't sounded as if Leatha would make it in time for supper. I would slice some leftover turkey for sandwiches, and there were mashed potatoes that I could use to make potato soup. And there was leftover pie. I smiled, thinking of Mack's "Pie fixes everything." I could almost believe that, especially if the pie was topped with a scoop of vanilla ice cream.

When I got back to the house, though, I was surprised when I didn't see Sue Ellen's red Ford Focus, surprised and more than a little worried. Where was she? What was keeping her? According to Patsy, she had left Three Gates a couple of hours ago. It didn't take two hours to drive from Three Gates to Bittersweet—more like thirty or forty minutes. I was feeling cross, too. I hoped that Sue Ellen wasn't going to make it a habit to leave without an explanation or promise to be here and then not show up. My mother needed somebody she could depend on.

And then—of course—I felt cross at myself and guilty for feeling cross at Sue Ellen. My mother ought to be able to depend on her daughter, rather than on a friend, oughtn't she? And she couldn't. On Sunday, I had to go back to Pecan Springs, where I worked and lived. And my mother would be here, with a man with a bad heart. Or here alone, if the worst happened and Sam didn't make it.

Thinking about all this, I sliced enough turkey for several sandwiches and got ready to make the soup. I was spooning the leftover mashed potatoes into a big pan when I heard a car drive up. *At last, Sue Ellen*, I thought, with a gritty satisfaction. *It's about time.* Or maybe Leatha, back from the hospital with news about Sam. I went eagerly to the window to look.

But it wasn't Sue Ellen's Ford, and it wasn't the Impala that Leatha was driving. It was a black SUV with dark-tinted windows. The next minute I heard someone frantically pounding on the front door and a woman's voice shouting, "China! China, it's Amy! Come on, open up, please! *Please!*"

And when I opened the door, there were three of them on the porch,

Amy, Chris, and Sharon. All three were panicked, wide-eyed, white-faced, and disheveled, and they all began shouting at once.

"We have to show you something, China," Amy cried breathlessly. "On the iPad." She was holding it up.

"Yes!" Sharon blurted, waving her arms. "You need to see this!"

"Right now," Chris exclaimed, pushing forward. "There's no time to mess around! You're not gonna friggin' believe this!!"

"Whoa," I said, and held up my hand. "Get a grip. You guys are *not* charging into my mom's house until you settle down and tell me what this is all about." I turned to Amy, whom I knew. "Okay, Amy. Why are you here?"

"Because we've just seen something really . . . bad," Amy said. "Really horrible. We came to you because we're afraid to go to the cops."

"Because of what we were doing," Chris added.

"What we were doing when we saw it," Sharon amended.

"So we need your legal opinion," Amy concluded.

My *legal* opinion? I rolled my eyes. "Of all the ridiculous—"

My cell phone chirped. I pulled it out of my pocket and saw that it was Mack.

I opened the door. "Okay," I said. "You can come in while I take this call. But no more shouting or screaming. And no more talking all at once. Got that? Amy, there are cold soft drinks in the fridge. Take what you want. And the three of you choose one person to tell me what's going on and why you're here. *One* person. No interruptions."

They filed meekly into the living room while I stayed in the hall and answered the call. Mack spoke quickly and tersely, the way cops do when they're conveying information.

"China, listen. I was heading south on 187 when I picked up an

11-79—code for an accident with an ambulance on the way. I wasn't far from the scene, so I headed over. I'm here on the Three Gates ranch road, about four miles off 187, with Ethan, the volunteer fire department, an EMS crew, and Jack Krause. We're looking at what's left of a red Ford Focus at the bottom of a very steep hill. Krause says that the car belongs to his wife. If she was driving it, she did not survive. It burned."

I couldn't speak. Sue Ellen was . . . *dead*?

"China?" Mack asked urgently. "China? You there? You got that?"

"I . . ." I sucked in my breath. "Yes. I've got that, Mack. Did Krause see it happen? You're sure it's Sue Ellen in the car? Do you have a positive ID?" I was clutching at straws. Patsy had already said that Sue Ellen was leaving Three Gates, heading to Bittersweet. It had to be her.

"No witnesses," Mack said. "Krause wasn't here when it happened. The wife of one of the Gates brothers—the owners of the ranch—drove along and saw the smoke and called 9-1-1. But she couldn't get a cell signal until she got out on 187, and after that, it took fifteen or twenty minutes to get a deputy here. The car had been burning for some time." There was a murmur of voices in the background and the spitting sound of tires spinning on gravel. "There's no ID yet, either, China. The wreck is too hot to get the body out."

"Just one body?" I asked. "What about passengers?"

Shouts, and a motor revving up. A door slammed. Mack raised her voice. "Can't be sure yet, but it looks like she was alone. Probably going too fast and lost control." A pause. "Didn't you tell me that she has a sister?"

"Yes, Patsy. Patsy Wilbur. She lives with her parents. Jack Krause should be able to give you their address." I swallowed, thinking how this was going to hurt others. Sue Ellen's sister, her parents, my mother. "Will the sheriff—"

"Yeah. Somebody will handle the notifications." More doors slamming, another shout. "Sorry, gotta go, China. Ethan is yelling at me. I thought you'd want to know, since you were expecting her." Mack clicked off.

I stood there for a moment, staring at my phone, trying to catch my breath. Sue Ellen, *dead*? How had it happened? I'd only been on that ranch road a couple of times, but I remembered the steep drop-offs, first on one side, then on the other, and the hairpin turns as the road slanted up the hill. If you were going too fast, if you got into a skid around one of those curves—

Yes, if you got into a skid there was nothing to keep you from sliding right off the road. If that happened, you could die. Even if you were a cute, bouncy cowgirl with high hopes and big dreams. I suddenly thought of my mother, who had come to depend on Sue Ellen's willing helpfulness and high spirits—and who was expecting to be able to count on her, now that Sam was out of commission. How in the world was I going to tell her that her young friend was dead?

Soberly, I pocketed my cell phone and went into the living room. Amy and Chris were perched uneasily on the sofa and Sharon on a nearby chair, cans of soft drinks in their hands. Gulping a deep breath, I dropped down onto Sam's big round hassock, at one end of the coffee table.

"Sorry," I said, and heard my voice catch. I cleared my throat. "I've just had some bad news. There's been a car crash. A young woman who was here for dinner yesterday—who has just moved into the guest lodge. Her car went off a road and down a hill and caught fire. She's . . . dead."

"We know," Amy said. Her voice was trembling, and her hands were squeezed into tight, hard fists. Her iPad was on the coffee table in front of her. "We saw it."

"But we didn't know it was a friend of yours," Chris put in.

"Shut up, Chris," Sharon said sharply. "We agreed. Amy is the one who's supposed to talk."

"Sorry," Chris muttered. "Tell her, Amy."

I was staring at Amy, astonished. "You *saw* it? What do you mean, you saw it? I just got off the phone with Mackenzie Chambers. She was calling from the accident scene. She said there were no witnesses. Somebody happened to drive by and see the smoke and called 9-1-1, but by that time it was too late." I could hear my voice rising. I was out of control and I didn't give a damn. A young woman was dead and these kids— "You don't mean to tell me *you* were on that road when it happened? You saw it happen and you didn't stay around to help? Do you know that you can get twenty years for failure to stop and render aid?"

Amy shook her head so hard that her red curls bounced. "*We* weren't on that road, China. We didn't see the wreck happen, either. But our drone was there. It saw both vehicles. And recorded what it saw. We've got the video."

My stomach muscles tightened. I couldn't believe what I'd just heard. "*Both* vehicles? There was another vehicle involved—a *second* vehicle?"

"A pickup truck," Sharon said grimly. "It was the truck that did it. On purpose."

"And it wasn't us!" Chris slammed his hand down on his knee. "We had nothing to do with what happened. You'll see, when you look at the video."

"Just look." Amy pushed her iPad toward me. "Just *look*, China. You'll see what happened."

"No," I said, pushing it back. "Hold on a moment." I took a deep breath, clenching my jaw, forcing myself to think. This was a tricky situation, for them and for me. I needed to handle it right, from the get-go. I glanced from one to the other. All three of them were white and scared. I thought they were telling the truth. And I thought that their story was essential. I let out my breath between my teeth.

"Okay," I said. "Who's got some money?"

The two girls looked at Chris. "I do, I guess," he said uncertainly. "Why are you asking?"

"Give me a five or a one, whatever." I was impatient. "Come on, Chris, hand it over."

"Ah," Sharon said wisely. "She wants us to put her on retainer. So she doesn't have to tell."

"Of course," Amy said, snapping her fingers. "Attorney-client privilege. We see it all the time on TV. Chris, give her something so she'll be our lawyer. If we're in trouble with the cops, she can get us off the hook."

She can get us off the hook? That wasn't exactly what I had in mind, but it was close enough. I wanted their information. But I wanted to protect them, especially Amy, Ruby's daughter. And I wanted to protect the video. If Amy and her friends were telling the truth, it would be evidence. The police were looking at Sue Ellen's death as an accident, but this video could change that. It could be evidence that could convict a killer.

Chris fumbled for his wallet and took out a ten-dollar bill. "Here. It's all I've got." He put it on the table. "But now I won't have any money for supper."

"Thank you. I'll give you your change and a receipt when we're done here." I turned back to Amy. "Now, about that iPad. I'm going to look at the video, yes. But before I do, you are going to tell me how you got it. How and where and when. And why."

Amy slid a troubled look at Chris.

I pushed Chris' ten-dollar bill back toward him. "We're not playing games here, Amy. This is serious. If you don't answer my questions—*all* my questions, and truthfully—you can count me out." I hardened my voice. "Now, how did you get that video?"

Sharon squirmed in her chair. Beside Amy, Chris nudged her. "Tell her, Amy."

Amy gulped. "Okay. We were at Three Gates Ranch, spying on a pigeon shoot."

"*Pigeon* shoot?" I shuddered. How could people actually— But now wasn't the time for that.

"Yeah." Amy made a face. "It's pretty awful. PETA has been trying to call attention to these things, wherever they occur. We wanted to get video of this one to put on YouTube, so everybody can see what goes on. Fourteen states have made it illegal. We think Texas should, too. That's really why we came here today. Not so much to demo the drone to Warden Chambers, but to video the shoot."

"I see. So you were on ranch property when you were conducting this aerial surveillance?"

"Yes," Amy said, and added defensively, "It was the only way we could see what we needed to see. The game ranches set up these shoots by invitation only, no public notice, no advertisement. We only found out about this one by accident. A cousin of one of the hunters—"

"They're *shooters*, not hunters," Sharon put in heatedly. "No self-respecting hunter would want to be involved in something like this."

"Don't bet on it," Chris growled.

I cleared my throat.

"Anyway," Amy said hastily, "a PETA member sent us a copy of the invitation. That's how we found out. If you want to see it, it's out in the SUV. It has the directions on it. Otherwise, we wouldn't have been able to find the shoot."

"Is pigeon shooting legal or illegal in Texas?" I asked.

"Legal," Amy said. "The birds are rock doves or collared doves. Both are open season, which means that they can be shot at any time. At the shoot, this guy grabs one and throws it up, sort of like a clay pigeon, and a shooter tries to drop it. There's an entry fee—a thousand dollars. And several prizes, around fifteen thousand dollars total."

"So you were trespassing on private property to film a lawful process," I said. "And interfere with the ranch's lawful business operation."

Chris scowled. "Wait a minute. I thought you're supposed to be on *our* side."

"I am," I snapped. "This is what being on your side sounds like." I turned back to Amy. "So where was this pigeon shoot, exactly? Where were you in relation to it?"

"A little more than four miles inside the ranch. The ranch road makes a Y about four miles in from the highway. The main road, the right-hand leg of the Y, goes off to the ranch compound. The pigeon shoot was on the left-hand leg, maybe a quarter of a mile past the Y, on top of a hill. We drove as close as we could get without being seen and pulled off behind some trees."

I pointed to the iPad. "Show me. On Google Maps."

"Oh, good idea," Amy said, and pulled the iPad toward her. She typed something in, fiddled with the screen display for a moment, then turned the tablet toward me. It displayed a map. "Here's Route 187, and here's the ranch road. Here's the Y. We took the left fork, drove up to about here, and pulled off." She pointed. "This is the track that leads up to the hill where they were holding the pigeon shoot. Chris flew the drone pretty high and off to one side, hoping they wouldn't notice it. For a while, they didn't, and we got several minutes of pretty good pictures. But then somebody shot at it. The drone was hit by some buckshot—"

"Birdshot," Chris put in authoritatively. "You don't shoot birds with buckshot."

"Whatever," Amy said. "Anyway, Chris swung the drone away fast, over this way, toward this other road." She moved the map display so I could see what she was describing. "See, the main ranch road makes a Y down here. The right leg goes to the ranch compound. We were parked here, on the left leg. The drone was pretty high up. The camera was still running, and Sharon and I were watching on the iPad, trying to figure out where it was. That's when we saw what . . ." She stopped, swallowed hard. "What happened to the red car."

"You were watching this, too?" I asked Chris.

"On the control panel, yes," he said. "I was starting to fly the drone in, back to where we were."

"So then what?" I said to Amy, and added, "I don't want to know what you saw on the iPad. We'll get to that in a minute. I want to know what you *did*, after you landed the drone."

Amy looked puzzled, but she answered. "Well, after we saw what happened on the road, we got really scared. I mean, we were scared for whoever was in that car, of course. From what we could see, it looked really bad." She glanced at Chris and Sharon, who were both nodding. "But we were scared for us, too. We weren't sure what was going to happen next—whether somebody from the pigeon shoot was going to hassle us, or whether the guy in the truck might come after us. So Chris flew the drone in as fast as we could, and we put it in the SUV and got the hell out of there."

"As you were leaving," I asked, "did you drive past the wreck?"

"No." Amy pointed to the map. "See? It happened on the other fork of the Y. We could see it because the drone was so high."

"Did you call 9-1-1?"

"We tried." Amy met my eyes. "We *tried*, honest, we did, China. But the country is rugged and there aren't any towers on the ranch, so we couldn't get a signal. When we got off the ranch road and onto Route 187, we saw a sheriff's truck with the lights and siren on, making a turn onto the Three Gates road. So we figured that somebody else had already called it in. And since we . . ." She stopped, swallowed hard, and went on. "And since we'd been trespassing and shooting that video on private property, we thought we could be in trouble. So we decided to come straight here and show the video to you. We know that it has to be turned over to the police, but we figured that you'd know the right way to do it."

I looked from Sharon to Chris. "Is that the way it happened? Amy hasn't left anything out, or misrepresented anything? If she has, now's the time to tell me. This is on the record."

"That's how it happened," Chris said emphatically, and Sharon nodded.

I nodded. "You can turn on the video now, Amy. Let's see what we've got here."

Amy left the map and went to the drone display. "We'll skip the footage from the pigeon shoot," she said. "I'm starting with what we saw after Chris swung the drone away from the shooting area. As you can see, there's a time-and-date stamp running across the bottom of the video."

I saw, and knew that it would be important, if a jury ever saw it—

which was by itself an open question. A picture might still be worth a thousand words and a video worth even more. But whether it would be admissible in court was still a matter of opinion. The *judge's* opinion.

The drone was flying at an altitude of about sixty feet. The road, a narrow gravel lane, crossed the iPad screen diagonally left to right. On the left, the rocky hill, pocked with prickly pear and yucca, fell away steeply into the ravine below.

"Now, watch what happens." Amy's voice was taut. "See? Here's the red car, going along at a pretty good clip. It's almost to the place where the road turns and starts to go down the hill to the Y. Now, watch the truck. It comes up from behind, fast."

Leaning on my elbows over the coffee table, I watched as Sue Ellen's red Ford came into view, moving along the road from left to right, above a steep drop-off on the driver's side. A blue pickup entered from the left, some eight or ten car lengths behind the Ford and closing fast. It pulled even with the passenger's door, then suddenly and deliberately swerved into the front right fender, so hard that I felt myself flinch. I bit my lip, imagining how terrified Sue Ellen must have been as she struggled to keep the car on the road, feeling panicked and helpless with the truck like a battering ram on one side and the ravine on the other.

The car kept moving forward. The truck slammed into it again, hard. The car veered sharply to the left, out of control, and catapulted over the edge of the road. It smashed into a rock outcrop and bounced into the air, somersaulting once, then rolling over and over, the doors flying open, boxes and bags scattering across the hillside. It settled at the bottom, wheels up, and an instant later exploded into bright flames.

The truck, meanwhile, had braked hard, skidding in the dust. A guy wearing a green army field jacket and an orange baseball cap jumped out, a scoped rifle in one hand. He ran to the edge of the road and stopped, raising the rifle to his shoulder and aiming it at the burning car. He stood that way for a moment or two, then lowered the rifle and raised a fist in an exultant gesture. I was holding my breath. Was it . . . was it Jack Krause? Had he just murdered his wife?

Then, so suddenly and unexpectedly that I blinked, the camera zoomed in close. The orange baseball cap had a big UT on it—the University of Texas. The man was thin and dark, with a scar on one side of his face. The truck was an older model silver gray Dodge. In the bed there were three bags of what looked like feed and a red gasoline can. The resolution was so good I could even see the brand name, in big letters, on one of the bags. Big & J Deer Feed. On the back bumper, there was a red bumper sticker—"Gun Control Is Being Able to Hit Your Target." And below that was the license plate.

Amy stopped the video, freezing the man in the act of getting into the truck, and I could read the license plate. *I could actually read the license plate.*

"Wow," I whispered. "Amazing." It was like viewing through a surveillance camera, a *mobile* surveillance camera, out there in the wilderness. The license plate, the video—this crime had an eyewitness. It was documented, beginning to end.

Chris cleared his throat. "When I realized what we were seeing, I reacted, sort of by instinct, I guess. I zoomed in fast. That guy had no idea he was on camera." His voice took on a sharply bitter edge. "The son of a bitch caused that wreck and he was celebrating!"

Amy started the video again. The man got back in the truck and drove off, fast. The camera followed the vehicle for a moment, then the screen went blank. All four of us let out our breaths, all at once, all together, in one long, sustained sigh.

"That's it," Amy said. "Except for the footage of the pigeon shoot."

Sharon made a whimpering noise. "We're not going to be arrested for trespassing, are we?" she asked plaintively.

"Under the circumstances," I said, "I doubt if the owners of Three Gates will press charges." Sharon sighed in relief. I frowned at her, thinking that of all the outcomes of this episode, their arrest for trespassing would be the most trivial. "But they might," I added. "Just to make sure that you don't try that stupid trick again."

Chris tilted his head, frowning, looking at me. "So what happens next? Do we go to the cops? Do the cops come to us? Are we going to jail? What?"

"Good questions." I fished my cell phone out of my jeans pocket. "We're about to find out the answers."

Chapter Ten

When Mack thought about it afterward, she remembered things happening so fast that the action was like a speeded-up movie, blurry, with chipmunk-like voices. But at the time, everything seemed to happen in slow motion. She was in her state-owned truck heading south on 187 when she heard Dispatch sending Ethan—off duty but on call—to the Three Gates ranch road on an 11-79. She was close, so she put on her lights and siren and drove to the scene to give Ethan a hand. Not long after she got there, EMS showed up, and then the Volunteer Fire Department's tanker truck with three volunteers from Utopia, and a few moments later, Jack Krause, a big, burly man with thick brown hair, dressed in a camo jacket and jeans. Looking stunned and disbelieving, he identified his wife's Ford. That was when Mack decided to call China and let her know what had happened.

And then, some twelve or fifteen minutes later, China called back.

"It wasn't an accident," she said tersely. "It was a homicide. The PETA crew with the drone was out there making a video. They've got surveillance camera footage—drone footage—of the whole thing, start to finish. And a clear image of the man driving the truck that forced Sue Ellen off the road."

"Homicide?" Mack was dumbfounded. "*Drone* footage? You mean—"

"Right. You and whoever is working the wreck need to take a look at this, Mack. I'm temporarily representing this trio. Do you want to come here to see it and question them, or should I load them up and bring them and the video to where you are?"

"Bring them here," Mack replied. If this was going to be a homicide investigation, they were shorthanded. Ethan had told her that Sheriff Rogers was attending a meeting in Austin. Two deputies were attending a training seminar in Houston. One deputy was on vacation, another out sick, and two others—Davenport and Murphy—were working a meth lab situation on the other side of the county. She and Ethan were the only law enforcement officers immediately available.

Thinking fast, she added, "If you've got video, can you see whether Krause was involved? When he showed up here at the scene, he said he was running some kind of shooting event nearby and heard the sirens and—"

"A pigeon shoot," China interrupted dryly.

"Yeah," Mack said, surprised. "How'd you know?"

"Tell you later. He's still there?"

"He's down at the wreck." She glanced down the hill where the men were working, three VFD men in firefighter turnout gear, two EMS guys in white, Ethan in uniform, Krause in camo. "They got the car cooled down. Looks like they're trying to get the body out now." She turned away. It wasn't a pretty sight.

"Detain him," China said grimly. "Put him somewhere and keep an eye on him."

Mack was surprised. "I can do that, but—"

"Just do it," China said. "I don't know what Krause looks like, so I can't tell you if he was the one driving the truck. Maybe, maybe not."

Mack climbed down the hill, pulled Ethan aside, and told him what China had said. He gave her a startled, questioning look, then made a quick decision. When Krause and the EMS team got up the hill with Sue Ellen's badly burned body in a Stokes basket, he pulled Krause aside, patted him down and took his driver's license, then instructed him to wait in the rear cab of Mack's truck while they "sorted things out."

Looking confused, Krause complied without objection—until Ethan took his cell phone. "What the hell you doing that for?" he demanded angrily. "I gotta call my boss and tell him where I am and what happened. And somebody's gotta break the news to Sue Ellen's family. Oughta be me."

"Warden Chambers will make the call for you, and we'll handle the notifications." Ethan tossed the phone to Mack. "When you're done," he said in a low voice, "lock him in your truck, Mack. And don't give him his phone back."

"Hey, wait!" Krause protested heatedly. "My wife ran off the road and killed herself and you're acting like *I've* done something wrong. What's this about?"

"Just a few things we need to clear up," Mack said, and slipped the phone in her pocket and said to Krause, "We'll get back to you as soon as we've cleared up a few things." She closed the rear cab door and locked it.

The EMS crew left with Sue Ellen's body. Most accident victims would be taken directly to a funeral home, but Ethan told them to take her to the county morgue in Uvalde. If this turned out to be a homicide, there'd be an autopsy. The VFD hung around a little longer, making sure that the fire was completely out. They were just pulling out when China arrived in her red panel van, leading the black SUV containing the three members of the PETA squad. She left them in their vehicle and walked over to where Mack and Ethan were standing beside Ethan's white truck. She was still wearing the gray fleece hoodie, green tee, and dirty jeans that she'd had on this morning. She was carrying an iPad.

"Attorney China Bayles, Deputy Ethan Conroy," Mack said, introducing them. "She's a friend from Pecan Springs—and she's temporarily representing the kids who made the video."

Ethan's eyes were narrowed. "Warden Chambers says that what we've got here isn't an accident. What do you know about it, Ms. Bayles?"

Mack listened as China swiftly and economically sketched out the story that Amy, Chris, and Sharon had told her, using the iPad map display to show them where the three drone crew members were when the video was taken. Then she played the surveillance video.

Mack was astonished. As she watched, she thought about the driver of the red car and the sheer panic she must have felt, fighting for control as the truck deliberately sideswiped her car and sent it over the edge. She felt a swift, hard-burning flash of anger as she watched the man with the rifle lift his fist in celebration, and a distinct jolt of pleasure as she jotted down the clearly visible license plate. That guy was going to pay for what he had done. Big-time.

But he wasn't Jack Krause. That much was clear. And that's what she said in answer to China's question.

"No. Krause is over there, in my truck. He's a big guy, burly. This is somebody else."

"Let's see that again," Ethan said. China handed him the iPad, and he replayed the video, freezing it on the zoom. "The video looks legit," he said, shaking his head. "There's even a date and time stamp."

"You can match up this display with the video that's still in the drone camera," China said. "The drone owner has volunteered to turn over this iPad and the camera, as well, so it can be used to document the crime when the case goes to court. You may not have an eyewitness to this murder, but you've got the next best thing, an eye-in-the-sky witness." She grinned crookedly. "All I need is a receipt for whatever you're taking. The owner will want it back when this is all over."

"He'll get it." Ethan shook his head, still half-disbelieving. "Don't know what the county prosecutor is going to say, though. She'll have a lot of questions, for sure. This whole thing is a pretty bizarre coincidence."

China chuckled. "She may have questions to start with, but when push comes to shove, she's going to tell the jury that the drone team may have been trespassing, but they were at the right place at exactly the right time. She may even hint at divine intervention. And when the verdict is in, she'll thank the kids for helping her get a conviction. Of course, you've got to catch the guy first, before she can prosecute. Any idea who he is?"

Ethan squinted at the image. "Don't recognize him. You, Mack?"

"No, I don't," Mack replied, and added wryly, "Too bad it wasn't Krause. That would have made it easy."

"Just because Krause wasn't driving doesn't mean he wasn't involved," China said. "He could have arranged to be at that pigeon shoot to give himself an alibi, while somebody else did the dirty work."

"True thing," Ethan agreed. "Let's play this video back to the zoom. I want to run that plate."

"I've already copied it," Mack said, and handed it to Ethan.

While Mack and China stood by, Ethan unhooked his mike from his epaulettes and called Dispatch. "I'd like a ten-twenty-eight on Texas bravo kilo niner alpha three two three. And while you're at it, a ten-twenty-nine on the owner of that vehicle and on"—he took Jack Krause's driver's license out of his breast pocket—"John Russell Krause."

"Ten-twenty-eight gets us the registration information," Mack said to China. "Ten-twenty-nine, outstanding wants and warrants." China raised one eyebrow and nodded, and Mack said, "Guess you knew that, huh?" They both chuckled.

In a couple of minutes, they learned that the 2001 Dodge pickup was registered to Thomas Perry, at an address on Route 1051, who was wanted for parole violations. And that Jack Krause had an outstanding misdemeanor warrant—he hadn't paid his speeding fines.

Mack and China exchanged startled glances. "Thomas Perry," China said. "He's one of the men at the Bar Bee ranch, isn't he?"

"It's beginning to add up," Mack said.

"Bar Bee?" Ethan asked.

Mack replied, "I went to the vet clinic this morning to check the billing records and try to find out where Doc Masters saw those tattooed fawns. After some digging, the office manager found out that Masters had been at the Bar Bee Ranch, on 1051, north of Reagan Wells. A couple of guys named Ronald and Thomas Perry live there."

"Ronald and Thomas. Brothers?" Ethan asked.

"Maybe. I did a quick search in the state criminal history database. Ronald is thirty-seven years old, Thomas, thirty-three—could be brothers, or maybe cousins. Ronald is mostly clean here in Texas, just a DUI and a contested speeding ticket, both local and both in the past couple of years. Thomas—he goes by the nickname Lucky—is another matter. Killed a guy in a barroom brawl over in Corpus, which got him seven years. He served five. The probation violations are probably related to his release from prison."

"Lucky!" China put in. "That's the name of one of the men Jack Krause was involved with, according to Sue Ellen. She called the other one Duke. What do you want to bet that Duke and Ronald Perry are the same?"

"Hold it," Ethan said, putting up his hand. "Too many moving parts. Let's back up." His expression was tense. "Tattooed fawns, Mack. Those are the fawns you were telling me about yesterday? The ones you and the doc thought were stolen?"

"Yes," Mack said. "Doc Masters told me he was pretty sure that the tattoo had been altered. The number he saw was four-eight-two, but it looked to him like the eight had originally been a three. He told me that Three Gates Ranch holds the permit number four-*three*-two. I think he'd pretty much decided that the fawns originally came from there."

"Ah." Ethan got out of the truck and straightened, hitching up his duty belt. "Now we're making sense. So these two guys at the Bar Bee are holding some stolen animals that came from Three Gates. And the guy who just slammed Sue Ellen Krause off the road could be one of them. One of the Perrys."

Mack turned to China. "Tell Ethan what Sue Ellen Krause told you, China. That helps confirm what we're dealing with here."

China nodded. "Her husband was involved with two men—Duke and Lucky—in a plan to set up a game ranch. The two men already had the land—the Bar Bee, I suppose. They were stocking it, and paying for the fencing they needed to get the permit, with deer they were smuggling in from Oklahoma."

"Lacey Act violations," Mack put in, speaking to Ethan. "Like that case over in East Texas."

"Got it," Ethan said. "Go on, Ms. Bayles."

"According to Sue Ellen, Jack was helping with the smuggling and buying into the business with stuff he was stealing from Three Gates. We were interrupted before she could tell me exactly what that was, but it likely included those fawns the vet happened to see. Possibly semen, as well, and maybe equipment. If that's true, you might be able to find the stolen items somewhere on the Perrys' ranch."

A thought occurred to Mack, and she pulled Krause's cell phone out of her pocket. She scrolled to recent calls, and there it was. Perry, with a long string of recent text messages. She held it up. "May be something here to document some of their transactions, meet-ups, plans." She handed the phone to Ethan.

"Good thought, Mack." Ethan looked inquiringly at China. "If Ms. Krause told you all this, she must have been thinking of going to the police."

China nodded. "That's right. She was asking me for advice. She knew Jack was stealing and was afraid he'd be caught. She felt she needed to protect herself from being charged as an accomplice. She tried to get him to pull out of the relationship with these guys, and when he refused, she told him she was getting a divorce. In fact, she was in the process of moving into the guest lodge on my mother's ranch." She gestured toward the boxes and bags scattered on the rocky hillside. "That's why her car was loaded with all that stuff. If you ask me, she was killed to keep her quiet. And the vet was killed for the same reason."

Ethan asked, "Do you have any reason to suspect that Krause was involved in either death?"

"No idea," China replied. "I could see it going either way. He may be involved only in the thefts and the smuggling. Or he could have been involved in one or both of the murders, as well."

Ethan looked at his watch, then squinted up at the sky. "It's nearly four, and we'll be losing the light pretty quick. We can arrest Krause on that misdemeanor warrant and hold him overnight for questioning in his wife's murder." He nodded toward the black SUV. "We also need to take statements from the drone bunch and secure the surveillance video and the camera. And the two Perrys have to be picked up—probably at their ranch—and brought in for questioning."

"I can see that the drone team gets down to the Uvalde sheriff's office to leave their statements," China offered. "I'll drive down there with them and stay until it's done."

Mack grinned at her. "I guess you don't trust us to treat them right. You're thinking rubber hoses, maybe?"

"Just doing my job," China said with a laugh. "When that's done, they can be on their way. If you need them again, I'll make sure they're available."

"That'll work. Thanks," Ethan said. "Mack, take Krause down to the county jail and book him on that warrant. That'll give him some time by himself to think about what he's been up to. If he gives you any trouble, tack on a charge of obstruction. Oh, and you take the iPad, the video camera, and Krause's cell phone and log them into the evidence locker. We'll want to go through all that before we question Krause and the Perrys." He paused. "And can you take the witness statements from the drone people?"

"On it," Mack said promptly. She wasn't sure who he meant by "we," but for the moment, she was going to assume that she would be involved. She eyed him. "And you?"

Ethan pulled out his cell phone. "I'm going to call Sheriff Rogers and tell him I need approval to assemble a criminal apprehension team to go after the Perrys. It has to be done tonight—the border is just an hour away, and I don't want to risk flight. I'll follow you as far south as Sabinal and get the justice of the peace there to issue an arrest warrant for Thomas Perry on the parole violation charge, and for Ronald Perry on suspicion of multiple Lacey Act violations. I'll throw in conspiracy, as well."

"Get a search warrant for the Bar Bee, too," Mack said. "We may not be able to prove Lacey without documentation, but the fawns are evidence of theft. Semen, too, if we can find it."

Ethan nodded. "I'll talk to John Coxey—he's the Sabinal chief of police—and see if he'll round up a couple of his officers and meet me in the Baptist church parking lot over in Reagan Wells. By that time, Davenport and Murphy should be available. Six of us ought to be a big enough team to corral the Perrys."

"Seven," Mack said firmly. "I'm in, too, Ethan." She handed him Krause's cell phone. "And if we're going after the Perrys, you'll want to take this. It's got their number—and the call will display Krause's caller ID. They'll think it's their partner and will pick up."

"Shoulda thought of that myself. Good idea." Ethan took the phone and slipped it into his uniform pocket. Shifting uncomfortably, he shook his head. "But I'm sorry, Mack. You're not in on this. We don't know these guys or what kind of arsenal they've got stashed at their place. We don't know the lay of the land, either. That's pretty rugged country over there, and it'll be dark by the time we go in. They won't expect us until we're on top of them, but serving that warrant will not be a piece of cake. Could be trouble. Could be shooting." His eyes were on hers, dark and troubled, and she knew that he would have reached out and touched her if China hadn't been standing there with them. "Please understand, Mack," he said more softly. "I don't want you to get hurt, that's all."

Mack stepped back, out of reach and unmoved by his appeal. *Damn!* He might be trying to soften it, but bottom line, Ethan was telling her that she couldn't handle a tough job, that he didn't trust her to do her part along with the male officers, that she'd just be in the way. Well, he could forget that. She wasn't going to let him get away with it. And if she pissed him off, so be it. His response would be a measure of *him*, not of her. He could accept her as a professional or not, his choice. But she was a conservation officer, a law enforcement officer, and a woman, all at the same time. If he couldn't accept her as a professional, there was no future in their personal relationship.

She pulled herself up to her full height and put her hand on her holster. "Knock it off, Ethan," she said in a level tone, meeting his eyes. "You tell Sheriff Rogers that Warden Chambers will be the Parks and Wildlife member of your team, to secure any stolen animals and take custody of whatever deer semen she can locate." She narrowed her eyes, willing him to understand just how much was hanging on his answer. "Nonnegotiable. You got that?"

Holding himself stiffly, his jaw working, Ethan studied her for a long moment. Then he relaxed. "Top dog, I guess," he said ruefully, and chuckled. His glance went from China back to Mack, and he threw up his hands in mock despair. "What are we going to do with you pushy broads?"

"Get behind us," China said promptly. "Then we won't have to push."

Mack tilted her head and pursed her lips as if she were thinking through a puzzle. "I could come up with a suggestion or two. Maybe involving 'exceptional circumstances.'"

Ethan's eyes lit up and he grinned at her. "Yeah, okay. I got it." His mouth tightened, stern. "If you're on my team, you're taking orders. I'm assuming you have a ballistics vest. Right?"

She nodded. "In my truck." Parks and Wildlife had made the vests standard issue a while back, after a game warden got shot when he was making an arrest. She wore it whenever she thought there might be trouble, and when she wore it, she always thought of her father.

"Good." He looked at his watch. "Six thirty, Reagan Wells, Baptist church parking lot. If you've got night-vision goggles, bring them." And then, with a half-defiant glance at China, he pulled Mack to him and kissed her quickly.

"Wear that vest," he hissed in her ear.

"Yes, sir," she said.

JACK Krause, cuffed and under arrest, did give Mack a hard time, not just screaming profanities but pummeling the seat with his feet. The front and rear cabs were separated by a cage-wire panel and a sliding-glass bulletproof panel, so when she got tired of listening to his rant, she slid the glass panel closed. And when she got to the county jail, she booked him on two charges—misdemeanor violations *and* obstruction (noting that it was not just verbal obstruction)—before she turned him over to the officer behind the desk for processing. She took the iPad and the video camera to the evidence locker, where she checked them in and got receipts for both. China came in a few moments later, and they sat with Amy, Chris, and Sharon, one at a time, to make a digital record of their statements. It would be transcribed by a secretary and faxed to them for their signatures. That done, she walked with China out to her panel van, which (China told her) was called Big Red Mama. It fit, she thought, and had to smile at the psychedelic swirls painted on the sides.

"You're heading back to the ranch?" she asked, hunching against the cold wind blowing down from the north, clearing out the clouds. Her heavy jacket was in the truck. She was going to need it tonight, she thought.

China nodded. "Mom should be there by the time I get back." She sighed. "I'm not looking forward to telling her about Sue Ellen, Mack. She'll be devastated."

"I'm sorry," Mack said inadequately. Death was like a stone cast into a river, the ripples moving out in all directions, encountering rocks and hidden snags and distant shores. Sue Ellen's death would be making a great many ripples, for a very long time. "What's going on with Sam?" she asked. "Is he better, worse?"

"I don't know what's going on. Leatha wouldn't tell me. She just said we'd talk it over tonight." China reached into her van, took out a nylon Windbreaker, and began pulling it on over her hoodie. "Sounds pretty serious, Mack. I'm afraid . . ." She didn't finish her sentence.

"Yeah. It does. Sound serious, I mean." Mack paused. "I need to thank you for all you've done in the past couple of days."

"Done?" China's eyebrows went up and she smiled crookedly. "Not me. I'm just a bystander. You guys are doing the heavy lifting."

"Hey, come on," Mack protested. "You're the one who got Sue Ellen to tell you what her husband was up to. You listened to me and to the drone crew, and you put everything together. If you hadn't connected all those crazy dots, Ethan and I might still be scratching our heads and wondering which way to turn next."

"I doubt that," China said with a wry chuckle. "But if you want to hand out a little credit—sure, I'll get in line. Next time I need a favor down here in Uvalde County, I'll know who to ask. You." She grinned. "And that hunky deputy of yours."

Mack thought of objecting that Ethan wasn't *her* hunky deputy, at least not yet. But all she said was, "You do that, China. We owe you."

"It's a deal." China got into her van and rolled down the driver's-side window. "And don't forget to do what Ethan told you."

"What's that?" Mack shivered. It was really getting cold.

China started her van. "Wear your vest. Arms and legs can be repaired and put back in service. I don't want to hear that my game warden buddy was taken out by a big one in the chest."

IT was five forty-five and getting dark by the time Mack finished up the paperwork in the sheriff's office and looked in on Krause in his holding cell to remind him that he was being monitored. Checking for a change in plans, she called Ethan on his cell phone to keep their arrangements off the radio (you never knew who had a police scanner and was making a career out of listening to the dispatches). He reported that he'd gotten the necessary search and arrest warrants and that they were on track for a meet-up at six thirty. "Vest," he added. "Wear it. And get something to eat. We may be out there for a while tonight."

"How about you?" There wasn't much in the way of fast food at the north end of the county. "I'll stop at the Dairy Queen. Want me to bring you a burger?"

"Hell of a deal. Bacon cheeseburger with extra jalapeños, onion rings, double catsup, large Coke."

"Roger that," she said. "Man after my own heart."

"Damn straight," he said with emphasis, and she laughed.

She went through the Dairy Queen's drive-in lane, getting Ethan's order and a burger, onion rings, and Diet Coke for herself, then headed up U.S. 83, enjoying the rich, fatty fragrance of the food and eating with relish as she drove. Burger and rings (always with about a quart of catsup and more salt than was good for her) had been her comfort food since she was a teenager, and tonight she could use a little comfort. She had a healthy fear of what might go down, up there at the Bar Bee. She'd been shot at before, and she'd even been hit once, in the shoulder, painfully but not seriously. But that came with the badge. It happened—it was part of the job when you dealt with people with guns, some of whom had no idea how to manage their weapons. She was more afraid that she'd screw something up, that in spite of the brave face she had put on, she wouldn't be able to hold up her end. It was always important to do the work well, but more important now, with Ethan there, watching.

The thought of Ethan and that last impetuous kiss made her heart race—and yes, the chemistry was definitely working. She couldn't think of him without wanting him, wanting him to hold her, make love to her. But that wasn't going to get in the way of doing her job. And she wasn't going to let him down in front of his colleagues, or give him a reason to be concerned about her safety. Period. Paragraph. End of story.

She stuffed the napkin in the paper bag, wadded it up, and turned on the flasher lights and siren, the road opening up in front of her truck like a lighted tunnel bored through the heavy dark. There was no traffic, the highway was clear, and she loved driving flat out, although she watched for the kamikaze deer that were known to dash across the highway. She made it the rest of the way to Reagan Wells in seventeen minutes.

The village had never been very big—a population of fifty at the most, in the days when wealthy health seekers came to stay in the two-story frame hotel, soak themselves in the restorative mineral waters, and saunter along the river, breathing in the clean, sage-scented air. Back then, before automobiles, the town boasted not only a post office but a sorghum mill, a fruit cannery, and a general store that provisioned the dozen or so cattle and sheep ranches in the grasslands along the river and up the tributary creeks.

The river was still there, of course, the Dry Frio, which sometimes did and sometimes didn't have water in it—mostly it didn't now, because the drought had hit the area hard. Like the river, the town had shrunk down to a single church and a few houses strung along the asphalt road and a historical marker celebrating the first settlers, the Heards and the Bohmes and the Joneses, who had arrived after the Civil War. It was full dark now, and you couldn't see the houses, just the lights in the windows and an occasional mercury vapor light casting its icy blue glow over a barn or a driveway or somebody's cluttered yard. But Mack knew from her patrols in the area that Sycamore Mountain rose to the west, between the Dry Frio and the Nueces, and that there were a number of small resorts and vacation cabins along the river, ranging from the primitive and rustic to the palatial. And somewhere to the north and west, on the flank of Sycamore Mountain, was the Bar Bee Ranch, and the Perrys, and some stolen fawns and smuggled white-tails.

The church, a small brick building, stood on the outskirts of town. When Mack pulled into the graveled parking lot, she saw the vehicles—two white sheriff's pickups, an unmarked SUV, and a marked police car from Sabinal—all parked to one side, headlights off. The SUV doors were open, a Maglite was hung on the door, and six men in cowboy hats were gathered around, peering at a laptop screen. From the stiffness of their movements, Mack guessed that at least some of them were wearing their vests. She took hers out from behind the seat, pulled off her jacket, and put it on, fastening the Velcro bands. It was cool and tight and constrained her movements, but the heaviness gave her a reassuring security. She put her jacket back on, pulled up the collar against the chill wind, and grabbed the sack of Ethan's still-warm food. Then she thought better of it, put the sack back in the truck, and walked toward the SUV. She didn't want the other men to think she was running anybody's errands.

"Hey, Chambers," Ethan hailed her. "Meet the team. Guys, this is Warden Chambers." He pointed around the small circle, and in the glow of the Maglite, Mack saw that all of the men were wearing badges. "Davenport, Murphy, Coxey, Jackson, Davies. Davenport and Murphy are sheriff's deputies," he added. "Coxey is the Sabinal chief of police, and Jackson and Davies are his officers."

There were grunts and half grins and skeptical glances, and Mack felt the weight, once again, of being the only woman in a group of law enforcement officers, some of whom weren't accustomed to working with a woman. She straightened her shoulders and nodded, meeting the eyes of each man briefly, committing their names to memory. Deputies Davenport and Murphy were both large and burly, Davenport with an unlit cigar in his mouth, Murphy pulling on a cigarette. Uniformed and in full duty gear, they looked confident and at ease, as if they did this every day. (They probably did.) Chief Coxey, white-haired and with a white mustache, was also uniformed, but didn't look quite so comfortable. Jackson had a nose that had been broken at least twice, while Davies had the mild and slightly bemused look of a Sunday School teacher. Both were in jeans and jackets, and Mack got the idea that Coxey had probably pulled them away from a quiet family evening. All of the men wore holstered sidearms.

Ethan made room for her, and she joined the circle beside him. They were looking at a Google map on the laptop. "Before we get into the map, let me fill you in," Ethan said. "We have warrants for the arrest of Thomas Perry on probation violations and Ronald Perry for suspected Lacey Act violations and conspiracy to commit theft. They are persons of interest in two homicides." He paused. "Warden Chambers will execute the search warrant. She's looking for stolen white-tails and other items, as well as deer smuggled into the state."

"Are they brothers?" Coxey asked. "Father-son?"

"Brothers," Davenport replied, around his cigar. "Lucky is the badass one—that's the name Thomas goes by. I served a protective order on him six or seven years ago, out there somewhere around Sycamore Mountain. It was some woman wanting him to keep his distance. Couldn't say I blamed her. The guy's got a quarter-inch fuse."

"What about the other brother?" Ethan asked. "Ronald."

"That would be Duke, if I recall." Davenport scratched his nose thoughtfully. "Seemed like a reasonable sort. Tried to tamp down his brother, without a lot of success."

Ethan nodded. "A man driving a truck registered to Thomas Perry forced a woman off the road on the Three Gates Ranch. She died when her car burst into flames. We have a surveillance video of the homicide. We also have reason to believe that one or both Perrys were involved in the murder of Doc Masters on Thursday. Both homicides appear to be cover-ups for a deer-smuggling scheme and thefts of animals and semen from Three Gates." He paused. "Oh, yeah. We've got one other man, Jack Krause, already in custody. It was his wife who died in the car wreck."

"Krause, huh?" Coxey said. "I know him. He's a big guy. He give you any trouble?"

"Dunno," Ethan said. "Chambers took him in and booked him." He turned to Mack, dark eyebrows raised, a half-amused smile at the corner of his mouth. "He give you any trouble?"

"A little mouth, but nothing I couldn't handle," Mack said carelessly, and a chuckle went around the circle.

"You don't want to mess with Chambers," Ethan remarked, and the chuckle went around the circle again.

"Did I hear right?" Murphy asked. "You got a surveillance video out there at Three Gates?" For a heavy man, he had a high, squeaky voice. "How in the hell did you manage that?"

"Drone," Ethan said.

"What? What'd you say?" Murphy piped. "*Drone*?"

Ethan grinned at Murphy. "Yeah, I know, Murph. The latest gimmick. Next thing you know, we'll all be conducting aerial surveillance. Just the next tool in the box, is all."

Murphy shook his head with a now-I've-heard-everything expression. Davenport gave a skeptical harrumph. "This I gotta see," he muttered.

"You will," Ethan promised. He turned to the group. "So here's the deal. The Perrys live on a ranch on the east flank of Sycamore Mountain.

We'll take all vehicles and caravan up 1051 to where it forks." He traced the route on the map on the screen with his finger. "We'll follow the left fork for about three miles, until we cross Bee Creek. After that, there's a mailbox. That's where we'll turn right." He looked around the circle. "Anybody know this area? Is the bridge marked?"

There was general headshaking. "I been out there several times," Davenport said, giving his duty belt a hitch. "But I never noticed a bridge. You sure about that?"

Mack said, "It's not a bridge. It's a low-water crossing with a white-painted five-foot flood gauge on each side. As I remember, it's the only low-water crossing on that fork of 1051. The mailbox is marked 'Perry' and 'Bar Bee.'" In a lower voice, she added to Ethan, "There's a gated community on the right fork of 1051. Could be there's a cell phone tower in the area. Maybe use Krause's phone? See if the Perrys are at home?"

Ethan nodded briefly. "Smart idea." He raised his voice. "Y'all get that detail about the low-water crossing? We'll pause there to let everybody catch up, then make a right at the mailbox just beyond. At that point, turn on your handheld radios, turn off your headlights. We'll run dark. The ranch house is maybe two miles back and up, and they may have a scanner, so we won't use the county radio. Here's the layout. Give it a good look. I don't want anybody getting lost."

He brought up Google Earth and zoomed in tight enough to see that the ranch house was a small, compact dwelling with what looked like a gray metal roof. The ranch road crossed an open area and led up to the house, ending in a parking area to the left of the house. There was a cedar brake to the right of the house and a cluster of outbuildings and fences behind it. Farther to the left, down by Bee Creek, lay a narrow green strip, cleared of trees and shrubs, and mowed, with a rounded-roof structure—a Quonset hut—at the end closest to the compound.

Ethan tilted the image, and they could see that the house and outbuildings were set against the side of a hill, and that the mowed strip along the creek was level. He zoomed back out and they could see Route 1051, a thin white line looping through the light green velvet of the Frio valley and the darker green corduroy of the hills, and then the thinner white thread of the ranch road unraveling from it.

Ethan pointed. "From the mailbox on 1051, here, parking lights only, no headlights. We'll caravan slow and dark, bumper to bumper and quiet, with the lead vehicle spotlighting the road only as much as necessary." He glanced up and over his shoulder, where the moon was just coming up over the hills to the east. "With that moon, we might not need a light. Or goggles."

"We taking all the vehicles in there?" Coxey asked nervously.

Ethan nodded. "With luck, we won't be seen until we get up to the house. And when they do see us, I want them to see *all* the vehicles and realize that we're not just a couple of guys with big mouths. So we'll do it this way. When we get about here—" He pointed to a spot where the ranch road came out of the woods and into the meadow in front of the house. "When we get here, I'll stop and pull around to use the truck as a shield. You pull off, park where your vehicle is visible, and leave it. No lights, no noise, no talking, weapons ready. Davenport and Jackson, you circle around to the left to cover the back, make sure nobody gets out that way. Coxey and Davies, hang to the right. Murphy, you're with me. Chambers, you stay behind your vehicle and keep the front of the house covered."

The thought came to Mack that he was keeping her out front with him because he was worried that she could get herself into trouble, and she bridled—then put that aside. Ethan would be where the action was, and that was where she wanted to be.

He went on. "I've got their partner's cell phone, and I'll call them, see if I can get them to come out the front door, unarmed, and surrender. If they don't answer, or if they cut off the call, I'll use the PA system on the truck. Everybody, keep your handhelds on. We'll communicate that way."

"You think it's just the two brothers?" Coxey asked, even more nervously. Mack got the idea that this wasn't something he did very often.

Ethan shrugged. "No way to tell. For all we know, there may be a woman or two in that house, even kids. Could be dogs penned up outside, or loose. And we have no idea about their arsenal. Hold your fire unless I give the command." He looked around the group and his voice hardened. "Everybody got that? We don't want another Ruby Ridge here. And for God's sake, no friendly fire casualties."

There was a subdued chorus of "yeahs." Jackson pointedly nudged Davies. "Got that, Bert? Don't shoot yourself in the foot again."

"Up yours, Jackson," Davies growled. "That's a lie."

"You guys be quiet," Coxey said. "You're embarrassing me."

"Just funnin'," Jackson said, and subsided.

Mack was leaning toward the screen, frowning in concentration. She manipulated the mouse pad, zooming in at a spot behind the house.

"Looking for something special?" Ethan asked.

"That paddock," Mack said, pointing. "It was empty when Google made this flyover, but that's got to be where Doc Masters saw the stolen white-tails. There may also be some smuggled deer in there, too." She raised her voice. "If the animals are still penned, let's make sure that nobody turns them loose. They may be evidence of theft." She peered closer and pointed to the long, narrow green ribbon, in the valley along Bee Creek. "And get that. A mowed airstrip, looks like, with a Quonset hut that might be a hangar, at the end of the strip. The Perrys have a plane up there?"

"Davenport, you know anything about that?" Ethan asked. "I can ask Dispatch to do a search on pilots' licenses, but we probably wouldn't get the results until—"

"Seems to me I did hear something about that," Davenport said. "Like maybe both of them had licenses. But I wouldn't let it worry me none. It's not like they're going to take off and fly away in the dark." Murphy squeaked an assenting laugh.

"Not likely," Ethan agreed. "Okay, let's do an inventory. What do we have in the way of armament and equipment?"

They were fully armed with both long guns—AR-15s and tactical shotguns—and sidearms. Mack wasn't too sure about men with guns tromping around out there in the dark, falling over who knows what and discharging their weapons accidentally. But it was what it was.

"Radios? Night-vision goggles? Vests?" Ethan asked. There was another chorus of yeses, with nos from Davies and Jackson. Coxey said, half defiantly, "Radios, yes. But we're not budgeted for goggles or vests."

Ethan nodded. "If there's fire, better stay down, then." He looked around the group. "Any questions?" Silence. He closed the laptop and picked it up. "When you get into your vehicles, check your weapons. If you're not loaded, do that now—and then turn off those overhead cab lights. When you're locked and loaded, turn on your headlights. When we're all lit, we roll."

Mack got Ethan's sack of burger and rings and quietly put it in his truck, smiling when he saw what she was doing and gave her a thumbs-up. As they drove out of the parking lot, she found herself in the middle of the five-vehicle pack, behind Ethan and the second sheriff's truck but ahead of Coxey's SUV and the Sabinal police car, which brought up the rear. By the time they got to Bee Creek on 1051, the moon was high and bright enough to cast shadows. The caravan paused at the low-water crossing, and Mack took the opportunity to put on the headgear that supported her night-vision goggles. She tightened the straps and flipped the eyepieces up and out of the way. The apparatus was uncomfortable—there was a reason it was called a "face prison"—and she didn't need it now. But the moon was fickle, and without it, the night was a black conundrum. Later, she might be glad she was wearing it. When the police car caught up, Ethan cut his headlights and made the turn onto the Bar Bee ranch road. Mack switched down to her parking lights, and the others followed suit.

There was enough moonlight to see the gravel two-track curving up and down through the trees, then down across another low-water crossing and up into an open field. Still running dark, Ethan pulled to the right and stopped. Davenport pulled off to the left and Mack followed, the other two vehicles pulling to the right of Ethan. The house sat on the side of the hill slightly above them, a narrow, verandah-like porch running across the width. There were three windows, two on the left side of the front door, one on the right. The first window to the left of the door was curtained and dimly lighted, the light flickering and bluish, probably a television screen, which was good, Mack thought. Whoever was inside was watching TV and would be surprised. In the parking area beside the house on the left were two pickups, one black, the other silver. The light-colored pickup looked like the Dodge that had forced Sue Ellen Krause off the road and to her death. There were no other vehicles, so it seemed likely that the men were alone. To the far left, about a hundred yards away at the foot of the steep hill, she saw the hulking shape of what she had guessed was a hangar. From its curved silhouette and the moonlight glinting on it, she saw that it was, yes, a Quonset hut. A square window in the side facing her displayed a light.

Taking her AR-15, Mack got out, silently closed her door, and took up a position facing the house, with Ethan's truck off to her right. The air was rich with the fragrance of burning cedar, and a curl of smoke drifted from the chimney. Overhead, the sky was a deep black, the stars were pinpricks of faraway light, and the moon was intermittently clouded over. Behind her the trees were dark and still. She unsnapped the keeper on her holster and loosened the Glock, then pulled back the bolt on her rifle, sliding a round into the chamber. She raised it to her shoulder, steadying her left arm against the cab and sighting the scope on the front door. To her left, Davenport and Jackson got out of the other sheriff's truck and melted into the shadows, heading for the back of the house. To the right, on the other side of Ethan's truck, Coxey and Davies were doing the same.

Murphy, who had been riding with Ethan, had taken cover behind Coxey's SUV. Ethan was out of his truck and standing behind it, using it as a shield. In the shimmering moonlight, Mack saw that he was holding a cell phone to his ear—Krause's, she presumed. After a moment, somebody apparently answered, and he spoke slow and level, loud enough for Mack to hear what he said.

"This is Deputy Sheriff Conroy. I am outside your house, and my men have the place surrounded. I have warrants for the arrest of Thomas and Ronald Perry and a search warrant for this property. Come out with your hands up. Now."

He stood for a moment, listening. But the person he'd been talking to must have clicked off, for he closed the phone and tossed it into the truck. At that moment, the television in the living room went off and the window went dark. A second or two later, a mercury vapor light blazed at the left side of the house, near the parking area, bathing the grassy space in front with a cool blue light. At the same time, the curtain in the window twitched. Somebody was looking out. Whoever was inside could see the ring of vehicles parked across the field in front of the house and could only guess at the number of armed officers somewhere out there.

Mack tensed, scarcely breathing, holding her rifle steady, half expecting a barrage of shots from one of the front windows. For what seemed a very long time, nothing happened. The silence lengthened. From the left side of the house, she heard the clink of a boot against a stone—Davenport and Jackson, moving around to the back. Somewhere off to the east, a coyote yipped and then another, a cacophony of coyote voices, singing to the moon.

Ethan had picked up the mike to the PA system in his truck and keyed it. He stood, waiting, then spoke into the mike, his voice startlingly loud and deep. "Thomas and Ronald Perry, you're under arrest. Your house is surrounded. Come out with your hands in the air."

Another long silence. Out of the corner of her eye, Mack caught the flicker of the light going out in the building she thought was a hangar.

Whoever was down there must have heard Ethan on the PA. Then her radio bleeped softly and she heard Davenport: "Rear's secure."

"Secure back here, too," Coxey chimed in.

Ethan spoke into the mike again. "We're not messing around. I'm counting down. I want you both out here, hands up, before I get to one. Ten . . . nine . . . eight . . ."

The front door opened a crack, and Mack tensed, watching the other windows for any sign of movement, her finger on the trigger of her rifle. "Don't shoot," a man called. "I'm coming out." He stepped onto the porch, both hands raised above his head.

Ethan switched on his spotlight, illuminating the man on the porch, who was dressed in jeans, a denim jacket, and cowboy boots. Mack knew at a glance that he wasn't the man she had seen on the drone video.

"Your name, sir?" Ethan said through the PA.

The man cleared his throat. "Ronald. Ronald Perry." His voice was high and threadlike, frightened.

"Your brother. Thomas Perry. Where is he?"

"Not here," Perry said. "He's . . . he's down in Uvalde. He won't be home until late."

Mack keyed the mike on her handheld. "Negative," she said. "There are two trucks parked to the left of the house. The silver Dodge is registered to Thomas Perry. He's here. And the light that was on in the hangar has just gone out."

"Roger that, Chambers," Ethan said.

Mack flipped her goggles down and turned toward the trees, startled, as always, by the sudden change in her vision. Everything was bathed in an eerie green light, patched with darker gray green shadows. She searched the area behind them visually, watching for movement. Where was the other Perry brother? Still in the hangar? Or moving up the hill toward them?

Ethan turned off the PA system. "Down the steps, Perry," he ordered loudly. "Hands clasped behind your head. Now, turn around backward and walk toward me." A few moments later: "Stop. Cover me, Murphy. I'm taking him." He closed the distance to Ronald Perry, pulled his arms down behind his back, and fastened a pair of plastic flex cuffs on him. "You're under arrest." He began a quick pat down.

Perry stood motionless, head hanging. "What's . . . what's the charge?"

"Suspicion of Lacey Act violations," Ethan said, straightening. He turned Perry and began marching him toward the truck. "There'll be other charges." He opened the door of the rear cab. "Get in," he said brusquely, and shut the door. He pulled out his radio and keyed it. Into it, he said, "Ronald Perry in custody. Davenport, go in through the back. Murphy and I are going in the front. Coxey, you and Davies check the buildings out back. Chambers, you stay where you are until we've secured the house and the outbuildings, then you can start your search."

Mack heard the curt "Rogers" from Davenport and Coxey but said nothing. Her stomach muscles tightening, she thought that "stay where you are" sounded like another effort to keep her out of trouble, out of harm's way. Was it because she was a game warden, not a deputy? Because she was a woman? And then, another thought: because Ethan was beginning to care for her?

But she had reported seeing the light in the hangar go out. There had been somebody down there, most likely Thomas Perry. The building should be checked out, and since nobody else was available to do it, she would.

She waited, covering Ethan and Murphy until they had safely crossed the open space in front of the house and gone inside. Then, carrying her rifle, she slipped out from behind her truck, dodged behind Davenport's vehicle, and headed diagonally downhill toward the Quonset hut, now dark. Her goggles allowed her to see everything quite clearly, the shadowy trees to her left, the hill rising steeply to her right as she moved swiftly forward and down. Behind her, she could hear Coxey and Davies stumbling among the outbuildings, Davies cursing as he crashed into what sounded like a metal trash can, and hoped that they didn't see her and take a shot at her. Not much chance of that, though, she thought with some relief. The moon was clouded over, the hillside had gone dark, and they didn't have any optics.

In the green glow of her goggles, the building, its curved metal skin dappled with green gray rust, bulked large and ominous. There was a door on the side toward her and a square window, where she had seen the light. She ignored the door, ducked under the window, and moved silently forward along the wall, to the front of the structure. Looking ahead, she could see that the rectangular area had been regularly mowed so that the grass was short and matted, and there were five or six markers at regular intervals on both sides, each topped with saucer-size plastic reflectors. To the right was a large white-painted metal fuel tank with a pump and hose apparatus at one end. No doubt about it—this was an airstrip.

Inside the building she heard somebody moving around, and a moment later, a door closing. She flipped the safety on her rifle and took a step forward. Then, to her surprise, she heard the deep-throated roar of a motor turning over, then a blustery *rrhumph-humph-humph*, escalating to a deafening thunder inside the metal drum of the Quonset hut. An airplane engine revving up, a propeller winding up to top speed.

She stepped around the edge of the building just as the airplane—white with a wide blue stripe, its registration number painted in large letters on the fuselage—emerged through the open doors of the hangar and started down the runway, accelerating faster and faster. A light in the plane's nose illuminated the dark turf ahead and flashed from the reflectors. Mack knelt on one knee and raised her rifle, aiming at the closest tire, but even though she was a good marksman, she knew the shot was futile. The plane was moving away from her, and moving too fast, at full power. The flaps were a better target. She fired three quick shots and thought she'd scored a hit, but the target was rapidly moving out of range for anything but a Hail Mary. She lowered her rifle and grabbed her radio.

"Single-engine aircraft taking off on the grass strip. Registration number bravo-one-seven-romeo-hotel." But even as she spoke, she could hear the shout from the top of the hill. Somebody else was seeing what she was seeing.

And then something happened that Mack would marvel at for the rest of her life. The plane seemed to have nearly reached its lift-off speed when the light on its nose illuminated a huge white-tailed buck as large as an elk, wearing an enormous rack of antlers. It was standing still as a statue in the middle of the grassy strip, head turned toward the onrushing aircraft, unafraid. The pilot must have seen it at about the same time, for the plane nosed up, then swerved sharply to the left, its left wing dipping down. The left wingtip caught the ground, and the plane swung violently around. Above, on the hill, more shouts.

And then, as Mack sucked in her breath, the right wing rose up and the plane cartwheeled, the left wing crumpling under it. It landed with a loud crash, upside down, and burst into flames.

Antlered head high, the buck stood watching, then trotted briskly toward the trees, its white tail a proud flag.

Chapter Eleven

American bittersweet (*Celastrus scandens*) is not just a pretty plant. It has a long history of use by Native Americans and by the colonists who copied their medical practices. The root was boiled and pounded into a poultice or made into an ointment to treat burns, skin sores, eruptions, cancers, and rheumatism. A tea was used to treat liver ailments and dysentery. A stronger tea was used to cause uterine contractions during and after childbirth, and as an abortifacient. Bark extracts are thought to be cardioactive, so modern herbalists generally avoid the use of this plant.

Oriental bittersweet (*Celastrus orbiculatus*) has its medicinal uses as well. In its native Asia, it is employed for the treatment of paralysis, circulatory problems, headache, toothache, and snake bites. Ongoing research is exploring its possible antitumor activity.

Both vines are highly decorative. But do remember that Oriental bittersweet is an invasive pest. Please hang out the UNWELCOME sign and don't let it move into your neighborhood!

China Bayles
"Native Plants for Wildlife Gardens"
Pecan Springs Enterprise

"And then what?" Ruby dropped her duster and stared at me over her shop counter. "Come on, China—you can't stop there! What happened to the pilot? Was he *killed*?"

"You bet," I said. "And if you ask me, that was poetic justice. He died in a crash-and-burn, just the way Sue Ellen died. And that white-tailed buck—" I shook my head, marveling. "Quite an amazing coincidence, that deer showing up on the airstrip just as the killer was about to take off. Mack was astonished at the way the buck behaved. She couldn't stop talking about it."

"That was no coincidence," Ruby said, very seriously. "That was the universe, which has its own ways of settling scores."

I regarded her, both eyebrows raised. "I hadn't thought of it that way."

"Well, do. Everybody knows how long it takes to work through the justice system, and even then things don't always turn out the way they should."

"Yes," I replied, with irony. I pulled Ruby's stool out from behind the counter and sat down, hooking my heels over the rungs. "Sometimes diabolically clever defense attorneys derail justice, don't they?"

It was the Monday after Thanksgiving, and we weren't open for business, but that didn't mean we had the day off. Both Ruby and I were working, even though we weren't waiting on customers. I had gone in about eight thirty to make out book and herb orders, stocking up for the holiday season. I had just gotten started when the UPS delivery guy came, bringing me an entirely new shipment of bittersweet—the *right* bittersweet, this time, with the apologies of the Michigan wreath maker and a promise to never again substitute Oriental for American bittersweet.

Miss T dropped in right after the UPS guy, to see if we were going to want her to work that week. She is short and chubby and loves bright colors. Today's outfit was a bright chartreuse sweatshirt over dark green pants, and her hair (pulled up and twisted to keep it out of her way) was a soft burnt orange. "In honor of Thanksgiving," she said with a laugh. "And of course, the Texas win over Texas Tech. Wasn't that a great game?"

I shanghaied her immediately, and the two of us spent a pleasant hour hanging wreaths and making the shop pretty for the winter holidays. That kind of creative work is one of the reasons I love Thyme and Seasons—it's almost like play, rather than work. And being able to share it with a friend and helper, like Miss T, makes it all the more interesting and fun. When we finished our work, the shop looked and smelled like the holidays, and Miss T went on her way with a hug and a smile—a great start to the week for both of us.

I returned to the task of ordering, but not for long. When I heard Ruby come in, I poured two cups of hot tea, put a half dozen of Cass' chai tea cookies on a plate, and carried everything into the Crystal Cave. Ruby—dressed in purple pants, a purple and blue psychedelic sweatshirt, and a purple bandana tied over her crinkly red hair—was starting on her Monday chores.

She disregarded my comment about diabolical defense attorneys. "So the universe took the judgment out of human hands," she said with satisfaction. She leaned both elbows on the counter, picked up her teacup, and sipped. "What happened when Mack went to look for her fawns? Did she find them?"

"They aren't *her* fawns," I replied. "They belong to the state of Texas—at least, that's what the state claims. But yes, she found them in the high-fenced pen where Doc Masters had spotted them. She was able to confirm that the tattoos had been changed and that the animals had originally been registered to Three Gates. She also found a box of semen straws in the freezer, a couple of pieces of Three Gates equipment in the barn, and enough fingerprint evidence to tie Jack Krause to the thefts. DNA will likely confirm that the semen was stolen from Three Gates."

"What about the smuggled deer?"

"There were several animals in the pen that didn't come from Three Gates. It's impossible to say where they might have come from. But Mack found invoices that appear to document the transfer of deer to several trophy ranchers in South Texas. She'll track those down, and if there's enough evidence, the appropriate charges will be filed. The Lacey Act is a powerful tool for prosecution. A good thing, too. Takes the case into federal court."

"And the murders?"

"Both Krause and Ronald Perry are cooperating with the sheriff's office. By which I mean," I added, "that they've confessed to theft and Lacey violations, but they're blaming both homicides on the dead Perry brother. Jack Krause is claiming that he doesn't know diddly about either murder. Ronald Perry is claiming that he was in the dark about both killings until the cops told him, and that his brother was a paranoid psychopath whose behavior was completely unpredictable."

"A paranoid psychopath who was taken out by a mysterious buck with magnificent antlers," Ruby said with a lofty satisfaction, munching on a cookie. "The goddess was seeking justice."

"Maybe," I conceded, not wanting to get into an argument over whether the buck was or was not a tool of celestial intervention. "It turns out that Doc Masters had been a good friend of the Perrys' father. He seems to have held off on telling Mack where he had seen the stolen fawns because he wanted to talk to Ronald Perry first—maybe try to get him to go state's evidence on the theft, which would have meant a lighter sentence for both of the Perrys."

"But the psychopathic brother preempted that by shooting Doc Masters," Ruby said.

I nodded soberly. "The ballistic evidence is still out, but a twenty-two caliber semiautomatic pistol with Thomas' prints all over it was found in the Perry house. I'm guessing it'll be a match for the twenty-two slug the autopsy surgeon dug out of the old vet." I sighed. "And as for the murder of Sue Ellen—well, we've got that crime on the drone video, thanks to Amy and her friends. What we don't have yet is evidence that Krause and Ronald Perry either knew about the murders or were somehow involved."

But the investigation, as they say, was ongoing. Perry and Krause were lawyering up and would probably bail later in the week, and their trials, of course, were still to come. It seemed like an open-and-shut case to me, and in this matter, I was on the side of the angels. If there was any evidence at all of collusion, I wanted to see those guys charged with conspiring to take the lives of a perfectly lovely cowgirl and a much-admired veterinarian.

But Ruby was right. Justice doesn't always work the way it's supposed to, and it's usually about as slow as molasses in December. And even if the prosecuting attorney manages to get the convictions she's looking for, the wily defense attorney will almost always file an appeal, with the aim of delaying justice as long as possible. Except, of course, in the case of Lucky Perry, who'd gotten the final verdict swiftly.

"Thanks to Amy and her friends," Ruby repeated. She shook her head, deeply troubled. "I can't get my mind around the fact that Amy was *there*, doing *that*. She didn't say a word to me about where exactly she was going or what she was planning. She told me that she was taking a couple of days of R and R in San Antonio." Her voice rose. "And *I* was keeping little Grace!" Her shoulders slumped. "It feels like she doesn't trust me, China."

I was sympathetic. "But look at it this way, dear. If Amy hadn't been *there*, doing *that*, Thomas Perry might have gotten away with Sue Ellen's murder."

Ruby pulled down her gingery eyebrows and pursed her lips. "I really don't see—"

"It's like this," I said patiently. "Amy insisted to Chris that they bring the drone video to me, because she was hoping I could keep them out of trouble. As it happened, I was the one who knew about the thefts at Three Gates and could put that information together with Mack's information about Doc Masters and the fawns at the Bar Bee ranch. Which gave Mack and her hunky deputy the ability to consider all the moving parts and figure out what had to be done. Amy's role was absolutely crucial." I smiled. "You might credit the universe or the goddess or whatever for arranging that little piece of synchronicity, as well."

"Maybe." Ruby sighed. "But that's not the only issue here, China. What was Amy doing there with Chris? Is she . . . is she involved with him? Romantically, I mean. And why didn't she tell me what she was doing, where she was going?"

"I don't know," I said honestly. "She was definitely surprised to see me, and uneasy, but I couldn't begin to guess about her relationship with Chris. And I don't know why she didn't tell you about the drone project—unless she thought you would disapprove of her trespassing on private property in order to get photos of that pigeon shoot. Would you?"

"I suppose," Ruby conceded. "It's one thing to carry a sign and join a protest march. It's another to do something you can get arrested for. Especially if you're a mom."

"Well, I don't know about that," I said. "There are some things worth getting arrested for. And as far as Chris is concerned, aren't we getting ahead of ourselves? I mean, for all we know, this little episode was exactly what it seemed—three young people with a big idea, a powerful new tool, and a mission. Nobody would have found out what they were up to if they hadn't somehow managed to video a murder-in-progress. That was a coincidence they couldn't have imagined."

Or maybe it wasn't a coincidence. Maybe it was just another piece of the universal design that was put in place to make everything work out okay in the end. But if that was true, why did the arrangements have to include the deaths of two very good people? Whoever was in charge of such things must not have been paying attention when that happened.

"The real truth," Ruby said disconsolately, "is that I would hate to see anything or anybody come between Amy and Kate, especially for little Grace's sake. The girls are the only parents she's known."

"That's not true," I protested. "Even if Amy and Kate split up, she'll have you. You're an important part of her life. And a stable part. You'll always be here for Grace." I eyed her. "You know, you could always just *ask* your daughter what's going on. Maybe she'll tell you."

Ruby pulled her mouth down. "I already know the answer," she said glumly. "Remember when I said I wasn't getting good vibes about Amy's weekend plans? That I didn't like the guy she was going to meet in San Antonio? The guy who turned out to be Chris? I was right, China. He has dangerous ideas—dangerous for Amy, that is. There's going to be trouble. Serious trouble."

"I'm sorry," I said, understanding. Ruby's gift—the crystal ball she carries around inside her head, or her heart—had given her another glimpse into the future. And she didn't like what she saw.

"I'm sorry, too," Ruby said simply. "And there's not a damn thing I can do about it." After a moment, she added, "You haven't told me about Sam. How is he? What's your mother going to do for help there at the ranch?"

My turn to be glum. "Two problems. He developed a blood clot in his leg and an infection in his lungs. He's still in the hospital, under treatment. Leatha has found a place to stay in Kerrville so she doesn't have to drive back and forth. And they agreed, both of them, to delay the opening of their nature sanctuary. Leatha and I emailed the people who made reservations and explained the situation. While we were working on it, I realized how hard it was for her to do. She's really invested in the idea. And who knows? Maybe Sam will recover enough to allow them to go on with their plans. The guest lodge is finished and waiting whenever they're up to it."

I paused, wanting to say that things were changing for me: that I was beginning to accept the obligations of an only daughter, to realize that the next chapters of my life might include my mother in ways that would likely alter our relationship. The change might be a while in coming, but it somehow seemed massive to me, on the order of the San Francisco earthquake, and I was having a hard time putting it into words.

But even though I didn't speak, Ruby seemed to understand, in that intuitive way of hers. She reached out and patted my hand. "It's hard to see our parents moving into their later years and not know how to make it easier for them without compromising their independence." She paused. "And ours."

"Exactly," I said. "Thank you."

Ruby nodded. "Been there, done that," she said, and I knew that was true. Her mother's Alzheimer's is a hard thing to cope with. But she didn't want to linger on the subject. "What about Mack and her hunky deputy? What do you think is going to happen there?"

I laughed. "Hey, I'm not the one who's living with a crystal ball. That's another story, isn't it? They've only just begun. How they're going to end is still a mystery."

Ruby peered into her empty cup, where a few microscopic bits of tea leaf had escaped the strainer. "Maybe," she said. "But the leaves suggest that the future looks promising." She twinkled. "Very promising."

"That's good," I said. "Mack needs a special guy—somebody who can live with the work she wants to do." I paused. "Which leaves us with just one more question. How did your yarn bombing go this weekend? I saw the results when I came in this morning. The trees are quite . . . amazing."

And they were. Amazing. All along our entire block, the trunk of each sidewalk tree had been wrapped with flamboyant knitted stripes. Turquoise, yellow, navy, fuchsia, mulberry, tangerine, lime, shamrock, periwinkle.

"I'm glad you like it," Ruby said modestly. "The permit says we can leave it up until after New Year. Next weekend, we're putting up the fairy lights, so it'll be even more eye-catching. And the kids at Sam Houston Elementary School are painting a big plywood sleigh and Rudolph and candy canes."

"Santa Boulevard," I said.

"Something like that." Ruby smiled. "I just love it when Christmas comes and everybody gets creative. Don't you?"

I nodded. "As long as Rudolph isn't wearing monster antlers, I'm fine."

To the Reader

When we talk about herbs, most of us think of the green plants growing in our gardens or the little jars of dried plant material on our pantry shelves. These are the herbs that appear in traditional European cuisines: parsley, sage, rosemary, thyme, bay, mint, dill, and oregano.

But in recent years, ethnobotanists have broadened our understanding and appreciation of the many human uses of plants. Ethnobotany is the study of native peoples and cultures and their relationship to plants, as food sources and in medicine, cosmetics, dyes, clothing, construction, ritual, and magic. As an amateur botanist, I treasure my well-thumbed copy of *Native American Ethnobotany*, anthropologist Daniel Moerman's extraordinary compilation containing descriptions of over 44,000 native uses of more than 4,000 plants, documented by hundreds of firsthand studies of Native Americans made over the past 200 years. (An edited version of this information is also available in a searchable format online at herb.umd.umich.edu/.)

Moerman's valuable work is the main source of my information for most of the American herbs that appear in *Bittersweet*. For example, Moerman cites studies documenting over two dozen different uses of the book's signature herb, *Celastrus scandens* (American bittersweet), by a dozen different Native American tribes—forty-four citations in all. Among other applications, bittersweet was used as an analgesic, an abortifacient, a diuretic, a fever and cough remedy, a treatment for cancer and tuberculosis, and a ritual body paint. Our modern society, in contrast, has reduced this versatile plant to only two uses: as a robust decorative vine for the back fence and a colorful wreath for the front door.

Bittersweet also has an invasive look-alike, Oriental bittersweet (*Celastrus orbiculatus*), that is wreaking havoc in many states. But it is only one of the many introduced invasives (kudzu is probably the best known of these, but there are literally hundreds of others) that pose an enormous threat to native environments. More and more gardeners are learning that our native plants are preferable to these imported exotics. This is important because introduced species are all too often capable of outcompeting and hybridizing with our mild-mannered natives, possibly to the point of extinction. Once established, native plants often require less care and attention than exotics. As self-sustaining plant communities adapted to the climate and soils of local regions, they tend to resist damage from freezing, drought, and disease. Because they have coevolved with other species, they coexist in a companionable way with them. They provide food and habitat for native wildlife, serve as an important genetic reserve of native plant species, and make our world beautiful.

There are invasive animal species as well. Not long ago, my husband was surprised to see a large axis deer grazing on our Hill Country property. In the 1930s, these beautiful animals were imported from India for Texas sport hunting. Unfortunately, they escaped confinement and moved into the Hill Country to stay. Finding themselves at home, they are outcompeting our smaller native white-tailed deer for scarce forage. It was that sighting that prompted me to begin the research that led to one of the major plotlines for this book: the development of commercial game ranches here in Texas and the treatment of wild animals as agricultural commodities, like cattle and sheep.

While the story in *Bittersweet* ends with justice more or less served, the rapid growth of Texas' commercial deer-farming industry continues, with many unhappy consequences. The game ranches are expanding their efforts to offer genetically modified bucks with enormous racks, while wealthy "sportsmen," eager to display the trophy antlers on their walls, are forking over even more outrageous sums to participate in canned hunts for captive animals. That story seems destined to continue, because there are too many Texas-size egos at stake, too much money to be made, and too much political influence to be bought and bartered.

As China Bayles might say, in the real world justice sometimes isn't served. And sometimes, that's just the way it is.

SEVERAL last-minute thoughts . . .

About herbal medicine. My reports of traditional medicinal uses of plants are not intended to suggest treatments for what ails you. Some folk uses of therapeutic herbs are not supported by modern science, while others are completely ineffective or may have potent and unwanted side effects, especially when combined with over-the-counter and prescription drugs. Respect these powerful plants. Do your homework before you use any plant-based medicine, and consult the appropriate authorities. China and I value our readers and friends. We'd hate to lose you.

About place and people. Uvalde County, where most of the action of this book takes place, is a real county, located in the Brush Country of South Texas, a biologically diverse eco-region that is bordered on the north by the Edwards Plateau, on the south and west by the Rio Grande River, and on the east by the Gulf Coast prairies and sand plains. Utopia is a real town, too— the setting for a recent movie, in fact (*Seven Days in Utopia*). The Lost Maples Café and the general store are real, and you can visit them when you go there for the rodeo, which is also real. But the people in this book, including the residents of Utopia and its environs, are all entirely fictional. They are not modeled on any individuals, living or dead, so please don't go to Uvalde County and start looking for them. You'll be disappointed.

About thanks. I'm grateful to the many journalists who have been following the Texas trophy ranch situation and writing about it in state and national publications. This is a developing story, so if you're interested in following it, the Internet is your best source. Try searching on Google for a combination of terms such as *Texas canned hunts, genetically modified deer, deer breeding*, and so on.

I'm grateful, as well, to Sharon M. Turner of Pflugerville, Texas, who appears as a cameo character in this book. Sharon is retired from a career as a teacher but leads a busy life full of fascinating projects: she teaches reading to adults and landscape painting and cooking to kids, tends her herb garden and her roses; makes rose sachets and herbal soaps; reads a book a day; and is always available to give China and Ruby a hand in their shops. And yes, she really does change her hair color often!

Thanks, too, to Peggy Moody, my extraordinary cyber-assistant and webmistress, without whose able assistance I would be in serious trouble at least once a day. And as always, to Bill Albert, for his unfailing support and his willingness to drive all over Uvalde County through a chilly January rain.

Yes, it does rain—occasionally—in South Texas.

Susan Wittig Albert
Bertram, Texas

Recipes

Leatha's Venison Chili

If venison isn't available, or if you prefer, substitute beef stew meat or ground beef.

4 tablespoons oil
1 large onion, chopped
4 cloves garlic, minced
4 tablespoons dark brown sugar
4 cups red wine
4 tablespoons red wine or balsamic vinegar
1 (6-ounce) can tomato sauce
1 (14.5-ounce) can diced tomatoes, undrained
1 teaspoon ground cumin
½ teaspoon cayenne pepper (or more, to taste)
½ teaspoon chili powder (or more, to taste)
1 teaspoon cinnamon
1 teaspoon oregano
6–8 dried juniper berries
salt to taste
4 tablespoons oil
10 slices cooked bacon, diced
2 pounds venison stew meat, trimmed and finely diced
2 (15-ounce) cans black or red beans, with liquid

Heat the oil in a large pot over medium heat. Stir in the onion and garlic and sauté for 3–4 minutes. Stir in brown sugar, red wine, vinegar, tomato sauce, diced tomatoes, cumin, cayenne pepper, chili powder, cinnamon, oregano, juniper berries, and salt. Simmer for 15–30 minutes, until reduced by about half. Meanwhile, heat the oil in a large skillet over medium-high heat. Stir in the diced bacon and fry until browned. Add the venison, mixing with the bacon, and sauté until the venison is cooked through, about 15 minutes. Transfer meat to the tomato sauce. Stir in beans, mixing thoroughly. Simmer for 20–25 minutes. Serves 8.

China's Cabbage and Sausage Soup

4 tablespoons oil, divided
1 onion, diced
2 garlic cloves, sliced
1 carrot, diced
½ green pepper, seeded and diced
½ medium head cabbage, chopped
6 cups water
1¼ tablespoons dried juniper berries, finely crushed, or substitute 3–4 fresh whole berries
2 bay leaves
1 pound mild Italian sausage, crumbled
¼ cup chopped parsley
salt and pepper to taste

In a medium-size, heavy-bottom pot, heat 2 tablespoons oil. Add onions, garlic, carrot, green pepper, and cabbage. Sauté until the vegetables are tender, about 5 minutes. Add water, juniper berries, and bay leaves, bring to a boil, reduce heat to medium-low, and simmer for 20 minutes. In a skillet, heat 2 tablespoons oil. Add crumbled sausage and brown. Add to cabbage mixture. Stir in parsley, salt, and pepper to taste. Simmer for 10 minutes. Remove bay leaves and whole juniper berries (if used). Serves 4.

Sue Ellen's Lemon-Rosemary Sticky Rolls

1 7.5-ounce tube refrigerated crescent rolls
1 cup granulated sugar
¼ teaspoon allspice
zest of 2 lemons
1 tablespoon minced fresh rosemary
2 tablespoons lemon juice
3 tablespoons softened butter or margarine
2 ounces cream cheese, softened
1 tablespoon lemon juice
½ cup confectioner's sugar

Remove the crescent rolls from the package and open each one. Mix the sugar, allspice, lemon zest, and rosemary with a spoon or your fingers. Add the lemon juice and margarine and mix very well. Spread evenly over the opened rolls and reroll each one, not too tightly. Bake at 375 degrees F for 11–13 minutes, or until brown. Glaze with lemon–cream cheese glaze.

To make glaze: mix cream cheese, lemon juice, and confectioner's sugar. Drizzle over rolls.

Orange-Ginger Carrots

¾ cup water
1 pound peeled baby carrots
1 tablespoon butter or margarine
¼ cup orange marmalade
1 teaspoon ground ginger
⅛ teaspoon ground nutmeg
3 tablespoons candied ginger (optional)

1 tablespoon chopped fresh parsley
Salt and pepper

In a medium saucepan over high heat, combine ¾ cup water and carrots. Cover, bring to a boil, then reduce heat to medium-high. Shake pan occasionally until carrots are tender, about 7–8 minutes. Drain. Return carrots to pan over medium heat. Add butter, marmalade, ginger, nutmeg, and candied ginger (optional). Cook, stirring, until marmalade mixture coats carrots, about 5 minutes. Sprinkle with parsley, and add salt and pepper to taste.

Slaw with Pickled Beets and Apples

2 cups chopped green cabbage
1 Granny Smith apple, peeled and chopped
½ cup chopped sweet onion
½ cup diced sweet red bell pepper
½ cup chopped pickled beets
½ teaspoon caraway seeds, lightly crushed
1 tablespoon pickled beet juice
4 tablespoons mayonnaise

Place the first 5 ingredients in a bowl and mix well. In a separate bowl, stir together caraway seeds, pickled beet juice, and mayonnaise. Add to cabbage mixture and stir all together. Refrigerate at least half an hour before serving.

Rosemary Stuffing

This recipe makes enough to stuff a 10–12 pound turkey. It can be doubled for a larger bird.

4 tablespoons butter
1 cup chopped onion
1 cup chopped celery
2 tablespoons chopped fresh sage
2 sprigs minced fresh thyme
½ cup chopped fresh parsley
1 teaspoon minced fresh rosemary
1 teaspoon olive oil, if needed
1 loaf sliced bread, cubed
2–2½ cups chicken broth
½ cup dried cranberries
½ cup chopped pecans or walnuts
Salt and pepper to taste

In a large skillet, heat the butter. Add onion and celery and sauté for about 5 minutes. Add the herbs. If the mixture seems dry, add olive oil. Put cubed bread in a large bowl. Add sautéed mixture and toss. Add about half of the chicken broth and toss to coat as much as you can. Add the dried cranberries and the nuts and toss. Bit by bit, add most of or all the remaining broth until the stuffing begins to hold together but isn't soggy. Season to taste with salt and pepper. Stuff the bird loosely and bake. Place remaining stuffing in a greased casserole dish, cover with foil, and bake at 350 degrees F for 20 minutes. For a crispy top, remove foil and bake 10–15 minutes longer.

Leatha's Peach Pie

Unbaked shell and top crust for 2-crust 9-inch pie

4 cups sliced peaches
1½ tablespoons flour
¾ cup brown sugar
1 tablespoon freshly squeezed lemon juice
1 tablespoon minced fresh rosemary
1 egg, beaten
1 tablespoon coarse sugar

BOURBON WHIPPED CREAM
1 cup whipping cream
2 tablespoons brown sugar
1 teaspoon vanilla
1 tablespoon bourbon

Preheat oven to 400 degrees F. In a bowl, gently mix peaches, flour, brown sugar, lemon juice, and rosemary. Place in pie shell, cover with top crust, and crimp to seal. Brush top crust with beaten egg, sprinkle with coarse sugar. Transfer the pie to the oven and place a baking sheet in the bottom to catch any drips. Bake at 400 degrees F for 30 minutes. Reduce to 375 degrees F, cover the pie's edges with foil, and bake for about 40 minutes longer. Serve warm with Bourbon Whipped Cream.

To make Bourbon Whipped Cream, use an electric mixer to beat all ingredients together until cream is thickened.

Herb Quiche

3 eggs, slightly beaten
2 cups warm milk
salt and pepper to taste
¾ cup grated Swiss cheese
9-inch unbaked pie shell
½ cup cooked, drained, chopped spinach
½ cup sautéed mushrooms
3 tablespoons fresh snipped chives
1 teaspoon fresh thyme leaves, minced
1 teaspoon fresh parsley, minced
1 tablespoon butter or margarine
leaves of fresh greens (kale, arugula, lettuce) and fresh chive blossoms for garnish

Preheat oven to 350 degrees F. Combine eggs, milk, salt, and pepper. Spread the grated cheese evenly in the bottom of the pie shell. Mix the spinach, mushrooms, and herbs and spoon over the cheese. Pour the milk-and-egg mixture over all. Dot the top with butter or margarine. Place the pie plate on a cookie sheet and bake until set, about 30–35 minutes. Remove when the outside is set and the middle still jiggles when shaken. Let stand 10–15 minutes before slicing. Serve slices on beds of fresh greens, garnished with chive blossoms.

Cass' Chai Tea Cookies

"Chai" (or "masala chai") is a term that describes black tea brewed with a variety of aromatic spices and consumed in Asia and Africa. For this recipe, you may use any chai mix you prefer, purchased or homemade. If you use bags, just cut the bags open. The cardamom, cinnamon, and allspice will lend additional spice, but may be omitted.

1 cup all-purpose flour
¼ cup sugar
¼ cup powdered sugar
1 tablespoon chai tea mix, ground with a mortar and pestle or spoon
½ teaspoon ground cardamom, optional
½ teaspoon ground cinnamon, optional
¼ teaspoon allspice, optional
¼ teaspoon salt
½ teaspoon vanilla
½ cup unsalted butter, softened

In a bowl, combine the flour, sugar, powdered sugar, tea, salt, and optional spices and mix thoroughly. Add the vanilla and butter and mix until a dough forms. (Your electric mixer will make short work of this job.) Form the dough into a log 8 to 9 inches long and wrap in waxed or parchment paper. Freeze or chill for at least 30 minutes. To bake, preheat oven to 375 degrees F. Slice dough into cookies ⅓ inch thick. Place on parchment-lined baking sheet and bake until the edges begin to brown, 10–12 minutes. Cool on baking sheet for 5 minutes, then transfer to wire racks. Store in an airtight container. Makes about 30 cookies.